S.S. Huber

Rise of the Dragon

Bernadine D. Morris

Song of the Dragon Series

Available through Amazon
Online at indigo.com
And through www.songofthedragon.com

Titles in reading order:

S.S. Huber – The Dragon's Eye Crystal
S.S. Huber – Rise of the Dragon

Book 2

In Book 2 of Song of the Dragon series, Sybil and Simon Huber follow their hound Sirius back to Aquadria. They are drawn into conflict in Seventh dimension as the country descends into civil war. Aligned with northern forces, a tale of cross-dimensional effort and heroism unfolds as they discover the key to Aquadorus's power and solve the mystery behind the Duplicating Chambers. Transformational changes bring surprising results for family and friends. Sybil is disconcerted by, and resists a growing attraction that begins to develop between her and Dimondus. Coming to terms with their unique strengths and abilities Sybil and Simon learn to deal with bullying as they grapple with Wesley Peters in Third dimension.

S.S. Huber
Rise of the Dragon

Published in Chilliwack, British Columbia, Canada

Library and Archives Canada
Cataloguing in Publication
S.S. Huber – Rise of the Dragon/Bernadine D. Morris

ISBN 978-0-9948237-2-4

1. Fantasy 2. Science Fiction

Printed by KDP, an Amazon.com company
Available through Amazon, order online from Indigo, or through Author's website www.songofthedragon.com

UNITREE

I dedicate this book to those who endure and persevere through the nightmare of being bullied. You are not alone. Share your experience and seek help.

And, for those who feel the need to bully.

May you come to know and live from your innate nobility.

Acknowledgements

Thank you to my husband Ken, for your lifelong friendship, commitment, and ongoing belief in us. I love your loyal and brave spirit. I am especially grateful for your patient tolerance of long hours I have spent in front of a computer.

For our son Kevin who lost his life to brain cancer in 2016. You are never far from my thoughts and forever in my heart.

To my amazing daughters, Lindsay and Kimberly. Your many talents, caring ways and commitment to your chosen life's work inspire me daily. I love your strength of spirit and devotion to family.

For my grandchildren, Joshua, Venice and Sullivan. And for youth everywhere. Your playful and resilient spirits renew our hope for the future.

To Aaron Parrott for designing and creating an outstanding cover. Your artistic talent and creative abilities are beyond expectation and are deeply appreciated. Thank you for your valuable suggestions and assistance with the legend and map of Aquadria. You have a special place in my heart.

I am deeply indebted to Maxine Gadsden for her willingness to read the manuscript and for her meticulous attention to detail. Thank you for your editing skills and valuable suggestions.

My sincere appreciation to Gill Grigor, for your helpful comments and supportive friendship throughout the years. Thank you to Betty-Anne Pap for your encouragement and wonderful memories we have shared.

I am sincerely grateful for the generosity of The Book Man and Coles Books in Chilliwack; for their belief in, and assistance of local authors. I wish to acknowledge Margaret Evans for her continued support of writers in our community. To friends and family members; I appreciate your encouraging words.

Map of Aquadria

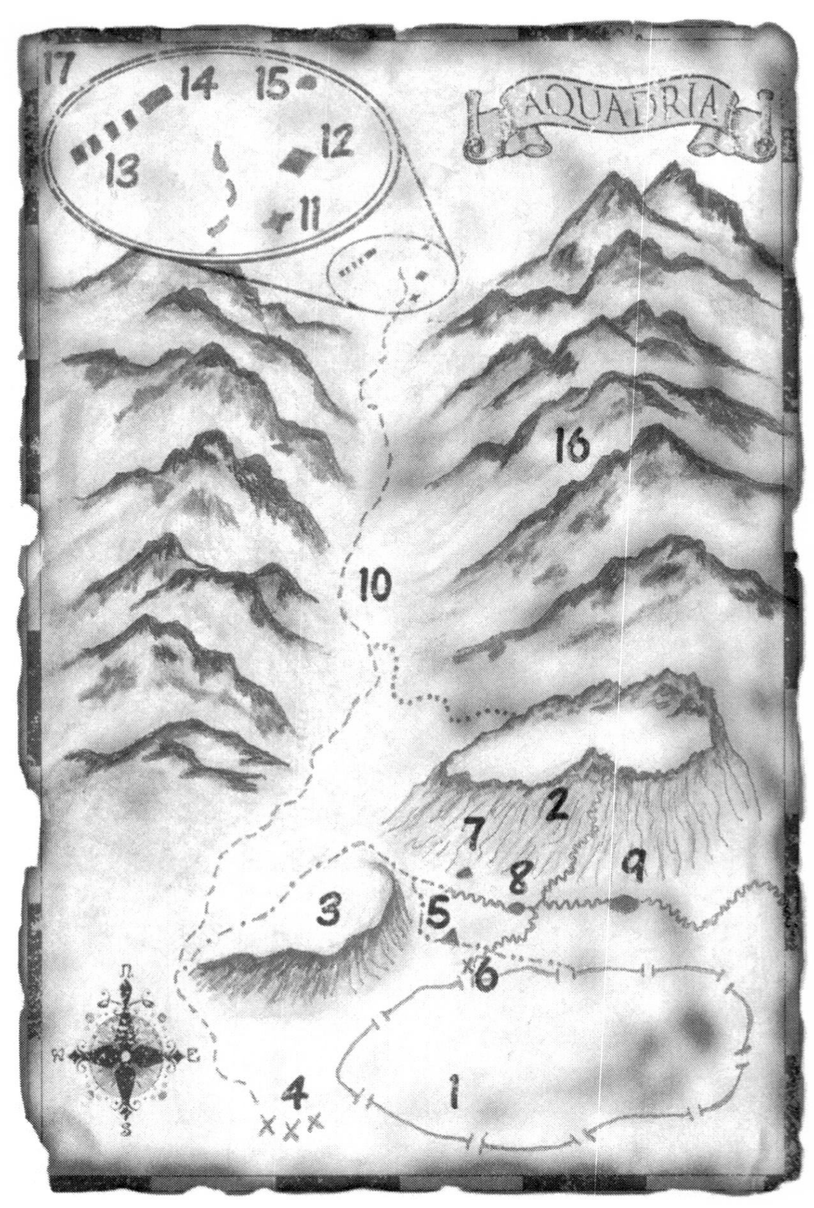

Wherever you go, go with all of your heart.

- Confucius

Legend

1. City of Aquadria
2. Opeggee Rookery
3. Plynthe Plateau
4. Refugee Camps
5. Pumping Station
6. Capture Point
7. Cave
8. Sinkhole
9. Hatching Grounds
10. Caliper Pass
11. Northern Headquarters
12. Mess Tents
13. Duplicating Chambers
14. Fifth Hall
15. Dragon Pit
16. Black Spine Mountains
17. Magnified Area

Rinaldo's Route

Sybil and Simon's first Route

Sybil, Simon & Rourke's Route

Route to Pumping Station

Back Route to Rookery

Contents

"Yesterday I was clever, so I wanted to change the world. Today I am wise, so now I am changing myself.

- Rumi

CHAPTER ONE
Chaos in Seventh

☆

"Courage is the power of the mind to overcome fear."

- Martin Luther King

Sybil patted her thigh. "Come, Sirius. Time to leave." The large hound capered to her side, licked her fingertips and whimpered. He turned and scuttled away, then came back and whined again.

"What's wrong, big fella?" She knelt and tussled his ruff. Letting her hands slide to the dog's ears, she turned his head toward her. The intelligent brown eyes reflected concern. There was tension in the depths.

Simon knelt beside her and stroked his back. "Something isn't right, Sybil. Sirius is trying to tell us."

The dog whined again, broke free, cantered off and stopped to look back.

"What's wrong, boy?" Simon asked. Sirius returned and nuzzled his leg, then ran off again.

"He wants us to follow," Sybil said. "Go on, boy. Show us."

Setting off on a fast trot, Sirius headed north. Simon and Sybil jogged after him. "Where is he going?" asked Sybil.

"Beats me," Simon responded. "Let's follow him and see where he's headed."

They'd been running behind the dog without let up for a good half hour when Sybil stopped. "He's making a beeline due north. You don't think he's headed toward the ozone portal, do you?"

"Sirius! Come back!" Simon shouted.

The dog kept running. "Sirius, stop!" commanded Sybil.

The big hound slowed, came to a halt and turned to look at them. Then he began to run again, barking loudly.

"Sirius, where are you going? Stop!" shouted Simon. This time Sirius came back and began running circles around them, whining and barking wildly.

"Something is definitely wrong," concluded Simon.

Catching hold of his thick neck, Sybil calmed him. "All right, all right. We understand. Lead the way, Sirius."

"Hold on, Sybil. We need to move faster than this. Let's use the mind net."

"But how do we know where he's taking us?" asked Sybil. "If it's back to Seventh dimension, I don't think that's such a good idea."

"Sirius is pretty wound up. I think we need to check this out. He won't come with us and we can't leave him," reasoned Simon.

"Okay, I see your point. But I don't like this," said Sybil. She joined Simon in creating the net. "Hop on, Sirius."

The big male climbed aboard and they sped away. "You have full control, Sirius. Take us where you want to go."

Streaking north, they soon encountered the aurora. Sirius knew the way. He'd found it before when he had followed them and was pulled into the abyss. The ozone hole loomed ahead. Before they could change their minds, they were drawn in and were hurtling down through the void. Veering right, they entered the oceanic trench.

"This is different than the first time we came!" Sybil whispered. "Where do you suppose he's taking us?"

"Trust him. He knows." In a short time they landed on high ground near the sea forest.

"The flooding has started!" gasped Sybil. All low-lying

areas were covered in sea water. The aerial tree roots of the old growth forest, just visible, dangled above the surface. Tops of buildings protruded from the water. Higher areas of the city remained dry.

"How long do you think we have?"

"Don't know. We'd better find Roark."

"But we're on the opposite side. The rookery is across the city."

"Can't get there on foot. We'll have to risk flying over."

Zooming high above the flooded areas, they headed directly to the cliff top rookery in the distance. "Look at that! Many have completed full transformation!" whispered Sybil, peering into the depths.

"The unflooded parts still have amphibious people," observed Simon. "Should we have a closer look?"

"First we need to see the Opeggees. Find out what's happening there. Maybe they can tell us more."

"Right. This time we can land on the cliff top."

Soon they were hovering over the settlement. There was a flurry of activity below. The Opeggees were in crisis mode.

"Roark!" Simon sent out a distress call. *"Where are you? Are you okay?"*

"Simon?" Roark's panicky voice could be heard above the frantic chaos.

"Roark. We're landing right now. Meet you at your place."

They set down safely in front of Meerak's home. Sirius leapt off the net before it could dissolve and headed off toward the cliff trail.

"Sirius, wait!" Simon and Sybil bounded after him.

As he neared the trail head, Roark's distraught face appeared around the bend in the cliff wall. The big hound slid to a halt in front of him, mindful not to bowl him over. He had learned that Opeggees were rather precarious on their feet. Their suction cups could let loose if he was too exuberant with his greetings. He gently nudged Roark's round blue form. It was all he could do to control himself. He began to lick his new friend all over.

"Sirius! Stop that," laughed Roark, giggling with mixed delight. "You sure know how to make a guy feel better!"

When the canine greeting was over, Roark ran to meet Sybil and Simon.

"Boy, am I glad to see you guys! What are you doing back here?"

"We got to the Fifth and saw Icelandia. DOU has returned to Ninth. We were about to leave for Hetopia and home to Third but Sirius was acting so strange. He took off and wouldn't come back to us. We knew something was wrong. He wouldn't stop, so here we are."

"Looks like Aquadorus has started to flood the valley. What's happened, Roark?" Simon asked.

"It began shortly after you left. But it stopped for some reason. It has only flooded part way."

"Do you know why?" asked Sybil.

"That's where I've been. I went down the trail to check the high water mark. Our nursery grounds are underwater. But not deep. I can still see the shrubs where I hatched."

"There must be something we can do!" cried Sybil.

"What's to become of you and the Opeggees?" Simon was thinking hard. "Can we evacuate you to the Fifth?"

"The Fifth?" cried Roark. "I don't think that's possible."

"Why not?" Sybil's frantic voice made him reconsider.

"Last resort, maybe. Seventh is our home. I don't see why we have to leave."

"Aquadorus is a tyrant. Who can stop him?" asked Simon.

"There are a few people in Aquadria who have nothing to lose by opposing him," said Sybil. "Maybe we can find some allies."

"Too risky," replied Simon. "It would be a long shot."

"What about Calazone and Hermaine? And poor old Rinaldo. No one cares about him. He doesn't seem to have one friend in all of Aquadria." Sybil's heart went out to him. She knew what it was like to be different.

"I wonder what happened to that woman Adelaide. She must be in big trouble with all this water—if she even survived the flooding," said Simon.

"And I'd like to know more about the far north, where DOU was. What else is up there?" asked Sybil.

"Hey! Maybe you have something there. Let's scope it out."

"What are we waiting for? Let's go north!" cried Roark.

He wanted to do all he could to save his colony. His mind wandered into visions of glory. The accolades he would have—if only he could do this.

"I'm all for that," agreed Sybil.

They hurriedly made their way toward Roark's home to advise Mother Meerak of their plans. Her worried frown indicated that she was anything but pleased by the prospect.

"Very well," she said hesitantly. "Get word to me if you can. Roark, Sybil, Simon, please be careful!" She gave them her farewell blessing.

Sirius let out a long, mournful howl. He was troubled by the distress he could smell on those around him. The people he loved; they were his responsibility. He was a guard dog after all. Fitfully, he settled on the mind net and they sped away.

"Easy, Sirius. You must be quiet if you come with us," said Sybil, stroking his back gently. She glanced back at the Opeggee settlement far below, wondering if they would ever see it again.

"Let's go high," suggested Roark. "Better chance of getting there undetected."

"You know the way best," replied Sybil. "Lead us in."

They left the flooded areas behind and were soon over the compound where they had discovered DOU the dragon. There was a heavy concentration of Aquadrian personnel on the ground.

"Still amphibious!" observed Sybil. "Maybe some of them are not able to change."

"That might account for the dissension among the Aquadrian folk. Dimondus is obviously hated by a lot of people in Aquadria," said Simon. "Maybe they don't like Aquadorus much either."

"Yeah, he does Aquadorus's dirty work. Thinks he's earned favours there. Maybe he has. Perhaps they need to cut the head off the snake. But how do we make contact? Who can we trust?" asked Sybil.

Checking for clues from the air, they flew on hoping to gather more information. Further along, they came to a conglomeration of halls set up in long, neat rows. The appearance of the buildings had a familiar contour.

"Simon! Look at those buildings! They look like the duplicating hall, the one at the lake bottom settlement!"

"Is that why the population seems to be doubling overnight?" cried Simon.

"Surely not! You think? This is all connected?"

"We've had our suspicions all along, haven't we?"

"We did. But this?"

"Beginning to make sense. If Aquadorus is planning on flooding the Fifth—but how do the Aquadrians fit in with Leanoria?"

"I don't think all of them agree with this. At least I hope not," replied Sybil, her thoughts racing ahead.

What about those who have already morphed? Were they being forced through the duplicator and set free outside the gel walls? Is Aquadorus amassing a huge army of Aquatics to do his bidding when the time comes? Are we too late? Can we still stop it? Should we try to destroy the duplicating halls?

She voiced all these fears to Simon and Roark. Roark hopped up and down with excitement.

"I can destroy those halls. You bet. Vulcan sacs. Poof!" he shouted eagerly.

"But first we have to know who is with us and who is not," cautioned Simon. "And exactly what is happening."

"We need to find Rinaldo first I think. He has nothing to lose and he seemed very grateful to us that morning he was hauled in," replied Sybil.

Her compassion for the underdog ran deep. She would love to see Rinaldo succeed for once in his life. Dimondus was a bully, and she was painfully aware, knew firsthand how that felt.

"How do we make contact?" asked Simon. His bafflement struck a chord in both Sybil and Roark. It was very risky.

"Now that we know what's up here, maybe we need to bring Profrak on board," suggested Sybil.

"No. We can handle this. The fewer involved, the less chance of being discovered." Roark's adamant reasoning made sense.

"Okay, but do you have enough vulcan sacs on hand?"

"Do I? I'm in charge of the stockpile. I can get in and out for as much as it takes to do the job."

"Good!" said Sybil. "Now all we need to do is make contact in the south if we can."

"Not so fast. I don't think we should destroy those halls until we know what we're up against," said Simon. "And we don't even know what the halls really are."

"He's right," said Roark. "Guess I'm a little trigger happy. Can't help it. All this water!"

"We certainly have our work cut out for us," replied Sybil. "How about we split up?"

"What? Go in different directions? You think that's wise?" asked Simon.

"We don't have much time. Lots to do. Check the halls, organize the vulcan sacs, see if we can find any allies. What do you suggest?"

"All valid points," replied Simon.

"Okay, then. I know about the duplicating chamber. It makes sense that job is mine."

"And I can handle the vulcan sacs," said Roark.

"So that leaves me with finding friends in the south," agreed Simon.

Sybil grimaced. The tasks seemed equally onerous.

Roark piped up, "With you two out of the picture, I'll need my two best buddies to help me. I can trust them."

"Give ourselves until mid-afternoon, say third bell and meet back here?" suggested Simon.

"Long enough, I hope," she said, turning toward the halls. "You'd better take Sirius with you. I can't take him into those halls with me. Be careful, Simon, Roark."

"You too, Syb."

She watched as they sped southward, then decided to hover from a distance and watch for clues. The crowds below were scurrying about frantically. A wedge of recognition slowly pried its way into her awareness. A familiar figure? She'd seen him before. Who was that? Slowly it dawned on her. It was that squadron leader she'd seen the first day when Dimondus marched them into the city. He had stood guard over them while Dimondus refreshed.

"Oh boy," she muttered, scratching her head. What was his

name? Helpin? Halcron? Herclan! That was it! She continued to watch. People were approaching Herclan who was set up at a field desk. He seemed to be consulting charts and giving directions.

I wonder if I can get into one of those halls. Maybe at night but that's too far off and they'd be heavily guarded. Crumbs! This was going to be a tough job. Well, who said life was easy? Then—another familiar figure! It was Rinaldo! What was he doing here?

She watched as he spoke with Herclan. His shoulders squared in an official way and he gave a sharp salute. Then he marched off smartly along the rows of halls, until he reached the last of them. What was he doing?

Sybil watched him unlock the double doors and enter. This is it. I can get in now! She accelerated, widely skirting the compound and swooped in from the opposite direction, landing in front of the open doors. She entered stealthily and proceeded through the echo chamber, willing her feet to tread lightly. It was the same so far! Sybil's excitement rose. Next should come the business section with office spaces, then the mirrored maze.

She crept forward until she entered the narrow hallway in the business area. Someone was rummaging around in one of the offices. Stealing closer, she saw Rinaldo, as expected. He was sorting through files and going through documents.

She was about to turn away, when something scuttled across the floor in front of her. It was tiny and quick. Out of the corner of her eye, she caught the form disappearing around the doorway into the room where Rinaldo continued to work. It launched itself at him and latched onto his ear.

Ears? Since when did Aquadrians have ears? Did he have them all along? Had she missed them? Sybil was flummoxed.

"Ow, ow, ow!" yelled Rinaldo, trying to pry it off. But it

held fast.

Without thinking, Sybil leapt into action. She rushed into the room and grabbed the tiny critter by the tail and squeezed. It was hard and crusty, some kind of shelled creature. It made a high-pitched shriek as its jaws let loose. It fell to the floor and Rinaldo stepped on it with his flipper. An ugly cracking sound and a final squeal signified the end.

"Sarah! What are you doing here?" cried Rinaldo, recovering from fright. "Where did you come from?"

He gaped at her, hardly believing his eyes. Then a gleam of satisfaction broke the tension on his face and he laughed and slapped his thigh with glee.

"Dimondus was fit to be tied! What an uproar when you didn't show up for work report at breakfast that morning. Hah! Old Dimondus got hauled up before Aquadorus. Serves that coward right."

Remembering their deception, Sybil was unsure of what to say but decided to play it safe for a little longer. She was enjoying his story about Dimondus. And she remembered how much she liked Rinaldo.

"What is happening, Rinaldo? Where is everyone? And what was that thing?" She pointed to the crushed, lifeless body on the floor.

"It's a rat crab. Vicious little beggars. But the least of our worries. It's Aquadorus. He's flooding the valley, taking over the whole of the Aquatic kingdom. His Aquatic clones govern the high seas. It's only a matter of time before they destroy the gel walls and we're all lost. Aquadorus means to turn us all into Aquamatons. Many are unable to change or don't want to. We've formed an underground. I've been leading a double life."

"Oh, Rinaldo!" Sybil's voice held a deep regard for his plight. "That's why you couldn't stay awake on duty."

“Yes. This is nasty business. I played the fool to maintain my cover.”

Sybil saw Rinaldo for what he was—a resourceful sort who would do what must be done for the cause. Her regard for him grew with each revelation.

Sizing him up, she decided on a course of action. Whether it was wise or not she did not know, but she made one of those leaps of faith and decided to reveal her true identity.

“I have a confession to make, Rinaldo.”

“Oh? What’s that?”

“You aren’t the only one who has been leading a double life.”

Rinaldo perked up. This was an intriguing bit of news. “How so?”

“My real name is Sybil. We didn’t fall overboard off a boat. We came through the ozone portal.”

“You and Dominic?”

“Yes, but his real name is Simon.”

Rinaldo’s surprised look was replaced by a grin that was growing wider with each disclosure.

“Say now! This is some new information—might be useful to northern forces. Came from where?”

“Now that’s a long story. We entered from the Fifth,” she replied, deciding to leave Third out of it for now. “Fifth is in dire straits.”

“Yes, we know about Aquadorus’s expansion into Fifth. He means to take over everything!”

“I’ve seen this type of hall in the Fifth dimension, Rinaldo. Aquadorus may not stop there. Could want more.”

“No doubt! He’s ruthless and power hungry.”

“What do these halls actually do?”

“Some of them produce clones, some new prototypes. They use existing life forms and transform them.”

Sybil was shocked. Her heart dropped into her stomach, fluttering like an injured bird. What if she and Simon had been sent through? Why weren't they? She thought about the Leanorians, the Namors Guardia, and the Graenwolven. Her jaw fell open as she contemplated the implications. Maybe they would have been, if they had not escaped from the Leanorians!

Afraid to ask the next question, she let an uncomfortable silence lapse between them. Rinaldo studied her face, saw the fear, the hopelessness slowly shutting her down. He rummaged his heart for something to say that would stem the tide of loss registering on her face.

Finally, he offered a feeble, "Sorry, Sybil. I wish I had better news."

Stunned by this information, she fought to get back on even ground. Her equilibrium had taken a dreadful hit. After several moments of horrified silence, she managed to revive enough to stammer, "Ca-can they be changed back to what they were before?"

"We're working on it. That's what I'm doing right now. Going through files. Everyone who has been through this is registered. So many!" His voice cracked with emotion.

"They will change back to their former selves?" she repeated, willing the answer.

From a distance she heard Rinaldo's voice. "Our scientists have been working on that. Right now it is not possible. But we are very close."

It wasn't what she wanted to hear. Very close. Too far, when so much was at stake.

"What is happening right now?"

"It's civil war. We're divided into two camps. Aquadorus in the south and us in the north. We hold the balance right now because we have control of the halls. Once we make the breakthrough, the Universe willing…" His thoughts stalled. The outlook was bleak.

"Simon has gone south to look for reinforcements. We had hoped to make contact with allies down there."

"Bad move, Sybil. Don't know how safe that is now. Most who have chosen northern forces have already fled and have linked up with us. Still, he may find a few. I can send help to him if you think…"

"Oh no. Thank you," Sybil interrupted. "I think Simon will turn back when he sees the situation. I will try to find him myself. You have enough to do. Who is in charge up here?"

"Herclan has assumed general responsibility. Hermaine, Calazone and I lead contingents reporting to him. We plan strategy as a united command, operating as a unified force. It works."

"Where are your scientists?" she asked. "How close are they to finding the solution? Can Fifth do anything to help? What can I do?" Her questions bubbled forth like hot lava. "What about the Opeggees?"

The blood left her face as she remembered Roark readying for battle. She must get to him and warn him to hold off on the vulcan sacs. He wouldn't go ahead without conferring would he? No, she didn't think so, but his two friends?

"Rinaldo, I have an urgent matter to see to. I must also find Simon. I'll leave you now, but we'll be back soon. Watch for us. If we aren't back by nightfall please send reinforcements. I'm heading to the cliffs near the Opeggee rookery. I think Simon will go there first. It's familiar territory."

"Most of the area below that is already under water, Sybil. Still, it won't hurt to scout it out. Good luck. May the Universe be with you! Hurry back."

Sybil left the hall and headed south immediately. Soon the

rookery cliffs were in sight.

"Where are you, Roark?" she said under her breath. She scanned the area. Where would they keep the vulcan armaments? She veered toward the back side of the cliffs. Below, she saw Roark struggling to load supplies on his own.

She dropped down swiftly, landing beside him. Sirius, who was left with Roark, gave a happy woof and bounded over to her. "Hi, boy," she said ruffling his fur.

"What are you doing, Roark? Where are your friends?"

"Couldn't find them, so I decided to get started on my own. I'll go back in a bit and recruit them."

"That won't be necessary right now, Roark. We have time." She told him about her meeting with Rinaldo and what she had learned.

"Lucky wing feathers! That is some good news for a change!" Roark did a skip-hop dance, popping his suction cups in a tap dance rhythm. "Where is Simon? Has he returned?"

"No. I'm on my way to find him. He may run into trouble in the south. Come with me, Roark."

"You bet! I'm your wing man." He laughed at his pun and Sybil couldn't help but grin, too. They were under a lot of pressure and a bit of humour lightened the mood.

"Oh, Roark. You truly are one of a kind."

"Yep, that's me. Only one Roark in all of the rookery."

"Where do you think Simon would go first?"

"I don't know, maybe the nesting grounds? But they're under water. Still, I think he would begin near there and follow the trail as far as he can."

"Okay then, we'll begin our search there. We can put out telepathic bulletins. Maybe he'll hear us."

Deciding a ground search was best, they set off down the

path. There was no guarantee that Aquadrian forces weren't still patrolling, but they had to take that chance. If they flew over the area Sybil's presence might become known. How had Simon chosen to travel? Was he still out there or had he been captured? Her heart rate increased.

"We have to find Simon fast. All this water. Flooding could resume at any time!"

CHAPTER TWO
Contact

"A room without books is like a body without a soul."

- Marcus Tullius Cicero

After he'd left Sybil, Simon made his way south toward the rookery, leaving Roark to deal with the vulcan sacs. Deciding it was safest to go on foot, he proceeded down the trail. They had risked flying over the flooded areas once before. If necessary he could always take to the skies again. At least he knew what he was up against. And Roark would be okay. But Sybil?

He was worried about her. She had the worst job. To check out those halls, she would have to go inside. The thought of it made his skin crawl. 'I hope she's okay,' was his last thought before the ground disappeared from under him. He slid, landing with a squelching thud at the bottom of a gaping sinkhole. Water had seeped up through the soil washing away the under layers. He was up to his knees in a quagmire of mud.

"Bollywocks!" It was going to take a bit of maneuvering to get out.

"Peeeuw," he held his nose and gagged. "What's that smell?" He looked around for a decent foothold. On his left he spotted a boulder protruding from the side. He slogged his way through the muck and leaned on it. It seemed solid enough. He pulled one leg out of the mud and used his knee to hoist himself up. His other leg released with a sickening *shlop*.

The next handhold was a long way up. He sat on the boulder with his back to the wall. "What if I'm stuck here? Careless fool, serves you right," he mumbled. The gloom at the bottom of the pit began to play mind games. He sat there for several minutes, the nauseating stench competing with dread, until full blown panic rose up his gorge and choked him. His stomach heaved and he vomited his last meal into the muck below. Wiping his mouth on his sleeve, his mind eddied in a whirlpool of panic.

Suddenly hearing voices, he tried to call for help, but the words stuck in his throat. A ligature of fear had seized his neck, choking the life out of him. He closed his eyes and imagined Sybil and Roark out there coming his way. Slowly, the noose around his neck eased. He willed his mind to be still and his heart slowed its frantic drumming. He was about to call out again, but caught himself. He held still, quietly trying to make out what they were saying.

The muffled voices drew nearer.

"Aquadorus is in a foul mood. He's ordered all those who won't or haven't completed transition, to be rounded up."

"We'll find the last of 'em and good riddance to that scum."

Simon shrunk back under the overhang in the wall. It was Dimondus! He'd recognize that snarling voice anywhere. His skin prickled with apprehension.

"What about you? How much time have you left?"

"Don't worry about me. I am almost complete. On my way north to make the final transformation now," said Dimondus.

"Seventh Dimension oaths! Would you look at that hole!" said the other one.

Two faces appeared over the edge.

"Can you see to the bottom, Sladus?"

"Nah, pretty murky. And stink, ugh!" Their two heads disappeared.

Simon held his breath. It was poor dumb luck to run into the guy he feared most in all of Aquadria—worse than Aquadorus. He and Sybil both agreed on that. Aquadorus was cruel and ruthless. Dimondus was that, and more. He was cunning and unpredictable. He was sly and sneaky. You avoided him at all cost.

"We'll have to go around," said Sladus, stepping off the trail and heading into the undergrowth.

"Go ahead, I need a drink. I'll be right with you."

Hanging back, he waited to see how far he would get before another sinkhole opened. Once he saw Sladus had made it safely to the other side, he gingerly left the trail, stepping exactly where he had trod. Sladus was expendable.

"We'd better get moving. It's a long way north. We're heading to higher ground, so there shouldn't be a lot of mud ahead." Dimondus was determined to get there and make his final transition. He needed to get back to Aquadorus to prove his loyalty before he was replaced.

At the bottom of the sinkhole, Simon let his breath escape in a long, ragged flow. Glad, only moments before, that the sinkhole was deep enough to hide him, he again felt trapped. He had to get out. If Sybil was still up north in those halls, she'd be in trouble when Dimondus arrived.

Feeling along the sides in every direction, he encountered a root. Tugging it free, he began to gouge out a foothold. It was tedious work, but at last he had another place to step up into. He found another root and used it as an anchor while he worked on a second step.

Tired and discouraged, he stopped for a breather and swore under his breath. Never one to use profanity—Mother

Josie would never allow it—in this situation, it relieved his rising desperation. "Okay, stop it," he told himself. "You've got to do this."

He stood up straight and resumed digging, clinging tenuously to roots, rocks, whatever he could find. The smell was unbearable and his arms were aching. There wasn't much rest on a precarious toehold in the side of a sinkhole, but he kept at it, making his way to near the halfway mark.

"Simon…"

He thought he heard his name.

"Now I'm imagining things." Shaking the cobwebs free, he hesitated. Again, he thought he heard it—a faint disturbance in energy waves.

"Sybil? Is that you?" No reply. *"Sybil?"*

Nah, he was hearing things. No use getting his hopes up. He kept gouging at the wall, sweat dripping off his forehead. His tongue was sticking to the roof of his mouth.

Resting his weary arms, he leaned into the wall, which had begun to slope outward. "I'd even drink stale pool water, right about now."

"Simon, where are you?" Roark's squawky voice floated in.

This time Simon was positive. Roark and Sybil, what were the chances of hearing both voices.

"Roark! Sybil! I'm here!" Relief flooded through him. He knew he could count on Sybil. And Roark was a steadfast friend.

"Where are you?"

"I followed the rookery path under the cliff. A long way west of the hatchery nests. Where are you?"

"Should be coming up to you soon."

Sybil's sigh of relief got translated into Telepath unintentionally. She was desperately worried. They had been scouring the east trail and had to double back because of flooding. Twice, they hid from Aquadrian patrols. One of them was Dimondus. Attuned to every sound, his blustering complaints were easy to pick up.

"Be careful, there are sinkholes opening up. I'm trapped in one."

"Simon, what are you thinking? Just fly out!" Sybil's annoyance was discernable, even in Telepath. Simon was hurt by the tone, but he saw the folly of his thinking and had to admit he hadn't even considered it.

"I'm losing it." His automatic default was set to 'victim.' He had been captive too long and too often—each time had worn a groove in his psyche.

"Okay, enough of this!" He powered up, but nothing happened. Try as he might, he could not lift off.

"I'm trying, Sybil, but it's not working."

"Oh, come on. Put your mind to it. Mind over matter, right?"

"Nope, not this time. Something's stopping me."

Sybil and Roark rushed on, running as fast as Roark's grips would allow.

"We have to get to Simon before another patrol goes through."

"You go ahead, Sybil. Don't wait for me. My feet are slowing us up."

"No, we don't split up."

"Go, Sybil. It'll be fine. I'll catch up in due time."

Sybil felt her leg muscles kick into overdrive. Simon ahead, Roark behind—she needed to get this done fast. Rounding a bend in the trail she skidded to a halt, teetering on the rim of a sinkhole.

"Simon! You down there?" She peered over the side. Yes, she could just see the outline of a human form. "That you? Pheeew. What's that smell?"

"I'm here," he said, his voice laced with frustration.

"What's stopping you?" She covered her nose. Something

was rotten in that hole. It was overpowering.

"If I knew, I wouldn't be down here."

"Sorry, Simon, guess I'm under a lot of stress."

"Yeah, well you aren't the only one."

She could tell he was near breaking point. It had been a long time since she'd heard that fragile tone. She would have to take care how she spoke to him.

"Hang on, Simon. I'll try coming down to you."

"No, that's crazy. If I can't fly out, do you think you can?" His strength was depleted from all the digging and his nerves were frayed.

"Guess you have a point there. Roark is on his way. Maybe he'll have some ideas."

"Are there any branches or vines long enough to reach me?"

"Stay there, I'll have a look."

"Like I'm going anywhere?" Simon exploded in disgust.

"Okay, okay. No need to be cross with me."

"Who's cross?"

"You are!"

"No, you are!"

"Nooo…" she stopped. Hearing her own whiny voice, she checked her feelings and bit her tongue.

"Never mind, Simon. I'm frustrated. I admit it. Sorry. Don't worry, we'll get you out." She ducked into the forest in search of vines.

Simon leaned against the wall and waited. Shortly, he heard suction cups popping along the trail and Roark's wheezy squawk. "Man, I hate this walking. Fly me anywhere and I'm a happy guy."

"Roark, buddy! Good to hear you. Can you and Sybil get me out of here?"

"Why don't you fly out?" Roark's matter of fact reply made

things worse.

"Oh, not you, too."

"Shhh, Simon isn't very happy right now," warned Sybil. She had made a precursory hunt for vines, returning when she heard Roark.

"I can see that," said Roark, his voice hard as rock. He, too, was getting a bit testy after slogging along the trail. Suction cups were meant for cliff dwelling not forest hikes. "It's a wonder we weren't discovered with all the noise I make."

"Did you say something, Roark?"

"No, just mumbling to myself."

"Wonder what's stopping him from flying out."

"Don't know. Maybe the soggy underground is shorting out the energy flow for whatever it is you guys tap into."

"Or maybe it has to do with that awful smell. We'll have to look for a long branch or vines to pull him up. I've been out looking that way," she pointed to the south side of the trail. "Do you want to look on the other side, while I go around this hole and scout ahead?"

"I'm not much good on feet, so I'll stay close."

"Oh, Roark. You're just fine the way you are. Not everyone can run. You can fly fast."

He brightened up when he pictured himself soaring over the countryside. "Go on," he grinned, hoping to hear more. But Sybil was already off the trail and skirting the opening where Simon was trapped.

"I'll make myself useful, then," he muttered, heading into the greenery. He found a game trail that began to slope upward. Stepping off the trail he waded deeper into the lush vegetation. It wasn't long before he came to a ledge draped with cascading vines. He brushed them aside and discovered a cavernous opening.

"Say, this looks interesting." He brightened at the prospects of what he would find. A scuttling sound coming from inside, stopped him short. He didn't relish the idea of checking this out alone.

"Just what I need. Some of these vines. Have to get back quick," he said, loudly enough to alert the cave dweller.

He tugged on several vines with his strong red beak until he had enough to braid into a strong cord. Slinging them around his neck, he set off the way he'd come, leaving a trail of bent fronds pointing the way back to the game trail so he'd be sure to find it again.

"Sybil, Simon. I found vines." When he reached the sinkhole, he looked over the edge.

"Yeah, Roark. I'm still here. Haven't flown away," Simon's stab at humour fell short.

"I found a lot of vines. We can braid a rope and get you out. Have you heard from Sybil?"

"No, not since she left."

"I hope nothing's happened to her." Roark had an uneasy feeling. "I don't like it when we split up."

"Well, start braiding and we'll go look for her as soon as I am out of this muck."

"Braid with these feather fingers? It needs more dexterous appendages than mine."

"Oh, sorry. I guess that's true. Never thought much about it, Roark."

"Believe me, I wish I had fingers sometimes. They look so useful."

"I suppose, but wings are pretty useful, too. Drifting on air currents, keeping someone warm, fully waterproof—much better than an umbrella."

"Hah, I nearly forgot. I found a cavern up there along the cliff face. When I pushed the vines aside, I heard something inside the cave. As soon as we get you out, we should investigate."

"Sounds intriguing." Simon loved a mystery.

"Where is Sybil? I wish she'd hurry." Roark tried a telepathic message, but there was no answer.

"Drat and blast! Now I have to go looking for her." He hated the thought of heading out into the undergrowth again. Taking no chances, he hid the vines under a shock of fronds clustered near the trail.

"Back soon. I'm going to find out what's taking Sybil so long."

Roark headed south of the trail and skirted the sinkhole, avoiding the soft edges. It was lower on that side and he didn't want to end up sink-holed like Simon. He looked for signs of Sybil, discovering every now and then, a bent frond, a broken twig and compressed blades of grass. He found a softly planted shoe print and was satisfied he was close behind her.

Periodically he sent out a message. *"Sybil! Where the blazes are you? I found what we need. You can come back."*

There was no answer and Roark began to dread what lay ahead. "Why doesn't she answer? She can't have gone too far," he grumbled, stamping his feet. The suction cups popped in protest sending a wave of irritability up his legs.

He trudged along as quietly as his noisy feet would allow. When he heard a soft moan, he stopped, cocking his head first one way then another, as birds often do. A groan, this time louder, came from his left. Someone was in pain.

He picked his way carefully through the undergrowth, muttering about his shape. It was not conducive to squeezing through tight places and thick vegetation.

"Is that you, Sybil?" Roark was undecided. He hoped it was, but was afraid of what he would find.

"Roark?"

"Yes, I'm here," he replied.

In a moment he was bending over her. "When you didn't come back, we got worried. Where are you hurt?"

"My head. I must have slipped."

Roark brushed his wingtip over her skull. "Nasty bump you have there." His concern deepened when he saw blood flowing unimpeded. "Do you have your first aid kit on you, Sybil?"

"Under my cloak." She reached for it, pulled out a pad of gauze and applied pressure. After several minutes, the flow of blood had been staunched.

"Can you get up? Try walking."

Sybil wobbled to standing position and walked a short distance. Feeling a bit woozy, she sat down with her head in her hands. "Just give me a minute."

Roark sat beside her. "You'll be all right," he soothed, patting her arm gently.

"I don't know how I tripped. One minute I was walking, next I knew, I was lying in the bush and I hear your voice. How long I was there, I don't know."

Roark got up to search the bushes. He backtracked on Sybil's route and found a wire leading to a stake. A snare had been set. She must have tripped on the lead wire.

"Who would set a snare in this country?" he asked, showing Sybil the wire he pulled up, stake and all.

"A snare? Why would anyone need a snare?"

"Whoever it is, we can't wait around to find out. We need to help Simon."

"Better hurry. He's probably fretting about us," replied Sybil, getting to her feet. She brushed off bits of twig and leaves. Steadying herself, she began working her way up the trail.

"You sure you're okay, Sybil?"

"Yes, just needed a minute to clear the brain fog. One doozer of a headache, though."

Arriving back at the sinkhole she called out, "Simon, we're back."

Roark retrieved the vines he had hidden and Sybil sat down to braid them into a sturdy rope. She stopped occasionally to run her hand over the bump on her head.

Once she had the right length, she made a loop around one end and tied the other end to a tree trunk.

"Okay, Simon, we're lowering it in. Put it over your head and cinch it tight around your waist."

Simon did as ordered. He'd had enough of the muck and stink. "Okay, pull me up."

Sybil pulled on the rope as Roark leaned his weight against her, slowly edging backward until Simon neared the top. He clambered out of the hole and let out a whoop of relief.

"Thanks, sure glad to be out of that stinking hole." He was covered in mud and smelled like rotten eggs.

"Smells like sulphur," said Sybil.

"Sinkhole, stinkhole." Simon attempted to lighten the mood.

"Stink or not, we had better get moving," said Sybil.

"Where's Sirius?" asked Simon, disappointed.

"Thought it best we leave him with Mother Meerak until we found you. We'll fetch him on our way back."

"Roark said he discovered a cave. Tell her, buddy."

"Where I found these vines. They covered the entrance. I thought I heard something inside. We should go check it out." Roark's excitement was hard to contain.

"Do we have time?" Sybil asked. "We need to go back up north." She told Simon what she had discovered.

"Doesn't sound good. Dimondus came past with another guy before you arrived. He was headed north, saying something about making his final transformation."

"Yeah, we had to avoid him earlier. Doesn't he know that it's in the hands of northern forces?" Sybil was surprised. "How could he not know?"

"If he hadn't transitioned when the flooding began, maybe he was afraid to show his face. Aquadorus would not be pleased with him," suggested Simon.

"We can return and scout out the cave later," said Sybil. "Going north is more important right now." Seeing the disappointment on Roark's face, she reassured, "We'll come back as soon as we can, Roark."

"We'd better hurry. Dimondus is way ahead. He's with a guy called Sladus." The urgency in Simon's voice ignited a fire under his friends.

"Let's fly," suggested a forest-weary Roark. Walking had taken a toll. He was beginning to limp. His feet hurt and the suction cups were losing their grip.

"Too risky," said Sybil.

Roark grimaced. Sybil made sense, but he was tired and didn't know how much further he could walk.

"If we gain altitude fast, fly very high, we should be well out of view. We're not looking for anything below us anyway," Simon countered. "We want to get there fast."

Roark let out a sigh of relief, sending Simon a grateful nod.

He flapped his wings, lifted off, and rose above the forest canopy. Happy to have a load off his aching feet, he let them trail behind, making a graceful silhouette against the blue backdrop. Before Sybil could object, Simon joined him, watching her from above.

"Oh, all right. Have it your way." She lifted off and they headed north, high over the Black Spine Mountains that lay dark and moody below. Looking back, they could see the extent of the flooding. It was worse than imagined.

"No time to lose," said Simon, powering up speed. In their frenzied haste, they flew onward, forgetting about Sirius. Shortly, they landed in front of the Duplicating Hall where Sybil had left Rinaldo. The door was still ajar.

"Rinaldo, you still working here?" asked Sybil, peering around the opening into the business office.

"Yes, it's tedious work. I'm gathering information on those who haven't made final transition. I see here, Dimondus, the slimy-hearted scoundrel, hasn't transitioned. Wonder what the hold-up is."

"Oh, there you are." Looking up from the desk, he grinned as Simon appeared in the doorway. "Sybil told me about your arrival from Fifth. Good to have you two back. Glad you are safe."

"It was touch and go there for a while. I was in a sinkhole until Sybil and Roark came along."

"Who's this with you?" Rinaldo asked, appraising their brightly-feathered companion.

"Sorry, Rinaldo. This is our good buddy Roark from the Opeggee cliff colony."

"Nice to meet you, Roark. Your people must be frantic. This flood would wipe everyone out."

"Yeah, there was no way of knowing when this would begin and no way to stop it."

"Not all Aquadrians want this. There's an uprising. Aquadorus needs to be stopped."

"There is hope, then," said Simon. "We'll do what we can to help."

"Our scientists are working day and night. They're looking for the sequencing codes to reverse the physical mutations. Some of us have not taken well to the changes forced on us. I already have unexpected complications. See here, my ears," he extended a long finger and flapped it against the pink appendage protruding from the side of his head.

"They look like our ears," said Sybil. The implications resonated with their growing suspicions.

"Yes, they do. I don't know what is happening. We think our memories have been erased during the process. There is no recall of what has gone on before."

"Is there anyone left who can sort it out?" asked Simon.

"Those among us with scientific acumen seem to grasp things better. Not me, sorry to say. I have joined the task force devoted to searching files in these halls. Would you be willing to help with that?"

"Of course. Show us where to start," said Sybil.

"Over here," said Rinaldo. Pulling out chairs, he seated them each next to filing cabinets. "I've been flagging those I know who have not made transition. But you won't know who's who, so just note anything you think might be useful. Look for information that might help discover the transformation process."

Bending to the task, their nimble fingers flew through the drawers.

"I'm not any good at this," said Roark, fiddling with his wing feathers. He gave up, engaged his pointed red beak and riffled through papers, first scanning with his two green eyes, then double checking with his purple one. It had amazing optic abilities. Not much escaped its scrutiny. "That's better," he sighed, pleased with his resourcefulness.

"When we finish with this hall, we'll move to the next one. Herclan has assigned these last two to me. These morphing fingers get in the way. Thank you, it's much faster with your help."

They worked into the late afternoon, stopping only briefly to have a bite to eat. When Sybil produced enough food for all from the BanquoeBag, Rinaldo was flabbergasted.

"How does that thing work?" He stared at it, open-mouthed, his gills sucking uselessly. He didn't need to immerse in water like many of the other folks in Aquadria. To be sure, he had made a pretense of refreshment, but he found it unnecessary. His double life sharpened his skills at deceit.

"Never had it explained to us. A reasonable explanation might be some special form of time travel, is our guess. Food is retrieved from pantries designed especially for field missions. It's from Hetopia in the west of Fifth dimension. Amazingly resourceful civilization. If we all worked together, think of what we could accomplish," said Sybil.

Rinaldo was beginning to see the wisdom of this. Their unique dexterous fingers, ability to fly, Roark's three eyes and youthful enthusiasm, coupled with his own good concentration and fearless work ethic, could indeed bring about change.

"Yeah, just imagine what could be done." He had always liked these two, back in the city before the flooding. They were intelligent and sensitive to others. He'd experienced it firsthand. He trusted them.

"What did you find in the south?" Rinaldo had meant to ask earlier, but with all the work before them, it slipped his mind.

"Apart from that stink hole…" Oh crud. He had forgotten to mention that Dimondus was on his way north with Sladus.

"How could I forget? When I was in the sinkhole, Dimondus and a guy named Sladus came by and looked in. Luck had it, they couldn't see me and the stench drove them back soon enough. I heard Dimondus say he was on his way north to make his final transformation."

"Doesn't he know northern forces are in control of the halls? If we can intercept them, maybe we can get some information out of him. He's a coward and won't put up much resistance. Now Sladus. Not sure where he stands," said Rinaldo.

"Dimondus, he's a mean one." Sybil shuddered at the prospect of meeting him again. "How are we going to capture him?"

"Leave it to me. I will take our best patrol guards. Roark, do you think you could fly surveillance for us? Those eyes of yours will spot him coming a long way off. Opeggees are all over the skies, nothing new there. He won't suspect a thing."

"Boy, would I!" Roark was aching to stretch his wings after bending over files all afternoon. "When do we leave?"

"Right now. Sybil, can you and Simon handle these files and move on to the next hall while Roark and I do this?"

"Yes, of course. We won't let up until the job is done. Best of luck and stay safe, you two."

After they left, Sybil looked at Simon. "Can we do all this? Before they get back?"

"We'll give it our best shot." Simon dove into the last drawer and riffled through files. "Nothing here. That's the last on this side. How are you doing over there?" He stood to stretch his back and walked over to help.

"I am working my way through the last file. Take a look. Nothing about information on codes."

"We're finished here. Now, on to the next hall," said Simon.

They made their way back through the mirror maze and the Echo Chamber.

"Say! What if someone has already found the information? It is encrypted when they pass through the Echo Chambers." Sybil recalled her first encounter with this secret coding system. "They could be working in circles and not even know it."

"This hall isn't powered up, but what about the other halls, do they have power?

"We may have to go through everything ourselves. How do we tell others? They don't speak Telepath?" said Simon.

"If the Echo Chambers are powered up in the remaining halls, no problem. The Echo Chamber doesn't encrypt Telepath. We can translate automatically. If they're without power, no problem."

"This is a colossal job." Simon's face furrowed, thinking of the work ahead. "We could sure use Roark here."

"As soon as they get back, we'll haul him in and let him know what we're up against."

Discovering that all halls were unpowered, they got seated once more to the task, working feverishly into the night. Herclan, aware of the urgent hunt, had ordered supplemental lighting until the task was finished.

By morning, Sybil and Simon had been introduced to the remaining halls and decided to work alongside other Aquadrians. Maybe they could discover some other useful information in the process.

At Fifth Hall, they stopped to take a break.

"Why is this hall so much bigger than the others?

"I wondered that," said Sybil. "About the same size as the administrative hall in Leanoria."

"A connection?"

"That's my guess."

Their eyes were tired, their backs ached from bending over files and Sybil's head had begun to throb.

"I'm going to close my eyes for a moment, Simon. My head feels like a bomb, ready to explode."

"Go ahead. I'll get us some tea." He led her over to an alcove and reached into the BanquoeBag. It was always tricky to retrieve hot drinks without spilling a drop or two. He set the BanquoeBag on top of a cabinet tucked in the corner and pulled forth two mugs of steaming-hot tea.

Dog tired and weary to the bone, he lowered himself to the floor and leaned against the cabinet. His gaze came to rest on a keyhole.

"Why is this one locked?" Feeling the back of it, he hunted for a key. Nothing. He slid his hand underneath and felt along the edge. There…something hard and unmovable. It was held fast by, what? Tape? Magnetic…was it magnetic?

"Sybil! Come here," he whispered, nudging her arm. She had dozed off.

"What?" His urgent tone alerted her instantly. "What is it? Did you find something?"

"Yes, maybe. This cabinet is locked. None of the others are. It looks the same except for the keyhole. I think there's a key underneath, but I can't budge it."

"Let me try!" Sybil's excitement caused ripples in the folk on the other side of the room.

"Shh! We don't know what this is."

"Yeah, and who knows about the people in here. What if there are spies?" They had come too far and worked too hard to have it all go sideways.

To provide cover, she pulled a jar from the BanquoeBag. "Let me try," she said again, making a pretense of opening the jar to allay suspicions.

They kicked back for a while, leaning on the cabinet drinking their tea. The people across the room resumed work.

Sybil reached under the front of the cabinet and felt for the key. It was stuck fast.

"How are we going to pry it loose?" she asked.

"You think it's magnetic?"

"Might be. Let's both try. I'll get my fingernail under one side and you try the other."

"Okay, you in position, Sybil?"

"Got it. Heave ho." Her nail bed ached as she pried her way under the edge. Simon worked at it from the opposite side. It popped off suddenly, falling to the floor with a clatter. She covered it with her hand and slid it out from under the cabinet, checking the room to see if they were being watched.

Handing it to Simon, she said, *"Here, you keep it in your pocket."*

"Not sure that's a safe place."

"Where else, then?"

"I don't know. I'd hate to lose it."

"Is my pocket any safer?"

"Point taken. How will we check this cabinet?"

"We'll figure it out."

"Okay, tea break is over. Back to work." Simon slid the key into his left pocket and patted it for safety.

Later that day, when the search teams had determined to move on, he and Sybil slipped back to Fifth Hall. Coming to the business section, they crossed the floor quietly and inserted the key into the locked cabinet. It turned with a click. When he tugged, the drawer slid open.

"What's in it?" asked Sybil.

"Usual files. Nothing seems different."

"Try the next drawer."

"Same, only these seem to have—what? A colour code?"

"Maybe. Why a colour code?"

"What else could it be?"

"It reminds me of the Great Hall in Fifth Dimension, those rainbow hues."

"Nah, no connection."

"I know, but it seems odd. Maybe it's a sign."

"A sign? Of what?"

"Check the red file."

Simon withdrew the red folder and opened the cover.

Inside was a holographic strip. He tapped it gently and the holograph opened before them.

"What is it?" Simon asked.

"Looks like DNA print outs. Or genetic codes…" In each file they found more of the same.

"Why are they colour coded?"

"Does each colour represent a different species or maybe another realm?"

"Don't know. Possible, I guess."

Moving on to the last drawer at the bottom, afraid of what they'd find, Simon slowly cracked it open. Blinding light streamed forth.

"Close it, quick!" cried Sybil, pushing his hand.

It snapped shut, but the room had taken on an eerie glow. The radiant energy permeated the space, then slowly dissipated.

"What was that?" Sybil's hands trembled with fear.

"Scary! This could be dangerous. Let's wait for Rinaldo to get back."

He locked the drawer, replaced the key in his pocket, and turned to leave.

"Listen! Someone's coming. Hide!"

"Where?" Sybil's desperate plea sent a surge of blood thumping through her aching head.

Simon shoved her in front of him toward the maze leading to the Duplicating Chamber.

"We can't go in there."

"Where else can we hide?"

There was no choice. They stepped into the mirrored maze and hovered near the edge, hoping whoever was coming would not follow.

"Who is it? Can you see?" Sybil asked.

"Not yet." He stepped back instinctively as the footfalls

neared. Someone had entered the room. He shrunk against the wall, shielding Sybil protectively behind him.

"Shh, not a sound. Someone is in there."

"What are they doing?"

Simon peeked around the doorway. There were two of them, but their backs were toward him and he couldn't tell who they were. *"They're rummaging around in file drawers."*

"Has to be in this hall. It's the biggest. It should be here somewhere," a frustrated voice rasped. "We've been through two already."

"Check that cabinet over there. It looks different," said the other one.

As they headed toward the back of the room, Simon peeked out again, this time catching a glimpse of a profile.

"It's Dimondus!"

"No!" Sybil went weak in her legs. She hated that feeling. Locking her knees, she managed to stay upright. *"What are they doing?"*

"Checking that cabinet."

"Supposed to be a key hidden somewhere," Dimondus said, sliding his long green fingers along the bottom front edge. "Hmm, I don't feel a key, but there is a place where one would have fit. It's not there, Sladus!"

"But we need the codes or we can't transform!" shouted Sladus.

"Quiet, you imbecile. You'll have the whole compound down on us."

"What are we going to do?"

"I don't know. How was I supposed to know northern forces were in control up here? Don't worry, we'll figure something out. We have to find a place to lay low for a while. Sladus, you can walk amongst them. They'd recognize me, but you; they don't know much about you."

"Me? Why me?"

"You're such a whiner. I told you, nobody will recognize you. You'll fit in. Keep your ears open and find out what's going on."

Sladus trembled. He wasn't sure which was worse, roaming about in enemy territory or suffering the wrath of Dimondus.

"Okay," he gave in weakly, shoulders sagging in defeat.

"We'll leave when it's dark. Hard enough making our way here in the daylight. Can't take any more chances."

"Where do you think they'll go, Simon?"

"Don't know. We'll have to wait."

After the gloom dissolved to inky blackness, Dimondus and Sladus slipped from the room and left the hall. Sybil and Simon moved out, discretely following their shadows weaving between the halls. Trailing at a safe distance, they soon realized the two were headed toward the pit where the dragon had been held.

"No one will want to check that pit," reasoned Dimondus. He had heard wild tales circulating in the city. Aquadorus was in a terrible rage over the dragon's escape. He opened the flood gates out of desperation, hoping to level the city before the balance of power shifted.

"I had no idea it would happen this soon, or I would have done the last transformation. Now I'm stuck. We have to find that key."

"Aquadorus doesn't care about us," whined Sladus.

"Silence! Don't talk about the Emperor that way. He's promised me a promotion."

"What if we can't find the codes?"

"Imbecile. Circulate among the crowds and keep your eyes and ears open tomorrow." Dimondus cuffed the back of his head. Then he grinned. "You can do it, Sladus. You have to."

Sladus slunk along beside him, chastised and fearful. Why

did he get mixed up with this guy? He should have heeded the warnings his friends had tried to give him. He kicked himself for not listening and wondered if it was too late to change sides.

Sybil and Simon watched as they approached the pit.

"You go first, Sladus. I'll keep a lookout."

"First? We don't know what's in there."

"Yeah, you go first. I'll keep watch outside."

With cautious trepidation, Sladus edged his way deeper into the pit. It was fearfully dark and he hated himself. He was being used, but he could not stand up to Dimondus. He feared him and could not resist.

"Okay," he hesitated. "It seems okay. I don't hear or see anything. Course it's awfully dark. Can't tell for sure, though."

"Well, make sure, you oaf. Can't count on you for anything."

"O-o-kay," his voice wavered. Then he took a deep breath and tiptoed deeper, feeling his way along the side. Soon he reached the back and realized it curved and was heading back the way he had come.

"Nothing down here," he called back. This time a measure of certainty satisfied Dimondus. It was safe to enter.

"Good job, Sladus." Dimondus slapped his back. He had to keep him under his control.

Sladus felt mollified, but he was getting fed up. Dimondus was not his friend. He knew that now. He was certain that his future with him was finite. He was beginning to think they didn't stand a chance. Aquadorus's time might be up, too. Then what? No, if given the chance, he would join northern forces. Settled in his decision, he lay back on the soft sand of the pit, while Dimondus snored loudly. There was no sleep for him. He laid awake waiting until morning.

Bleary-eyed, Sladus shook Dimondus. "Wake up. It's

morning."

"Hmmph! Let me sleep. You get up and see what's going on out there. When you find out something, come back and let me know."

Sladus emerged from the pit, found a stream of water west of the compound, refreshed, and washed the sand from his sleepless eyes. He crept into town, mingling with the crowds readying for battle. The determination on their faces reinforced his decision to join them.

CHAPTER THREE
The Trek

"I like nonsense. It wakes up the brain cells. Fantasy is a necessary ingredient in living."

- Dr. Seuss.

Once Dimondus and Sladus were settled for the night, Sybil and Simon retreated to the halls. Without sleep for two days and weary to the bone, they curled up under the sheltering overhang of the furthermost hall.

"What's keeping Rinaldo and Roark?" Sybil's worried tone stirred anxiety in Simon.

"Well, we know they haven't found Dimondus and Sladus. Must have slipped past them on their way south. I should've remembered to tell Rinaldo sooner. How could I forget that?"

"Or maybe Dimondus and Sladus…" cringing at the thought, she stopped in mid-sentence not daring to speak the unthinkable. "They'll be back soon—it's working out for the best. At least we know where Dimondus is right now."

Dread hung in the air between them. What if they *had* found Dimondus?

"If they aren't back by morning we'll go looking for them."

"Agreed, but we should alert Herclan about Dimondus and Sladus in the pit," said Sybil.

"Not tonight. I'm too tired to go any further," said Simon.

The first light of morning filtered through leaden skies when Simon made the first move. Cramped and stiff, they got up and stretched, going through yoga poses, followed by a few moments of gentle quiet time. After mornings at the Wellness Sanctuary, sitting in silence came naturally to them. The routine focused their inner resources, preparing them for the day.

"I'm starving. How about you?" asked Simon.

"Why don't we go to the mess hall this morning? See what's for breakfast."

"You know the way?"

"No, but a brisk walk will do us good. Follow the crowds. They'll be going there to eat."

Carried along by the sea of people, delectable aromas began to waft toward them.

"Crisp fish strips! I'd know that smell anywhere. I love those." Simon's stomach growled in anticipation.

Soon they were seated on benches beside other folks, eagerly devouring their breakfasts. Curious looks turned their way.

"Hey there, lass. Ain't ya ta one who shined up my flippers?" An old gentleman across the table gave her a grin. "Best'est spit polish ever. T'ya remember me?"

"Yes, certainly I do," Sybil smiled, brightened by the prospect of a familiar face. "How are you, sir?"

"Well ting's changed fer sure since den. S'pose can't git no worse. Maybe dey could. Hard times dese days."

Sybil nodded politely and went back to her breakfast.

When they had finished, they carried their trays, cleared their dishes and made their way through the throng of people.

As they were leaving, someone called out, "Sybil!"

Startled, she pivoted and searched the crowd. An older

gentleman pushed his way through the thronging mass.

"By golly! Been looking for you. Good to see you survived the flood." He patted her arm and gave her an unabashed hug.

Surprised and happy, she beamed at her benefactor. He had saved her life and she never did find a way to repay him.

"Dr. Teselwode! How wonderful to see you," she hugged him back. "How did you know my name?"

"I suspected you had a cover story when Simon, here, let your name slip. You know—that day when I treated you in the cells."

"I did?" Simon was aghast.

"Can't blame you. It was touch and go for a while. You were a pretty distraught young man. Old Dimondus was so worried about himself and what Aquadorus would do to him, well, I guess he never heard it."

"Wheeeew," Simon let out a whistle of relief. "Sure am glad of that."

"Oh, I sort of covered a bit for you. It didn't seem like much at the time, but a snort here and harrumph there, distracted him soon enough."

"Thank you, Dr. Teselwode. Now, I really do need to repay you."

"Harrumph. Nonsense, I am just glad you are here and safe. Lost track of what happened to you two after that."

"How did you know we were here?" asked Simon.

"Rinaldo told me, before he went south with that friend of yours. He asked me to make contact with you. So here I am," he grinned.

"Sure is nice to see you. Can't tell you how grateful we are—for Sybil I mean." Simon's face lit up at the memory of her recovery.

"Balderdash! That's my job; especially young folks. Good to see 'em back to life. I love it."

Meeting a second familiar face today was a bonus. Things were looking up. Now, if only Rinaldo and Roark would show up. Simon's present mood waned as worry set in.

"How about we meet here for dinner, say, around five bells?" Dr. Teselwode suggested. "I'd love to get to know you better."

"Sorry, Dr. Teselwode. We're worried about Roark and Rinaldo. About ready to head south to find them. They should have been back long ago," said Simon. "This doesn't feel right."

"Not necessarily. They could still be searching for Dimondus." Sybil's matter-of-fact statement cooled the turbulent broiler of doubt searing Simon's brain.

"Perhaps," said Dr. Teselwode. "It's best to be safe and check it out."

"If we are back on time, we'd love a visit," replied Sybil. "If we are late…"

Dr. Teslewode stepped in reassuringly. "I'll alert Herclan. He'll send reinforcements."

"We'll set off now, Dr. Teselwode. Thank you so much and we'll see you soon."

The kindly old gentleman wished them luck. He shook their hands, gave them a pat on their shoulders and urged them to be careful. "Come find me when you get back."

After finding Herclan, they reported what they knew about Dimondus and Sladus and told him of their decision to go south. Herclan offered the use of equipment and they prepared for the trip, packing necessary items.

Keeping in mind that Roark would probably touch base at the rookery, they left right after breakfast and landed in front of Meerak's home.

"Have you seen Roark?" The question, preceding social

greetings, tumbled out of their mouths in a cascade of nervous anxiety.

"He left here with that fellow Rinaldo two days ago," replied Meerak. "I never thought I'd live to see the day an Aquadrian would scale that cliff. Determined sort."

"He has cause to be concerned and is anxious to reassure the Opeggee nation. He will prove to be a reliable ally."

"Roark was very stalwart in his praise of the fellow. Good to learn there is opposition to Aquadorus. There is still hope for us."

"Did they say which way they were going?" asked Simon.

"It seems to me they were planning to check the surrounding area for pockets of resistance, people who may need help," replied Meerak. "Rinaldo was concerned about the far southern areas, past city limits. He was going to try to find a way across."

"He's pretty adept in water. Hasn't made full transition, but still..." A thought occurred to Sybil. His ears were changing. If he was losing aquatic ability, would he lose some of his prowess in water? The thought hung around the periphery of her consciousness, creating a deep sense of unease.

Though it would take longer, Simon and Sybil felt it was best to fly high, take a circuitous route west of the city and access the south safely.

"We'll call in on our way back, Meerak. Don't worry."

In their harried state, they had lost track of Sirius, who lay sleeping in a dejected heap in Roark's home. Confined, living the life of a house dog was more than he could bear. He longed to be free, roaming the countryside with his friends, following scents in long, grassy meadows, tracking for his humans. His ears perked up when he heard Simon and Sybil, but his will had been trammelled. He had been left too many times. When they departed, the heaviness of loss settled once more. He let out a soft whimper, as hope faded yet again.

"Don't fret, Sirius. They'll come back for you," Meerak brushed his head with her wing tip.

Her reassuring voice did little to alleviate his clouded vision. He plopped his head on his forepaws and let out a deep rumble of discontent.

"Did you hear that? It sounded like Sirius. We were in such a rush when we went north." Remorse washed over Sybil. "Roark must have left him with Meerak. Rinaldo could have taken to water, while Roark flew."

They did an about turn, calling out to Meerak, "Is Sirius still here?"

She poked her head around the doorway of her home, "Roark and Rinaldo left him. They were in such a state."

"We'll take him with us. Poor fellow. He likes to be free," said Simon.

Meerak disappeared and returned with the hound. "He's been a little despondent without you." The sad eyes held a glint of accusatory hurt.

"Sorry, boy." Simon knelt and caressed his head. "Being cooped up is not your style. That won't happen again."

Sybil crouched beside him, circling her arms around his torso. "You're with us now, for good." She pulled a peace offering, his favourite dried beef sticks, from the BanquoeBag and held it out to him. She caressed his ears as he snatched the treat. His tail began to wag. Soon, his whole body wriggled with happiness.

"Hop on, Sirius," said Simon. The hound, restored to good humour, needed no further invitation.

Making their way west, they flew over the sinkhole where Simon had been trapped. They could smell the foul odor even at the altitude they were flying.

"Must have been the gases in that pit. That's why you couldn't fly out. Can't think why else."

"I felt weak all over, no energy. Maybe it was the digging."

A hidden presence below watched as they passed over. Anxiety rippled the atmosphere, sending waves of discontent skyward.

"Do you feel that?" Sybil's sixth sense caught a waft of deep distress.

"It's as though we flew through a heavy, black cloud." Simon shook his shoulders, casting off the feeling that had sent shivers along his arms.

"Whatever it is, it will have to wait."

"Check it out on the way back?" Simon's raised eyebrow sent a query. "Ignoring things like that could be costly."

Sybil nodded in agreement. She'd had too many premonitions and knew better than to pass over them lightly. There was something to be known, something needed to be learned. It was always that way with her. It made sense Simon would feel the same.

"Yes, on the way back."

Arcing toward the southern shores of the submerged city, they soon discovered a lot of people had been caught on the other side. They had migrated south-west and were camped out in forest groves.

Gaining altitude they perused the lay of the land from a distance.

"Which camp should we make contact with first?" asked Simon.

"Let's take our time."

Drifting on the winds coming up from the south, they allowed themselves the luxury of a brief reprieve.

"Simon, do you think we'll ever get back to Hetopia?" She didn't dare think about Third dimension. Homesickness came in waves and it was all she could do to keep herself from abandoning the scene below. Why care about what happens here? It wasn't her business. She should just go home.

Resisting the dangerous line of thought that had been allowed to creep in, she steeled her nerves. Roark was down there. His family was in danger. He would never abandon her. The safety of Fifth and Third were at stake. She had to care.

"What's our next move?"

Simon didn't answer. His attention was focussed on a flash of bright blue in the landscape below. The lapis lazuli hue flitted in and out of view, darting here and there under the dense canopy.

"Sybil, look over there," he motioned. "Is that Roark?"

"Can't tell from here. Let's get closer," she said. Accelerating forward, they swooped in a gentle arc toward the treetops.

A blue figure scurried about below, talking to people, assuring them of support by the Opeggee nation. "If we can't get through, we can shelter many of you on the cliff top. We'll make room. You can join the northern force when it's safer."

Rinaldo appeared beside him. "Yes, folks. It's true. The Opeggees are trustworthy. We need all the support we can find and they need us."

"Then we're with you," said many in the crowd gathered around them.

Sybil and Simon let out a collective sigh of relief. Roark and Rinaldo were safe and what's more, they had found refugees willing to go north to swell the ranks of the uprising.

After nightfall when the camps were settled, Sybil and Simon made their way through dense bush where Roark and Rinaldo had bivouacked.

"Roark, are you there?" asked Sybil.

Roark's persistent training in self-discipline had paid off. The only sign that he'd heard her, was a slight dip of his head.

"Yes, we're here. Rinaldo is with me."

"Where are you set up?" asked Simon.

"Where are you now?"

"We're near a creek. Not far from the tallest tree in the area."

"Follow the stream and you'll find us. We're camped beside it."

Emerging into a small clearing several minutes later, Sybil and Simon loped toward the campsite. "Roark, Rinaldo! Thank goodness you're safe. We've been worried sick."

"We're fine." Roark disliked the slightest implication that he couldn't take care of himself. "Nothing to worry about."

"Sure, buddy. We hadn't heard from you, missed you. Can't help worrying." Sybil's calmness smoothed the situation. "Hi, Rinaldo. Good to see you."

"Sybil, Simon. You're a welcome sight! We can use some help getting organized tomorrow."

"Looks like you and Roark have found a lot of reinforcements," said Simon.

"We're about ready to pull up camp and head north. It'll take a while on foot. Tomorrow I'll introduce you and Sybil around. We divided them into groups of thirty and will move out a few minutes apart."

"Rinaldo and I think it's best to travel in small groups. There are women and children, so two men at the front and two as a rear guard for each group. We're going as far as the rookery," Roark beamed.

"The rookery? Up that steep cliff?" asked Simon.

"No, we discovered a better way. Rinaldo and I used it coming from the north. It means a longer walk, but at least it will be safer."

"There are people of many abilities. A lot of them won't make the north in one trip. Roark says we can rest up at the rookery and go on from there when we're ready." Rinaldo gave Roark a grateful pat on his back.

"I will fly as scout and warn the lead party if enemy patrols come their way," said Roark.

"We can help with that, Roark. But we'll fly at a higher altitude to avoid being spotted," offered Sybil.

"And you can send me Telepath. I can get word to the groups below. Bird's-eye view," Roark said, his chest feathers ruffling with pride.

"We'll swing wide to the west, away from civilization, then cut north and come in from the back of the rookery. With frequent stops for the children, it should take a little more than a week, if all goes well," added Rinaldo.

Pulling up camp in the morning was easy. In their desperate haste to flee, they arrived with very little and had settled in the open, huddling together for warmth. Women readied the children while Sybil and Simon shared out rations from their BanquoeBag. Although the food was a bit foreign to the Aquadrian palate, hunger took care of any dislikes and the children munched ravenously.

Setting off as intended, a few minutes between each group, they made steady progress, stopping frequently for rest breaks and snacks. Those who needed to refresh, immersed in nearby streams. The first and second day went smoothly. On the third, Roark spotted an Aquadrian patrol heading on a trajectory that would overtake the refugees. In order to avoid the point of interception, they would have to step up their pace.

He alerted Rinaldo at the head of the column, who issued orders. Roark flew down the line warning of the imminent danger, exhorting all to hurry.

The older children began to weary as the day wore on.

From above, Roark could see the advancing Aquadrian force closing on them. The last group was in danger. He flew along the line encouraging them. Men and women, already carrying the very young in their arms, bent to hoist older children onto their backs. Exhaustion was taking its toll and the pace slowed.

Overseeing progress, Roark was alarmed. It would be a close encounter.

"Do you see another route?" he messaged. *"Any other patrols advancing from a different direction?"*

Simon and Sybil, who had a broader view, were watching the dangerous scene unfolding.

"Maybe that last group needs to stop and let the Aquadrians pass," suggested Simon.

"I think that's best," agreed Sybil.

"Okay, I trust your judgment." Roark responded instantly, dropping low to the group once again.

"You're not going to make it. It's best to stop and take cover until the patrol passes."

"You sure about that?" asked Madonus, who was leading the group.

"Positive. Take cover in the underbrush. Keep the children quiet."

The weary group of stragglers backtracked to a densely forested area they had just come through and dove into the undergrowth.

Sheltering in absolute silence, they heard the advancing Aquadrians tramping through the brush. The low drone of voices, increasing in volume, became distinct conversation.

"A lot of 'em fled south; we know that for certain. Our Intelligence now tells us they've left. Making their way north. Have to step up our presence, catch 'em in between."

"Aquadorus has dispatched three more regiments. They're

spreading out along the frontier. They won't slip by on us."

A wave of dread shuddered through Madonus. If they were covering the frontier, it would be virtually impossible to make it through.

"Step it up, troops!" The voices receded and faded out in the distance.

Madonus summoned Roark. "What chance is there to get through? You heard 'em. They're closing down the frontier."

"Right now, we must catch up to the main column," replied Roark. "You get everyone moving and I will scout out the route."

He took to the skies, leaving the weary refugees to regroup. Roark could see the defeat setting in. Being cut off from Rinaldo's party was unnerving them. Some were clearly fatigued, still needing to top up oxygen levels regularly. They would have to find water soon or these folks weren't going to make it.

As he flew north, he spotted the last group of Rinaldo's column. Although they had stopped for a short break, they appeared in much better shape. Following the columns onward he found Rinaldo at the lead and dropped in beside him.

"Aquadorus is reinforcing the frontier. Troops are on their way now to cut off escape. The last group had to take cover to let an Aquadrian patrol pass and many of them need refreshment. We must find water," advised Roark.

"So, that *is* becoming a problem since we left the south," said Rinaldo. "I was afraid of that. It is why I organised them according to ability. Believed it was the best chance for success. Any suggestions?"

"I can scout the way," replied Roark. "I know water has reached our old nesting grounds. Could be streams or pools in the low areas on the way."

"Find water and catch up with us when you can. Keep in touch."

Flying off, he linked up with Sybil and Simon, alerting them to the problem. They flew in different directions with Sirius electing to remain with Simon.

From above, it was clear they were cut off from Rinaldo's group. More Aquadrians were advancing swiftly from the south. They must find water and take refuge. Simon reluctantly thought of the cave. It was shelter, but at what cost?

"Hey, Roark. Buddy, can you hear me?"

"I'm here, Simon."

"What about that cave you found? Think we should head in that direction?"

"Could do. Good place to hide. But what's in that cave?"

"I'd sure like to find out," replied Simon, curiosity overcoming his fear. He loved a mystery and exploring was in his nature. *"Let's ask Sybil, see what she thinks."*

Roark flew further north, putting out telepathic messages until Sybil answered.

Apprised of the plan, she agreed. "Might be worth the risk. I'll find Rinaldo and tell him."

Roark headed back to Simon while Sybil flew on, locating the column far ahead. Rinaldo had made good progress. Most of his people were more adept at moving across country. They hadn't morphed as easily and were able to remain out of water for longer periods.

"Rinaldo, people in our group are doing poorly. We need to find water and more troops are on their way from the south. We think it would be safer to take them to a cave Roark found earlier."

"Is there water nearby?"

"I believe so. We did pass flood water earlier down that

way."

"Right, then. It might be the best option for now."

"The countryside is crawling with Aquadrians. We really have no choice. If we make it to the cave, at least they aren't exposed."

"Are the three of you willing to take them into that area?"

"I suppose…" Sybil hesitated. "What are your plans, Rinaldo? Don't you want to come with us?"

"Our best chance is to push through. We're well ahead of the Aquadrian patrols. And the stamina of these people—well I think it's in their best interest."

"I hate to split up. We need you, Rinaldo."

"We are already strung out a long distance. I can't see doubling back with my group. If the frontier becomes impassable…" He sent a questioning look her way. "Instead of the Opeggee rookery, it makes more sense to go north with those who are capable of the distance. I will take these people to safety and rejoin you later with reinforcements. We can use their talents up north."

Seeing the logic in Rinaldo's reasoning, she reluctantly agreed. "We'll do our best here. Be safe, Rinaldo."

"Thank you, Sybil. I trust you and Simon. And Roark is a capable fellow. You'll make it work."

"I will alert the rest of your groups to the rear. Maybe it is best they join up with you, now. You are on your own, without us as messengers."

"Right, we'll need to stick together from here on. Hurry, Sybil, spread the word."

Anxiously waiting in thick undergrowth, Rinaldo fidgeted with his tunic sleeve. He did not know if he was making the right decision, but uncertainty lay in all directions.

Sybil returned shortly to inform him that his people were on their way.

"Do you want me to wait or see to the others?"

"You go, Sybil. We can manage from here. Your group is in more danger. Wishing you all haste and safety."

Now that she and Simon were to travel on land with them, many of the Aquadrians hung back, alarmed by Sirius. Roark alleviated some of the tension by entertaining them with tricks he had taught the hound. Once they saw that Sirius was a friendly sort who enjoyed attention, they realised he was harmless. When they learned he was a good tracker and could warn them of danger, they were reassured.

"Roark knows of a cave east of here," said Sybil. "I just came from Rinaldo. He thinks it is best to hide there until he can return with reinforcements. He is going to push north to safety before the frontier becomes impassable."

"He's leaving us behind!" said Sardonica. His voice held a fine tremor, betraying his fear. A look of anger crossed his face, but he held his tongue.

"No, he isn't *leaving* you behind," said Sybil. "This group can't keep up."

"Rather than wait for us and risk everyone, it is better he takes that group north," said Madonus.

"It's best to find safety. We can hide in the cave," said Simon.

"You sure you know where this is?" A restlessness swept through the crowd, fed by Sardonica's doubt. The children clung to their mothers, clearly aware of the situation.

"Roark can find it again," Simon replied. "Can't you, buddy?" He gave Roark an encouraging thump on his shoulder.

"You bet! I'm your wingman," he replied, flapping his bright blue wings. The children giggled, adding some levity to the dire situation. "It isn't all that far. You can do it."

Determined to march through the night to make safety, they conserved energy by trudging on in silence, concentrating on the way ahead. Stopping for short breaks alleviated their fatigue. Sybil was aware of the children who braved the situation with stoic faces. They were respectful of their elders and minded cautionary corrections.

It was nearing morning before a longer rest was called and snacks were distributed. They had made good progress and were at the west end of the trail that lead to the rookery cliffs.

Madonus approached Sybil. "Many of us are in need of refreshment. We must find water soon."

"Roark, will you make a quick search for a stream or low-lying areas for flood water?" asked Sybil.

"Right-o," replied Roark. "Back in a jiff." He flew off, circling the area methodically. The pale morning light illuminated the landscape below. To the right of the trail, not far along, he encountered the first of a series of shallow pools large enough for the Aquadrians to use.

Arriving back with a flourish of wings, he announced his findings. "Not far ahead, off to the right. I found water!"

A silent cheer went up from the Aquadrians, relief animating their faces. They were on their feet, moving in the direction Roark had indicated.

Submerging in the pools, they took in oxygen, storing it in reserve. After the much-needed refreshment, they regrouped, energized and ready to move on.

Advancing down the trail, a foul odour began to waft from ahead. They were nearing the sinkhole and Simon cautioned everyone to wait while he went on alone. Determining it was safe enough, he returned and motioned them to follow.

Stepping off the trail to his left toward the cliff side, Roark led the way to where he had gathered vines. He was sure he could find the way back, but it took him a while to pick up the trail of markers he had left. Although bent twigs had straightened out, a few remained crimped at an angle pointing in the direction of the cave.

He approached hesitantly, fearing the unknown. Sirius had stuck close to him and was part of the advance guard. Simon and Sybil flanked Sirius, one on either side. A low rumble in his throat warned them of something ahead.

"Steady, Sirius," cautioned Simon. "Easy, boy. We'll go in together."

Roark dropped behind, letting them lead the way. Standing outside the cave entrance, listening for evidence of presence within, they satisfied themselves it was at least safe enough to make a small foray into the cave opening. Brushing aside the vines, they entered and made a short scouting expedition. It was roomy and extended far enough back to house the Aquadrians. Sirius sniffed the floor and whined. He began tracking a scent around the cave interior. Simon caught his ruff and held him.

"Not now, boy. We'll check it out in a minute. First, we need to bring everyone inside."

Sybil returned to the entrance and waved everyone forward. "Come in, there's plenty of space."

Roark entered with a sigh of relief. "My aching feet," he muttered as he popped his suction cups and sat down with a thump on the nearest rock. "I don't know about you, but I am famished. I could eat the berries off a Snakebush. " He patted his rumbling stomach.

"You don't want to do that," said Sybil, telling him of her deadly encounter with the bush.

"Of course not. I'm being facetious. But I could sure use some of those delicious Hetopian rations."

"I am just about to distribute food. Can you give me a hand?"

"What? Me with these lovely blue wing feathers, give you a hand?" He chuckled at the idea. "Best if I watch them line up for food."

"You are my *wingman*," she corrected, laughing at her faux pas. She loved Roark and saw how easy he was in his own being.

"Yep, your wingman, not your handyman." He burst into a full-blown belly laugh. It was contagious and soon the whole cave was chuckling, especially when the joke got around.

Once the tired fugitives had eaten and chosen places to curl up for a nap, the cave settled for the afternoon.

"Let's explore this cave," suggested Simon. "Bring your illuminator, Sybil."

"I wonder how deep it goes. And what did Roark hear? He thinks it might be occupied."

"I know what I heard," said Roark, joining the conversation. "Could be the one who set that snare in the forest."

"Well, we won't find out anything by standing around here," said Sybil. "But first I will tell Madonus what we are up to."

"A real adventure!" cried Roark, his earlier reticence about the cave faded after his afternoon rest.

"Madonus said he'd come in after us if we're late," said Sybil. "He'll cover our backs."

CHAPTER FOUR
Spelunking

"I have not failed. I've just found 10,000 ways that won't work."

- Thomas A. Edison

Sirius set off at a fast trot, his nose to the cave floor, sniffing out a trail that led in haphazard fashion. His tail stood alertly skyward, his jowly face serious with concentrated effort.

"Atta boy," said Simon. "See where this goes."

The trail led deeper through narrow passages, eventually opening into a broad expanse. Flashing her illuminator across a large pool, Sybil cried, "Wow! Can you believe it?" High above, a cascading waterfall poured out of a fissure and plummeted into the churning froth below. "The Aquadrians can refresh here in safety."

"What a piece of luck!" agreed Simon, grinning from ear to ear. "Best thing we've found so far."

Sirius, anxious to be on the trail, skirted the left side of the pool, to where it emptied into a small stream at the far end.

"Do you think it will lead out?" asked Roark, stopping to get his bearings. "Could be a dead end if the stream goes underground."

"Let's find out," said Sybil, setting off after Sirius.

"Better turn back before Madonus gets concerned and sends out a search party," suggested Simon.

"Just try to turn Sirius around," said Sybil. "He's hot on the trail."

"We have to turn back now," said Simon.

"We could bring the Aquadrians to this pool in the morning and set out again from here," suggested Roark.

"Excellent idea, buddy," agreed Simon. "That's enough for one day, Sirius."

"You'll wear out your sniffer," teased Sybil, jostling his jowls playfully. "Come," she commanded, grabbing his ruff and propelling him back through the cave.

Sirius gave a discontented little snort and resigned himself to giving up the search.

Arriving back at the cave entrance, they told the Aquadrians of their discovery. A murmur of relief rippled through the crowd gathered around a small fire Madonus had started.

"Where did you find wood?" asked Simon.

"In that recess over there in the cave wall," Madonus replied, indicating a patch of gloom to the right of the entrance. "As long as we are here, we might as well have some comfort. Besides, it was easy to see that someone had a campfire before us, so I went hunting for the wood supply."

"So, there really are others in the cave. We'll have to be careful," said Sybil. A shiver slithered up her spine as she recalled the heaviness rising from the area when they had flown over.

"We have no choice. With all those Aquadrian forces about, this is the safest place for now," said Madonus.

"You're right, but no one stray off alone. Stay in small groups and be alert. Tomorrow we'll visit the pool and set up camp there," said Simon.

"Best to stay clear of the entrance in case Aquadrians come by and hear our noise," added Sybil.

"We'll post sentries outside and oversee the gathering of

more wood," said Roark. "Could be here a lot longer than we think."

*

After relocating to the pool, a meeting was called to discuss exploration of the cave.

"Sirius was tracking a scent yesterday. We'd like to go back and check it out," said Simon. "Sybil and I will take him in."

"I'll stay here with you, Madonus," offered Roark, just as happy to be off his aching feet. "We can get camp organized."

"We'll start gathering wood and see to security," said Madonus. "Who wants to take first watch?"

"I will," volunteered Roark, happy at the prospect of being airborne. "I'll do air patrols."

Three people stepped forward. A young Aquadrian named Cascious held up his half-morphed hand. "I'll take the west trail. I want to know if we were followed."

His younger brother Darius readily agreed to take the east trail. Both were unable to go through transition. Their family was adamantly opposed to Aquadorus and his political machinations.

"And I'll guard the cave entrance," volunteered their older sister, Cebelia.

"Roark, you can warn the outposts of anyone coming our way. That will give us time to alert those out gathering wood," said Madonus.

"I can see to the wood gatherers, too," offered Roark. "Easy for me to find them from above."

"Good," replied Madonus. "Thank you. Shifts will be relieved every four bells until we have enough wood gathered. Three bell shifts thereafter."

Madonus was genuinely proud of the young Aquadrians who stepped forward. Their parents had gone missing in the flood, and the family patriarch was a friend of his since childhood. Perhaps they had made it safely north or were still out there searching for their children. His hope was to find them alive, but until then he would do his utmost to help them. His protective instincts arose naturally, for he had worked as a sentry in the city and had suffered enough working under Dimondus.

"I will lead the wood gathering detail," Madonus said, setting off with a group of five. He gave Roark a wave of confidence.

"See you later," Sybil called. "Let's see what we can find in the cave, Sirius."

Retracing the trail he'd picked up the day before, Simon said, "He seems to wander a lot. Maybe there's more than one scent."

"Or the same one, but different trails," suggested Sybil. After tracking for some time, Sirius began to wander in circles.

"Looks like the trail ends here. What now? Turn back or see where this leads?"

"I say we go on," replied Sybil, heading out.

"Shame not to explore now that we're this far," said Simon. Their natural curiosity drew them deeper into the cave system.

"Further along, Sirius stopped abruptly and let out a warning growl. A strong odour wafted in from the left where the cave branched off into another passage. "Smells a lot like that sinkhole," said Simon. "Best stay out of there."

"You don't like that smell either, boy," said Sybil. "Nasty stuff." She pulled on his ruff and he forged ahead.

They proceeded along the main passageway. Well into the afternoon, they came upon a smaller opening that led to the right.

"Should we check this one out?" asked Sybil. "We can always backtrack and continue following the stream."

"Yeah, let's go," said Simon. He grabbed Sirius and hauled

him along. "This way, boy."

A noticeable incline drew them onward. The way became steeper and a waft of fresh air sifted in from ahead. Encouraged by the prospects of a way out, they stepped up their pace.

"Stop a minute," said Sybil. She switched off the illuminator and dim light seeped through the darkness. "We might be in luck."

"Cross your fingers," said Simon, following Sirius who rushed toward the opening.

"Stop him, Simon," warned Sybil. "We don't know what's out there."

Simon chased after Sirius and caught him by the ruff, bringing him to a halt. "Easy now, boy."

Sybil switched off the illuminator again as their eyes adjusted to daylight streaming in. They huddled at the small opening, cautious and alert.

"I'll go first," said Simon. "Keep Sirius here." He eased his way through the small exit into a thick undergrowth of vegetation. His heart thundered with fear and excitement as he scouted the area. After a preliminary search, he circled back.

"The stream empties out to the left and well below us there's a waterfall. Looks safe so far. Should we carry on or head back?"

"Madonus and Roark will be worried. It's already late afternoon."

"Now that we know where this leads, we can check it out another day."

About halfway back they met the search party. Madonus, carrying a smoky torch, called out as the three figures appeared around a bend in the cave wall. "Ho, we're sure glad to see you!"

"We were getting concerned," said Roark.

"Sorry," apologised Simon. "One branch of the cave led upwards and we couldn't resist. We found a way out."

Madonus gave a sigh of relief. "That's good news."

"Maybe, replied Sybil. "It depends on where it leads—north or south. That passage could turn around any old way."

"Suppose you're right," conceded Madonus.

"Roark, will you come with us tomorrow and scout out the lay of the land?" asked Simon.

"Would I? No problem," replied Roark. Cave life was not his forte. He longed to be over his homeland cliffs, catching the updrafts and soaring freely. Mother Meerak would be worried and his priority was to get word to her.

"We'll start out before dawn," said Sybil. "That should put us at the opening in enough time. We need to figure out where we are."

"Shouldn't take long," said Roark. "I know this land like the back of my wingtips."

Rising very early, the trio set off with Sirius in the lead. When they came to the malodorous cleft in the passage, his hackles rose. A deep rumble issued from his throat. He skirted the area, slinking by warily.

"Doesn't like that smell," said Simon. "Can't blame him. Can you imagine how strong it is? A bloodhound's nose can smell at least a 1,000 times better than ours. That's pretty amazing."

"Does it connect to that sinkhole in some way?" asked Sybil. "That's the only time we've smelled it before."

"Same stench, that's for sure," said Simon. "I don't want to go near it."

"Huh-uh, no way I'm going in there," agreed Sybil.

Roark hurried on by, relieved to be on his way. He was anxious to be out doing what he did best, scouting from above.

Arriving at the cave opening, he took to wing and disappeared over the forest canopy.

From overhead, Roark could just make out the patch of underbrush where he'd emerged. The entrance was well-hidden, assuring a measure of safety for the time being.

He decided to fly in concentric circles from that point, keeping a sharp eye out for Aquadrian patrols. All was going well, until he spied a small contingent coming in from the west. They would soon be upon the westernmost sentry standing guard. He picked up speed and swooped in low to warn Cascious, who abandoned his post and fled to the safety of the cave. Roark flew on to alert the eastern guard and check on wood gatherers. Realizing how valuable his skills were to the group, his chest feathers ruffled with pride. When he was satisfied the Aquadrians were safe, he continued his ever-widening surveillance.

"Say, this is beginning to look familiar," he preened, self-satisfied. "This looks very much like the route Rinaldo and I found on our way south."

He swooped lower and continued his search. "Yes, I remember that outcropping of rock along the cliff." Soaring in closer, he managed to locate the small trail he and Rinaldo had blazed. "Lucky wing feathers," he chuckled to himself. "We can bring the Aquadrians up the back way to the rookery."

He flew a beeline toward the cave landmark to break the good news.

"We're on the northern frontier," he gasped. "I found the trail Rinaldo and I used. We can get to the rookery from there."

"Will the children be able to make it?" asked Sybil.

"It isn't that hard. If they have any trouble, they can be relayed on backs."

Retracing their way back to the pool where the Aquadrians were camped, they were met with sighs of relief at the news.

"Best to rest up here at the pool for a while," Madonus suggested, aware of their fatigue. The flight north had taken its toll on the children. In consultation, the decision was made to stay a few days before moving on.

Sybil and Simon decided to explore further with Sirius, heading out again the following morning. Each time they passed the opening that reeked of sulphur, Sybil and Simon became more concerned. Although neither of them had voiced their intentions, a plan to check into it was beginning to take shape in the back of their minds.

Now they heeded the small urge growing within. "Simon, I have been thinking. I know neither of us really wants to check out that foul smelling area."

"Do you think we should have a look?"

"Yes, there have been too many times I did not heed a warning."

"I have the same feeling. But I think we need to get the Aquadrians to the rookery first. We can always come back."

"Agreed. We need to come prepared. Braid some more vines into rope. Can't take a torch in there, but we have the illuminator. Can you think of anything else?"

"We don't have much on hand. Maybe take a club with us. I get a bad feeling about it."

"Glad Sirius is with us," Sybil said, feeling a measure of security.

They headed back to the cave entrance. "Maybe we can find the vines you used to get me out of that pit," suggested Simon. "Let's have a look."

They made their way along the east trail to the sinkhole and searched in the undergrowth, careful to avoid the soft perimeter.

"Hey, watch out," said Simon. "See that wire?"

"It's another snare. Someone is trapping this area. Maybe a lone Aquadrian family got lost and decided to stick it out in the cave."

"It's creepy. Why don't they show themselves?"

"Just saying, by all those tracks Sirius picked up in the cave, there may be more than one person."

After more searching, Sybil called out, "Found it." She grabbed the tail end of a braided rope protruding from a clump of ferns and wound it around her arm. "Let's get out of here."

Near the cave entrance they stashed the rope and some clubs in the undergrowth for their return trip.

On the morning of the third day, the group headed out. When they arrived at the cave opening, it was hard to hold back. Fresh air and daylight held a strong pull. But it would have been unwise to attempt to make it to the rookery in one day and the decision was made to hold up just inside the entrance. In order to get to the rookery before nightfall, they would leave the cave at daybreak the following morning.

As dawn approached, Roark led the way to the trail. He set off as quickly as his feet would allow, the Aquadrian youngsters trailing along behind him. With his cheerful quips and tap dancing routines, he was becoming a popular figure. They giggled as his blue plumpness shimmied and pirouetted. The adults were delighted by his ability to keep them entertained. Although the children never complained, it relieved their fear and tension.

Stopping once for refreshment in a stream gurgling just off the trail, the group made good time. The children were in a merry mood, keeping their voices low on the occasions they needed to relay information. Secure in their trust, Roark decided to leave the group for an overall view of their progress.

As he became airborne, his wing feathers brushed the aerial roots of an old tree, causing him to falter. Crashing into a rock face, he muttered, "Drat and blast!"

His wing dangled helplessly and he cringed with pain. "Not an opportune time. That's what you get for showing off," he mumbled to himself.

Running to catch up with him, Simon asked, "You okay, buddy?"

"Yeah, oh yeah," replied Roark sheepishly. "Just a bruise I believe, but it sure hurts."

"Let me have a look," said Sybil, coming up beside him. She gently held his wing and asked him to flex his pectoral muscles. "Nothing broken, could use a sling to immobilise it for a day or two. Give it a bit of rest and it should be okay." She pulled out a triangle of cloth and Simon held Roark's wing in place while she bound it into a comfortable configuration against his chest.

"Dumb luck," grumbled Roark. "If I can't get a view from above, we might be heading into Aquadrians."

"We'll just have to trust," replied Simon. "Or, I can take a chance and go aloft to check it out."

"Pretty risky," said Roark. "Not much choice, though." He made a pact with himself to tone down his rashness and proceed with more caution. He was putting them all in danger.

"Okay," said Simon. "That leaves it to me." He lifted off and sailed over the area. In the distance, he could see the cliff top rookery. Satisfied they were alone on the trail, he swooped down and gave the all clear.

Sirius stuck close to Roark, sensing his disgruntled mood. He nudged him with his cold, wet nose every now and then.

Nothing seemed to work. He began to lick his long, red, skinny leg.

"Hey, that tickles," giggled Roark, his mood brightening. He reached out with his good wing and brushed the top of his head.

"Good dog," he smiled, feelings of love returning some bounce to his step.

As the incline increased, some of the children tired. Hoisting them on their backs, the adults' pace quickened and they reached the pond just below the rookery for much needed refreshment and a bite to eat.

Knowing that reassurance was needed, Roark addressed the crowd. "There are many families at the rookery who will gladly welcome you."

"We'll go ahead and prepare for your arrival. We don't want to alarm anyone," said Simon.

When they entered the rookery amidst shouts of joy, Mother Meerak descended upon them, her wings opened wide in a loving embrace. "Thank the Seventh Stars. So glad you're back!" Her glowing face did little to ease the tension that had taken up permanent residence around her eyes. "Where have you been? We were dreadfully worried. What has happened to your wing, Roark?" she croaked, in horrified alarm.

"Oh, nothing to worry about, Mother. I brushed the side of a cliff. It's only bruised. My friends took care of it," he said, looking gratefully to Sybil and Simon.

Sirius gave Meerak a gentle nudge and gave her wing a reassuring lick.

"Hello, Sirius," she smiled. "You sure have a way of cheering people up." She turned toward her house. "Now, come in and have a cup of nettle tea. You must be tired."

"No, Mother. We can't stay long. We must get back to the Aquadrian refugees. I promised them safe refuge with us here at the rookery."

Meerak's eyes widened in alarm. "Aquadrians, here on the cliff top?"

"Yes, nothing to fear. We came the same way Rinaldo and I did. Up the back. There are about thirty people, many of them children."

"Had a long and dangerous journey from the south. They are exhausted. We left them back at the pool, down the trail," said Sybil.

"That trail leaves us in danger. Could bring a whole army up," said Simon.

"Well, hurry then and bring them here. We can make room for people in need," assured Meerak. "I'll ask around. We'll find homes for them. Go now."

She turned toward home, alerting her husband Profrak to the situation. They called an assembly and together explained the need. The Opeggees, social by nature, welcomed the chance to help the unfortunate band of Aquadrians. They scurried about making ready.

When the group of tired and frightened people arrived, it was to a warm and open welcome.

"Madonus, you and your family can stay with us," Roark invited after making introductions.

"Yes," Meerak assured. "You have a safe refuge with us. We are people, no matter what our differences."

"It is our firm belief," added Profrak. "We all have a right to choose. We wish no harm to others and hope the same for ourselves."

Madonus nodded in agreement. "Thank you. So kind of you to take us in. We'll never be able to repay you."

"No need," assured Profrak. "Glad we can be of some help in these turbulent times."

"Who knows how this will end," said Meerak, her worried

frown reappeared. "We need to work together, all of us, in good faith."

CHAPTER FIVE
Life at the Rookery

"There are only two ways to live your life. One is as though nothing is a miracle. The other is as though everything is a miracle."

- Albert Einstein

Once the Aquadrian refugees were settled, life resumed at the rookery. Routines were established providing for the newcomers' needs. Gathering foragers were sent out daily to meet the increased demand for food supplies. The generosity of the Hetopian BanquoeBag helped provide nourishment.

Although some Aquadrians no longer needed daily replenishment and were content to maintain every other day, trips to the pool were a cause for concern. It was only a matter of time before the back trail was discovered.

"We should go north to alert Rinaldo, let him know we reached the rookery," said Simon. "He will be concerned."

"His plan was to return with reinforcements," replied Sybil. "We should wait. If he doesn't arrive in a few days maybe we can have a look."

"The Aquadrians could stay as long as needed. Mother has said as much," reassured Roark.

"Certainly good of her," said Sybil, remembering their first meeting and how welcomed she had made them feel.

Roark continued, "Madonus wants to join northern forces as soon as possible. Once they have rested and Rinaldo returns with an escort, they mean to move on."

"Probably safer for all of us," replied Simon. "Having to go down trail to the pool is dangerous.

"Yes, Father Profrak is concerned," said Roark.

"Profrak is your father?" asked Sybil.

"Yes, did I not tell you? So much happened after finding DOU, suppose I didn't have a chance."

"Well, that is not hard to see, Roark. You are very much like him," said Sybil. It was gratifying to know that he had such a wonderful lineage.

Roark beamed, for he venerated his father and emulated his steady, common-sense ways. He knew that he, too, would one day be a responsible adult. For the moment he was content to learn from the person he revered most.

Mother Meerak made every effort to see to the comfort of her guests and was mindful of Madonus and his wife Delania's situation. Having no children of their own, they had taken in the three teens: Cascious, Darius and Cebelia. Memories of their parents, who were lost in the flooding, crowded their waking moments and invaded their dreams at night.

Simon was keenly aware of their feelings, his own loss resurfacing. Darius, who was about his age, had taken a liking to Simon and the furry companion that shadowed him. Sirius's trait of comforting people was inborn. He had come from a long line of hounds known for the capacity to win people over. The ability to sense distress sent his inquisitive nose in search of their pain. He nudged and prodded, licking them with his soft wet tongue, as if to say 'There, there, you can rely on me.'

The Aquadrian youth were enthralled by the furry creature. They came to trust him, for he was a stalwart figure, always on hand to play or comfort.

One of the Aquadrian men who was sheltering at a neighbouring home arrived at the door one day, asking to see Madonus.

"Could I have a word with you?"

"What is it, Sardonica?" he asked, stepping outside. They walked toward the cliff access trail.

"Nothing much," he replied, trying to remain tactful. "I feel we should be moving along soon. Not staying here with the enemy."

"Enemy?" Madonus's eyebrows lifted in surprise. "Surely, you can't still think of them as enemies, after all they are doing for us."

"Well…" he said slowly, hesitating around his prejudice. He had been brought up to believe the worst of these 'three-eyed feather brains.'

"It's just that…well, they aren't like us," he ventured, hoping to persuade Madonus to leave the rookery. He was very uncomfortable living with blue feathers and popping suction cups. It made him squeamish. "Don't mean to seem ungrateful, but they can't really know what we know. Can they? I mean, they don't believe anything we do. They are just too different," he said lamely.

Madonus cast a sideways glance at him, wondering how trustworthy this man would prove to be. If a squadron of Aquadorus's men happened along, would he turn coat in betrayal?

"Sardonica, isn't that a little unreasonable? I mean, just look what they are doing for us."

"Yes, but, can we trust them?" he countered. "What's to say they won't turn on us in our sleep?"

Madonus silently shook his head. It always came to that—the deep distrust sown early in formative years. What had Opeggees ever done to the Aquadrians? If anyone had a case not to trust, it would surely be the Opeggees. It is we who hunted their fledglings for the soup that many considered a delicacy. Personally, he did not partake of it, always considered it a barbaric act. Such cruel aggression, for what? The sake of snobbery in the culinary arts?

"Well, our young are not ready to make the trek north," hedged Madonus. "It is best to wait until Rinaldo arrives with reinforcements. Too dangerous to try to make it on our own."

He needed to see what this guy was about and what he was up against. Sardonica was a fence sitter. Which side would he land on when the going got rough? There were far too many who could not take a definite stand. It was why Aquadorus rose to power in a short time.

"It ain't right. Aquadrians bedded down with Opeggees. Nothing good can come of it," said Sardonica, rooted in his stubborn beliefs.

"Once our people recover and we're ready to move, we will head north," said Madonus, hoping to pacify him. "At least we are safe and well fed."

"Well fed? How can you say that? Sea lettuce crackers, and seeds? Sure, the Hetopian fare is more to our liking, but that Opeggee slop? You call that food?"

"When one goes hungry, it sure does hit the spot," Madonus fortified his argument. "I can stand to lose a few rolls around the middle anyway."

"Not me, I like my own fare best, none of this foreign glop. It leaves a terrible aftertaste."

"Well, all I can say is, the Opeggees are very kind to share what they have. There will be shortages soon with all this upheaval. If Aquadorus means to convert us, he will have to take me out feet first. I can't and I won't live like that!" Madonus's ire got the better of him.

"Dangerous words, Madonus. You best be more careful."

He had let his emotions lead him into dangerous territory. To let this man gain privy to his true feelings was not the wisest move. He backtracked. "I'm just weary, Sardonica. You escaped the city when I did, surely you weren't ready to convert. We needed to go through transformation ritual first. Even if we had been ready, we weren't given notice or a chance to carry it out."

Sardonica took note of his words and had to agree. He hadn't been ready. Now what choice was there? If he went back south he would have to transform, if that were still even an option. If he stayed with this side, they risked being overwhelmed by Aquadorus's forces. And now to be living in Opeggee territory; he hadn't bargained on that.

"All I can say—it ain't right," he stubbornly reiterated.

"Perhaps," replied Madonus, hoping to keep him off guard. "We'll be going north in no time. Wait and see. Rinaldo will not leave us stranded."

"He'd better hurry," Sardonica replied tersely.

"If you have any more questions or suggestions, please let me know." Madonus was aware that it was more prudent to keep enemies close. His loyalties were in question, but he did not want to alienate this man altogether.

After that episode, he watched the man more closely. Sardonica seemed to accept what had been said, but his continued aloofness bothered Madonus. Occasionally, the slight look of revulsion on his face caught him off guard. It was obvious his aversion was deeply entrenched.

Life in the Opeggee rookery appeared to flow smoothly on the surface, but discontent was brewing. Sardonica had a way of stirring up trouble. It wouldn't take much to have others believing they were in danger from the Opeggees.

Madonus decided to call a meeting, asking all adult Aquadrians to gather at the pond on the back access trail.

When they had assembled, he began forthwith. "I sense there is some tension amongst our people. If anyone has something to say, they need to do so now." He made eye contact with all present. Some turned away, afraid to voice the small meanness that had begun to prickle under their skin.

Many believed Sardonica was right, they shouldn't be there. It was one thing to escape Aquadrian forces, but it was an altogether different thing to shelter with these blue-feathered folk; traditional enemies.

"No? Nothing to say? This is your chance, speak now or hold your peace."

A woman standing beside Sardonica ventured a feeble excuse. "This isn't right. We don't live on cliff tops with Opeggees. It is time to move on."

He could hear the echo of Sardonica's earlier words. He was behind this all right. It was best to cut the roots of this noxious weed.

"Anyone else here feel the same way?" Some of the adults looked to the ground, afraid to own up to such base feelings.

He stared them down. "This is appalling behaviour from Aquadrians. It is, after all, the kind of thing we are working against. We need to remember what life in the city was like back there. I don't recall any of you wanting to turn back when the trek north got to be too much. You were willing to carry on, and you know Roark. He is one of the best." He stopped to catch his breath. "If you want to turn around now and head south, I suggest you better do it, because northern forces won't welcome this intolerance. It is your choice."

Silence descended as the crowd dispersed. Sardonica, mumbling under his breath as he slunk away, headed up hill toward the rookery.

Simon met Madonus on the trail and asked if everything was all right. "Seems some folks are a little upset. What's happening?"

"Oh, it's nothing too much. I suspect they are just irritable after the long trek across country. Some folks don't know when they have it so good."

"Sardonica seems especially out of sorts."

"He can't get past his prejudice. We are lucky to have the help of the Opeggee nation. I suspect his folks had no use for them, or perhaps he's just weak-livered."

The words stung Simon as he thought of Roark and his family, a most gracious friend one could ever hope to meet. How unfair! How unkind! His immediate reaction was to call him down. But he realized, in so doing, he would be no better. The only way to combat prejudice was to expose the folly of such thinking.

If there was one thing he wished to accomplish during his stay on the cliff top; it was to promote understanding. With it, lasting peace was possible. Living beside Aquadrians and Opeggees in the same community was an opportunity. He'd met plenty of good people, both in Aquadria, and here in the Opeggee nation. Surely, those of good will can find a way. He knew Madonus was that sort of person.

"Thank you for sharing that. Maybe we can make a difference here, Madonus."

He loped off down the trail in search of Sybil. He'd had his belly full of hatred. The Namors Guardia, Dimondus, Aquadorus—I am guilty of it myself. Who can stomach any of those people? They lorded it over everyone. He was all too aware of Dimondus's ways. That man needed to lighten up and not take himself so seriously. Simon's brain was in turmoil. He couldn't sort out his conflicting feelings. He needed an ally, someone he could bounce ideas off, someone to work with, to help find peace in himself.

"Sybil, there you are!" said Simon. He pulled her aside and

related all he'd learned.

"Not going to be easy," said Sybil. "We know all too well how it feels, don't we? What did DOU say? 'From fierce warriors to Beings of Light'."

"Compassion for all," said Simon. His thoughts mellowed as he relived the glow of basking in DOU's brilliance. It was as though his mind had opened to greater possibilities. It was hopeful. Hope, that old bugaboo he always wrestled with.

All that week, the atmosphere in the rookery thickened. Tension was building. The children seemed not to notice, for they enjoyed capering around the settlement with Roark, Sybil and Simon. Sirius captivated their days, playing fetch and running after balls fashioned out of grass and mud from the pond.

As the Aquadrians grew restless, anxious to join northern forces, Simon and Sybil felt the undercurrents of division. Sardonica's incessant complaints were contagious. Many others joined the back-biting and fear-mongering that often go with intolerance and lack of understanding.

Madonus did his best to placate and keep things under control. He feared violence might erupt. Sardonica was a hothead and there was no telling what he might do if he felt provoked.

Profrak, too, was concerned. Although peaceful folk at heart, they would not stand by and watch the aggression get out of hand. They were prepared to defend themselves. Many had lost fledglings to these Aquadrians. Who was to say that one of these very people did not have a hand in that?

At last, Sybil and Simon approached Profrak and Madonus to voice their concerns. "Many of the children are coming to us. They are overhearing things and are frightened," said Sybil. "It isn't right."

"We know," said Profrak. "I am growing very concerned

about the way things are going in our village. I realize the magnitude of what is developing."

"Yes, said Madonus. "I, too, am aware. I have already called our people together to address this, but I see it has not improved matters. It is time to discuss the consequences of our actions if this is allowed to continue. I will speak with them again."

"I have already scheduled a meeting with all Opeggees," said Profrak. "You are our guests. Whether they feel provoked or not, it is common courtesy to be decent to people. Some of our citizens are getting a little testy, I must admit. We will be speaking about this. Our guests have a right to share what we have. It is our duty to show kindness to strangers and those in need."

"I can't say I blame them," said Madonus. "Some of our people have been downright rude. I am sorry for that, Profrak. We must overcome years of prejudice. Life under Aquadorus's regime has hardened many. If a leader shows such callous disregard for life, it gives them permission. It conditions them to see their own as entitled, the only ones that have rights. You know how leaders can sway others."

"Yes, it begins to feel right. Our people are not without fault," admitted Profrak. "It has been difficult for many because they have suffered hardships at the hands of Aquadrian folk."

"Yes, I admit that. I would feel the same if it were my family, my people."

"What can we do to promote better feelings?" asked Profrak. "We need to head this off before it boils over."

"It is a good start by calling people together and discussing the situation," said Simon.

"Once that has been done, it might be good to have a general meeting of us all. Let everyone hear what people want to say," suggested Sybil.

"And maybe that could be followed up with a concert and a feast," said Simon.

Following those meetings, things seemed to improve as good will began to show on both sides. Once Meerak got wind of Simon's suggestion, it began with an act of kindness from her. Well aware that music could improve everyone's spirits, she scheduled an open-air concert for all to attend. Her offspring, naturally talented, were well-known for their beautiful harmonies and gracious solos. Toward the end of the concert, she invited all to stand and join them in song.

"If you don't know the words, you can hum. It provides a mellow undercurrent. Men, your bass voices add a rich, deep tone. Best of all, children, your clear, young voices provide a lightness that is ethereal."

She was well pleased to see that all assembled joined the chorus, swelling the night sky with hauntingly beautiful music. The bonfire died away while Aquadrians and Opeggees sat in the stillness of the night. The ragged edges of the past days began to dissolve as tensions softened. By emphasizing the things in common, they had planted an idea. It was possible to create beauty together no matter who or what you were.

Everyone had a voice. Whether it was considered a pleasing voice or one that sang off-key; when you put them all together, it created a whole.

CHAPTER SIX
Discovery

"We accept the love we think we deserve."

- Stephen Chbosky

Discussion returned to the subject of the cave. "We don't have a lot of time, Sybil. Let's go back tomorrow morning."

"It will take time just to reach the cave. Do you think we can risk a flyover?"

"Either very high or very low. Not sure which is best," said Sybil.

"Very high," interrupted Roark, who had joined them. "You'll have a better chance. After all, your blue clothing is camouflage against the backdrop of the sky. And Aquadrian eyesight is changing, diminishing with mutation. I learned that from Madonus."

"Good to know," replied Simon. "We're going to the cave to check out the passage that smells like rotten eggs. We'll take Sirius with us."

"I knew you would," Roark chuckled. "You two can't resist an adventure. Oh, I wish I could go, too."

"It isn't adventure, Roark. It's more like we are *called*. There is something that needs to be done or something we need to know," said Sybil.

"The best way is to confront it head on," added Simon. "If we aren't back in a couple of days, send Profrak in for us."

"Maybe my wing will be mended by then. Sure would love

to go with you," said Roark. He popped his suction cups and kicked a pebble in disgust. "I miss all the good things."

They left at pre-dawn, darkness concealing their flight path. Landing at the cave opening above the falls, they gathered their wits and entered. Switching on the illuminator, Simon and Sybil descended deeper until they came to the foul-smelling passage.

"First, let's check out the front part of the cave. It would be good to know if they have returned."

Smouldering coals of a recent campfire near the entrance verified their suspicions.

"They're here again, we'd better be careful," said Simon.

"Let's go outside and watch," suggested Sybil. "They can't be too far."

"Sirius, you need to be quiet," commanded Simon. "Understand, boy? Quiet."

Sirius gave a soft "Woof" and licked his hand. A short distance away, they found a hiding place in the dense underbrush. It wasn't long before crackling twigs alerted them of approaching footsteps.

"Can you see anyone?" asked Simon.

"Not yet. Easy, Sirius," Sybil rested her hand on his neck.

A hooded figure pared its way through the vegetation, parted the vines and entered the cave.

"Did you get a look at his face, Simon?"

"No, he was too fast."

"I didn't see either."

"We'll just have to wait until he comes out again," said Sybil.

"Do you think there is anyone else living there? Could be two or three, or maybe a family."

"I doubt it is a family. Someone would have stayed in the cave, you'd think."

"Oh, oh. Can't get back inside now. Never thought about that."

"Hope he goes out again soon," said Sybil, vexed at the thought of spending the night in the underbrush.

"Yeah, I don't want Profrak to have to come looking for us," replied Simon. *"What a nuisance that would be."*

"He wouldn't stay in the cave all day, would he?"

"Nah, not likely. Could be a long wait, though. Did you see what he was carrying?"

"That, I did see. It was a rat crab," replied Sybil.

"A, what crab?"

"A rat crab. Nasty little beggars. That's what Rinaldo called them. He killed one that attacked him when I saw him at the Duplicating Chamber."

"Do you suppose he is going to eat it?"

"Not much else to live on out here, I guess."

Just then, the vines parted. The figure stepped out of the cave and threw back its hood.

"It's not a man!" cried Sybil.

"It, it's that woman from the city."

"It's Adelaide, Claire's old friend!"

"What do we do?" asked Simon, his voice shaking with anger.

"The first thing we do is get back in that cave and skedaddle," said Sybil. *"We can figure out what to do about her later."*

"Right," he said. Once Adelaide left, Simon scrambled toward the entrance. Sirius trotted after him, concerned about the strange new odour Simon was giving off.

They ran through the cave system, stopping only to catch their breath near the pool. Arriving outside the opening overlooking the waterfall, they collapsed, shaken by their discovery. The steady rush cascading over the falls below sent a soothing aura of peace. Letting their heart rates return to normal, they rested on the carpet of decaying vegetation in the thick undergrowth. Sirius laid his muzzle in Simon's lap. Sybil flopped over his torso and breathed in his dog scent.

"She's probably alone," said Simon. "I doubt anyone else would go with her."

"How did she get away, with all that flooding?"

"Maybe she came out here before the flood started. That cave was not easy to find."

"Did she know Aquadorus meant to flood the valley?" asked Sybil.

"Why would she come live here, if she didn't?"

"Right, that makes sense. So, Aquadorus duped her and now she has been double-crossed; just as I said would happen."

"Or, maybe she heard rumours around the city. Fearing for her life, she set out into the wilderness, found this cave and set up camp," said Simon.

"Pretty lonely life. She must be frightened," added Sybil.

"Do I feel sorry for her? Is that what you are wondering, Sybil?"

"Just making an observation, that's all. Still, one wonders. Put yourself in her situation."

"A predicament, that's for sure. Likely doesn't have one friend. Hard way to go, in times like these," said Simon. A shudder ran through him as he recalled his days in Leanoria and the Namors Guardia. He thought about the storm that took Benni and a stirring of pity went out to Adelaide.

"We don't have to make any decisions right now," said Sybil. "She's not going anywhere."

"Yeah, she'll stay put. Best place to hold up in these dangerous times."

"Let's hang out here until after sundown. We can get back easier then."

As they drank in the beauty of the hillside, the sunset streamed into their safe haven lighting their hearts on fire. The deep peace of the countryside, the gentle beauty all around, set them to dreaming of DOU. The dragon had said they were to discover; that it was up to them. The universe was within. That dream ignited compassion whenever they thought of it.

The fading sunset called them to action. "Better leave so we get back before dark," said Simon.

"I kinda hate to go back. It's so peaceful here. It is hard to face all the discontent Sardonica is stirring up."

"Maybe we can do something about it," replied Simon. "DOU has said there's much to do."

"Is that what DOU means?"

"That night in the pit when we looked into the eye crystal—it was there, open for all to see."

"It's more a feeling," said Sybil. "Like the *gift,* when we are about to know something."

"You're right. I never thought about it that way. The edge of it is there."

"Mystery, like that lavender fog in the Great Hall in Hetopia. No way of knowing. But in feeling, there is a sense of it."

"It's gentle, it's joyful. Oh, it's best to say nothing. Beyond words. Just let it be mystery."

"Right," agreed Sybil. "Just bask in the feeling."

"Sybil, you do have a way with words."

She was lost deep in thought and ignored his last comment. "Better go or we'll be very late."

Sirius agreed with an eager high-pitched whine, wriggling in all directions. "Up you go, buddy," called Simon. "We're off."

It was dark by the time they landed in front of Roark's home. The pale light of the moon illuminated the Aquadrian sky filtering through the gel canopy.

Roark greeted them at the front door, hustling them outside into the shadows. "Glad you're back. I was worried."

"What's up?" asked Simon. He could read the distress by

the way he held his head. His good wing jutted out from his body.

"How's your wing doing?" asked Sybil, as she patted the sling gently.

"Improving," said Roark. "I could manage without the sling, but it reminds me to rest it. Walk with me," he said in a hushed tone.

"What's wrong, Roark?" asked Sybil. "You seem pretty down."

"Oh, I shouldn't take it to heart, I guess. It's Sardonica; he's acting all high and mighty. Turns his nose up at our food. It's just plain rude the way he struts around here."

"We were afraid of that," replied Simon. "Madonus said there's a stubborn prejudice in him. After all the Opeggees are doing for them."

"Ungrateful," said Sybil.

"Can't help what other people feel," said Roark. "He has been brought up to believe the worst of us."

"Not everyone feels that way," said Simon. "Madonus and Delania are not like that, neither are the children."

"Look how much fun we have with them," added Sybil, trying to cheer him up.

"They *are* a lot of fun, aren't they?" said Roark, smiling at the thought of the boisterous youngsters.

"They give us hope," said Simon, surprised by his own thought. "It is up to us. It starts here," he tapped his chest. "One at a time. Allow the differences to die."

"Can find no better way than playing together," agreed Roark. He brightened at the thought. "Okay, then we carry on with that. Not hard to do," laughed Roark. He adored the little green faces who looked up to him, grinning at his crazy antics.

The following morning, after resolving to let it slide, they called the children together. "Who wants to learn a new game?" Roark asked.

"We do, we do," they shouted, swarming around his red legs.

"Okay, this is how it goes. Are you ready? Form a circle everyone."

Simon watched Roark's talent for showmanship developing. "He has a natural gift."

"It's fun to watch him," replied Sybil. "Come on, let's join in." The circle opened to allow them in; blue wing-tips, and small, pale green hands joining flesh-coloured human hands.

"First, we all sit down," Roark directed. "I am going to pick someone to be 'It.' " He closed his eyes, twirled around with his wing outstretched and stopped, pointing to a tiny girl. Her face lit up in delight and she jumped to her feet.

"What I do?" She looked up shyly at Roark, grinning from ear to ear, for she had not fully transformed. Two little appendages stuck out from the sides of her head.

"Carpetia," said Roark, bending over to brush her soft, green cheek with his wing tip. "You will walk around the outside of the circle and touch each head. When you touch a head, you say, 'glowfish, glowfish, glowfish.' Keep going and when you pick someone, you say 'ratcrab.' Then you race back to the empty spot you left. Whoever gets there first, sits down and the person left standing becomes 'It' and continues on."

Many rounds of 'Glowfish, Ratcrab,' were played. Sirius raced around the circle with the children until lunch was called.

"That was so much fun!" they laughed, as they scrambled to the village centre where the settlement was gathered for a communal picnic.

Their merriment soon spilled over on everyone. Even Sardonica seemed to be softening. A smile played at the corner of his lips. He was watching Roark engage the little girl Carpetia. He winked one of his green eyes, swivelled his head and winked with his purple eye, then back again to his other green eye. Back and forth, until the little girl dissolved in giggles, saying, "Woarky funny!"

"This is going well," said Sybil.

"Even Sardonica can see how much fun 'Woarky' is," laughed Simon. He caught his eye and gave him a smile and a wink of his own.

To his surprise, Sardonica winked back and laughed, popping a fish strip in his mouth. He was glad of the Hetopian fare Simon and Sybil had shared. His stomach dictated many of his moods these days.

"Children have a way of softening people up," observed Sybil. "And that little girl Carpetia is so sweet."

"She is a darling," agreed Simon. "Even Sirius allows her to ride on his back."

"He has taken a liking to that little one, that's for sure."

Days passed and still there was no sign of Rinaldo or an escort.

"Do you think we should go north and see what has happened?" asked Simon.

"He said he'd be back," replied Sybil. "If we miss him and he's halfway here, then what?"

"Okay, maybe we should stay put."

"I think we should make another trip to the cave and see if we can figure out what to do about Adelaide. If we make ourselves known, I doubt she will welcome us."

On their second excursion to the cave, all was silent. The campfire coals were cold. It looked deserted. At the cave entrance they saw many new tracks in the soft sand. They were Aquadrian flipper prints.

"Oh, oh! Looks like they caught her," said Sybil. "What will happen to her?"

"Can't go back to the city, most of it is under water."

"Nothing we can do for her now," said Simon, a bit of sadness hanging on his words.

"What if they come back and discover the exit near the falls?"

"We'd better go," said Simon.

He moved ahead, following Sirius through the cave system. When they approached the sulphurous passageway, Sirius stopped and sniffed the air.

They held their noses while he tracked a scent on the cave floor. It led into the opening.

"No, Sirius. You can't go in there," said Simon. The hound tugged against his restraining hand.

"We said we wanted to check this out, didn't we?" Crouched beside Sirius, she asked, "What is it, boy? You want to go in there?"

A muffled cry drifted through the damp air wafting from the opening.

"Did you hear that?" asked Simon.

"Yeah, I sure did."

"Someone is in trouble."

"Maybe it's the woman," said Sybil.

Wrestling with his conscience, Simon finally replied, "We can't just leave her there."

"Wouldn't be right," said Sybil. She hesitated, remembering what had happened to Simon and her grandmother. "What if it isn't her? Could be someone else who escaped the city."

Sirius tugged again and they followed him in. Her illuminator bounced off yellow walls laden with sulphur deposits. It reeked and the twins held their noses. A general malaise was overtaking them, but Sirius forged ahead and they followed.

"This is dangerous," said Simon. "We'd better head back."

"Can't just leave," said Sybil. She pulled out two slings and they fashioned masks to filter the air.

They hurried on and soon came upon a quagmire of mud and sulphur. Adelaide was stuck fast. She, too, had tied a rag across her face to filter the noxious fumes.

Approaching the exhausted figure struggling to gain traction, Simon called out gently, "Adelaide."

Startled, she turned toward the ghostly figures eerily lit by Sybil's illuminator. The terror in her eyes, at the sight of two masked human forms and a dog, softened their approach.

"It's all right, Adelaide. We mean you no harm," reassured Sybil.

She struggled more, sinking deeper, not speaking.

"Hold still. We'll get you out," said Simon. "I'll go find that rope. You and Sirius stay here."

"No, take him with you. He needs fresh air."

He turned and sped back to the main cave, Sirius loping on ahead.

"Easy, Adelaide. Be still and you won't sink any further." Sybil wanted to reach out to her, but she was too far in.

"How do you know my name?" asked the woman.

"It's a long story. Once we have you safely out of there, we can talk about it."

Adelaide seemed to accept that and settled down to wait.

"How long have you been living in this cave?"

"I moved out of the city quite a while ago. Conditions back there got too bad. Couldn't turn sideways for the crowding. Heard wild tales about transitions and Duplicating Chambers. And the rumours of floods scared me, so I moved to higher ground."

"The city is half-flooded, but it has stopped."

"Really? It stopped?" A fleeting look of relief softened her face.

"Ho, we're back," shouted Simon, rushing to them. "Grab this rope and tie it around yourself," he said, flinging it to her.

She did as instructed. They grasped the end and pulled, leaning their weight into it. A sickening squelch released her from the muck and she was pulled onto solid ground. She lay exhausted. Simon sat beside her while Sybil undid the rope, setting her free. Sirius slumped next to her.

"What am I going to do?" she asked, when she had revived.

"Why did you come into this part of the cave?" asked Simon.

"A patrol of Aquadrians came by. This is the only place I could think to hide."

"They wouldn't come in here, that's for sure," Sybil agreed.

"Usually I take a torch from the fire, but I didn't have a fire going. Good thing, or they would have hunted me down. Had to feel my way along. Smelled the sulphur pit and decided they wouldn't follow me in."

"Glad you didn't bring a torch in here. This sulphur would go poof!" said Simon.

"What are you going to do, Adelaide?" asked Sybil. "You can't stay here. The Aquadrian patrols know about the cave."

"You ready to travel?" asked Simon.

"Yes," said Adelaide, rolling onto her knees. Simon gripped her by the elbow and helped her stand.

"Thank you, young man," she said, moving ahead of him toward the main cave.

"Come with us," said Sybil."

"Where are you going?"

"First, we'll get out of here," said Simon, leading the way to the main passage.

"Let me wash some of this muck off in the stream." Adelaide waded into the shallow water, squatting to rinse away as much as she could.

When they came to the fork that led away from the stream, she said, "I haven't been this far back in the cave." Her breathing became more laboured as the incline steepened. Arriving at the cave exit, they stepped out into fresh air and sunshine.

"I should have explored this myself," said Adelaide, shaking her head. "I wouldn't have got stuck in the sulphur pit."

"Let's rest here for a while," suggested Sybil.

"I don't even know your names," said Adelaide. "And what are you doing in Seventh?"

Simon looked at Sybil. A flicker of concern in his eyes told her he wasn't sure how this would go.

She stepped into his hesitation and said, "My name is Sybil and this is my brother Simon."

A baffled look crossed Adelaide's face, followed by horrified silence. Her mouth worked in strange ways as an embarrassed stammer tumbled out. "S-s-imon and Sybil?" She looked at the ground, not knowing what to say next. A red flush crept up her face.

"We know the story, Adelaide," said Sybil.

"I, I don't know what to say," said the woman.

"How about telling us why," said Simon. The old feelings of anger stirred his gut.

Adelaide sighed. "Why? I often ask myself that. I was young when I lost Benni. I was angry. I was bitter and I carried that bitterness a long time. I hurt a lot of people."

Simon remained quiet, studying her face. There was a softness about her eyes. She no longer resembled the woman they'd seen in the earlier century.

"Living here has changed me. I came to realize I've made many mistakes."

"Aquadorus double-crossed you, didn't he?" said Sybil.

"He didn't hold true to his word, that's for sure. I was such a fool." Remorse hung about her shoulders, pulling them downward. "I don't think your grandmother will ever forgive me. Claire," she said her name softly. "I am so sorry."

Simon's anger slowly seeped away, leaving a softness that settled in his mid-section. Her sadness permeated the small clearing in which they sat. Sirius wriggled closer to Adelaide, whining softly, his sad eyes mirroring hers. He gave her hand a tentative lick. She responded with a gentle caress of his muzzle, an act of trust. "Who is this?" she asked.

"We call him Sirius, like the Dog Star," replied Simon.

"Sirius," she said, placing her hands tenderly on either side of his head. His eyes reflected her sorrow, understanding the compassion of forgiveness.

Simon reached out and covered her hand. Turning her gaze upward to meet his eyes, she saw that he, too, had forgiven her.

"Simon…."

"Let it be," he said.

She turned to Sybil who had covered Simon's hand. "No words," Sybil said past the lump in her throat, as her eyes welled with moisture.

They sat in silence, the warmth of their hands and softened hearts leading them to a deeper understanding. Sitting for several minutes, Simon finally stirred and said, "We have a long way to go."

"Where are you going?"

"We are staying with the Opeggees at the cliff top rookery."

"Will you consider coming back with us?" asked Sybil. "It's

not safe down here."

"It may be only a matter of time before the Aquadrians discover the trail up the back side," said Simon.

"Will they accept me?"

"Of course. The Opeggees are the most welcoming people we've met," said Sybil.

"Thank you. I have nowhere else to go."

"Then we had better start if we want to make it there before nightfall. Might be best to skirt the trail. It is already becoming worn and noticeable."

They set off on the steady climb toward the summit, stopping at the pool of water to allow Adelaide to scrub away the remaining sulphur muck. Satisfied she was relatively clean, they proceeded up the last incline to the rookery.

"Welcome to our humble abode," said Meerak, graciously. She dipped a small curtsy to Adelaide and smiled.

"Thank you," said Adelaide, staring at her. She had never been this close to an Opeggee before. They certainly were unusual folk.

"Where did they find you?" asked Meerak.

"At the cave we told you about earlier," said Sybil, filling in the details.

"Well, anyone who's a friend of Simon and Sybil is welcome," she repeated. Open-hearted giving was her most positive trait. "We have moved to two rooms and opened our other three to guests."

"You must be very crowded," said Adelaide. "I can sleep outside under the stars."

"Nonsense, you will stay inside with us."

Adelaide began to see the appeal Sybil and Simon had spoken of. Meerak was a comely shade of blue, very pretty in her own right. And her beautiful, kind heart enhanced this overall impression. She was a lovely woman.

"It is good to be among friends again," said Adelaide, responding to her gentle ways.

"Sybil and Simon can move in with me," said Roark, for he had taken over a single man's dwelling while they were away. His wing was mended and he no longer wore a sling. They can bring Sirius with them," he added, delighted by the prospect.

"Very well," said Meerak. "Come, I will show you where you can sleep. Then we'll have some refreshments. You must be very hungry."

"Indeed, my diet has been frugal. Rat crab and various vegetable plants I could gather."

"We have plenty to go around, especially with Sybil and Simon's BanquoeBag. A very useful Hetopian invention."

"Hetopian?" asked Adelaide. She'd heard of them in Ninth, but had never met one.

"Yes, said Simon. When this is over, we will return to Fifth. Come with us, I know you will be welcome."

"Could I? Is it possible?" After what she had done, the thought of being welcomed by other dimensions left a soft glow about her heart.

"No reason you can't come," reinforced Sybil.

"The uprising is gaining ground and there is much to do," said Simon. "Rinaldo is on his way here to escort us north. We can be of help."

"Rinaldo? Yes, I remember that nice young man I met at the fish market one day. He introduced himself."

CHAPTER SEVEN
Northward Bound

"Anyone who has never made a mistake has never tried anything new."

- Albert Einstein

The following afternoon a shout alerted the rookery. A party of Aquadrians approaching from the back trail had already reached the pool.

Roark took to the sky to investigate, returning with news that Rinaldo had arrived with a large regiment.

Dr. Teselwode, true to his word, had alerted Herclan when Sybil and Simon were overdue. A large force had been deployed, which met up with Rinaldo partway there. Fresh reinforcements escorted them on the final leg north. Rinaldo regrouped taking command of the regiment and headed south once more to rescue the remaining refugees.

The Aquadrians on the cliff top turned out to watch them troop into the village amidst cheers. Profrak and Meerak were on hand to welcome them, providing refreshments and food.

"Glad to see you made it to the Rookery," said Rinaldo. "Not sure we'd have been able to find that cave."

"We discovered a different way out and Roark found the back trail from there," said Sybil.

"How was the trip south?" asked Simon.

"We had a difficult time getting through. Southern forces

are all over the countryside. We'll rest up here a few days and decide what's to be done."

"Our group had a hard time," said Sybil.

"We just managed to get through," added Simon. "Roark, what do you think?"

"There'll be more eyes in the sky," said Roark. "We can send as many Opeggees as needed."

"Of course," said Sybil. "That's a plus."

"And we can harass them. Dive bomb 'em, keep 'em off guard. Our young commanders are very evasive and we'll have vulcan sacs."

"We are very grateful to the Opeggee nation," said Rinaldo. "Had you not brought our people safely here they may not have survived."

"What's happening up north with the Duplicating Halls?" Sybil asked.

"Our scientists are getting closer to solving it. We have only one code left to crack. If only we could get into the locked vault."

Simon patted his shirt pocket. He had forgotten about the key. "What vault are you talking about?"

"Hall number Five has a set of cabinets that holds the key. That much we have been able to establish."

"This vault thing is confusing," said Sybil. *"They keep calling it a vault. But it's only a cabinet."*

"Seems that way," said Simon.

"How did you figure that out?" asked Simon.

"Dimondus," chuckled Rinaldo. "We stormed the pit and captured him. Sladus turned himself in and is working with us now."

"How did that go?" asked Sybil.

"It didn't take long. That coward rolled over at the first threat. He doesn't stick with things for long."

Sybil grinned and Simon gave her a wink, as if to say, let's keep this quiet.

"Told us there was a key under the cabinet, but it was no longer there. It's missing."

Simon held his tongue. He would hold on to the key and tell Rinaldo later, once they were safely north. It was best if not too many people knew its whereabouts.

"I wish I'd been there to see that!" laughed Simon. "He is one scary dude."

"He deserves what he gets," added Sybil, grinning broadly. She felt badly for thinking that. But after his treatment of them in Aquadria, she wasn't so ready to cut him any slack. He'd made their lives miserable enough. Let him sweat.

Calling a general meeting, Rinaldo informed the Aquadrians of their plans. Profrak attended to offer Opeggee air support.

"If anyone feels they are unable to make the trip north, the Opeggees have agreed to shelter those who wish to remain here," said Rinaldo. It was nice to know they were still welcome.

"Yes," said Profrak. "We are honoured to serve beside you. It will take all of us working together to save Aquadria."

"Madonus, will you please do a head count of those who decide to stay?" said Rinaldo.

"Of course," he replied. "I'll have those numbers for you by tomorrow morning."

Turning to Profrak, he said, "I want to take this opportunity to express our appreciation, to thank our allies, our friends here on the cliff top."

A cheer went up from the Aquadrians. Even Sardonica saw the sense of these words and joined in. He was more relaxed now that Rinaldo's forces were present.

Within two days, preparations to leave were in place. All had decided they would risk going north to join the main force. Adelaide elected to go with them, walking with the women and assisting small children.

Roark and other young wing commanders laid in a store of vulcan sacs, prepared to use them if necessary. They would circle overhead, looping out far enough to provide feedback on approaching Aquadorian troops, those loyal to Aquadorus.

There were tearful goodbyes along with invitations and promises of return visits in better times. Waving farewell, the Opeggees watched as the last Aquadrians disappeared down the trail.

Sybil and Simon decided they could best serve by flying high aerial reconnaissance. As they flew escort, Simon said, "It has turned out better than I first thought. I had no idea whether these two nations would come together, not with all the unrest of the first few days."

"Look at Adelaide," said Sybil, pointing to her in the distance. She was toting a young boy on her back. Occasionally, she skipped along, making a game of it. "She is very helpful with the little ones. It's hard to believe she is the same person."

"I suspect she was not well tolerated in the city, maybe even shunned. Alienation can create a change of heart in most people."

"It was good she set out on her own when she did or she may not have survived," said Sybil.

"Past, is in the past. It can stay there," said Simon. He had forgiven her. Realizing there was still a reckoning with Claire to come, he resolved to help with that meeting.

The Aquadrian patrol escorting the refugees made good headway, sticking to lightly wooded areas along hillsides. Fearing ambush from above, they avoided the low-lying areas.

Periodically, they descended to refresh in the river that had carved the valley on its way south.

In the afternoon of the third day a contingent of Aquadorians appeared on the horizon. *"Roark, there's a patrol coming from the north in the valley ahead of them. They are moving pretty fast,"* said Simon.

"I'm on it," said Roark. He accelerated ahead to relay the information to Rinaldo.

"We'll stop until they pass by below us. Tell everyone down the line," ordered Rinaldo.

Holed up in a grove of trees, the hillside cover was adequate concealment. Once an all clear was given they resumed their long, slow trek northward.

After refreshment on the fifth night they camped near the river, too exhausted to climb higher.

Nearing twelve bells, Roark and two of his buddies who had remained on watch north and south of the river, alerted camp. A night patrol was approaching from the south. Groggy children cried out in fear as the adults scooped them up, scrambling toward the safety of the hillside. Shouts from the south meant an Aquadorian scout had discovered them and was raising an alarm to the main body behind.

"Roark swooped into action, dive bombing the scout until he turned tail and ran. He proceeded to drop vulcan pellets in his wake, messing up the trail with hot lava. He and his buddies would make the southern river trail impassable. When it was determined they had done enough damage, they rejoined Rinaldo.

"We bought you some time," he said, recounting the defensive tactic they had executed.

"I'm impressed, Roark. Good thinking and fast action," said Rinaldo. "It's what I like about you."

"All in a night's work," Roark beamed. He was maturing.

Praise didn't ruffle his feathers with pride as much as it once did.

The Aquadrians carried on through the night. Fatigue was a major concern for the older folks and for young children too heavy to carry. Rinaldo had weighed options carefully at the time and made the decision to bed down after they had refreshed in the river. Too late, he realized it had been a foolish gamble to stay in the river valley.

Simon and Sybil, who came into camp to spend their nights, were concerned. It wasn't like Rinaldo to take risks. He was usually very careful.

"Do you think Rinaldo is overly tired?" asked Sybil.

"He has been on the trail a long time, taking the first group north, returning south and now leading this group again. He hasn't had much rest."

"Certainly is unlike him. He normally uses a lot of caution, maybe more than is necessary sometimes."

"I don't think that's fair to say," said Simon. "Can anyone ever be too cautious?"

"Yes, I think we can be too cautious."

"Sybil, I never thought I'd hear you say that. You, of all people, have always been extremely cautious."

"I know, but lately I have been thinking. Is it caution or fear?"

"What do you mean?"

"Most of the time I am acting out of fear. That's what makes me so cautious."

"Isn't that a good thing?"

"Could be, I guess. But in the past it has held me back when I should have acted."

"That may be, but I am sure it has saved you from heading into dangerous situations."

"I suppose I'll never really know. Let's take Wesley Peters, for example. I am afraid of him. I avoid him as much as possible."

Simon acknowledged her fear and continued, "That's true, and I picked up on that. I'm scared of him, too."

"You came out of a fearful situation, though. I think fear stays with us. Like that worn old wagon rut on the way to Lenore Lake. It wears a groove in our brain."

"You're right, Sybil. The Namors and Wesley make me feel the same. Dimondus, too."

"Can anyone make us feel?" asked Sybil, shrugging her shoulders.

"How can *they* not make us feel? You're living in head space now."

"I guess it's more that I *wish* I could be strong enough to live without fear."

"I doubt it has anything to do with strength," said Simon. "A good healthy dose of fear can avoid trouble."

"Healthy fear? It sure doesn't feel healthy!"

"Maybe that's not the right word. How about wise?"

"I never thought about it as being *wise*. But yeah, that makes sense. It could be wise to fear something."

"One day Wesley might get carried away and hurt you," said Simon.

"I have wondered that myself. I did run into him once in the classroom. He was carrying a pencil. To this day I will never know if he *meant* to jab me with it or if it was an accident. I still have the scar. See here, this dark mark on my shin. She held her leg out for Simon to inspect.

"Your shin? That was not an accident."

"He made fencing motions with his pencil. I tried to deflect the advance. Could have been play-acting."

"Nah, if you ask me; that was deliberate. I think there's still a bit of graphite under your skin."

"I cleaned it in the washroom, but that dark mark never came out."

"Why didn't you go to first aid at school?"

"And have to lie about it? I wasn't getting him into more trouble. I'd done that in the past and it only aggravated the situation. No, I need to learn to handle this myself."

"That's not right, Sybil, and you know it!" Simon said, his face flushing with anger.

"Maybe so, but I know what's happened in the past."

"You won't be handling this by yourself anymore. You have me."

"I'm glad of that, but it is mainly up to me. I've faced a lot in Fifth and in Seventh. If I can do that, I can surely face Wesley."

"I understand what you are saying, Sybil. Still, I am right beside you all the way. If you need me I am here for you."

"Thanks, I know that, Simon. And I am here for you."

"A mutual admiration society, hah," laughed Simon.

"Come to think of it, I do admire you. After all you've been through. You are a strong person."

Simon blushed, not knowing quite what to say. Then he grinned and said, "Me str-o-o-ng, sista." He flexed his muscles in a manly way, making light of her compliment.

"No, I mean that, Simon. I am very proud of you. When we talked about fear, how much it has held me back, it has made me realize some things about myself."

"I know one thing. You're one of the bravest people I have met. You came to Leanoria. You found me. You never gave up."

"Fear ruled me all the way through. I should have thought better of going into Spoon Lake that night. I was afraid even then. On the flip side, if I hadn't gone for the midnight swim on Mount Cheam," she paused, "I wouldn't have found you.

None of this would have happened."

"So, what are you saying, Sybil? Do you think you should have been more cautious or not?"

"No, I was not cautious and I am glad I didn't let fear interfere with our destiny."

"In hindsight that's all well and good. But how are we to know?" asked Simon.

"We don't. We never know how things will unfold, do we?"

"It's like that hope thing. We just have to make a decision that seems best at the time and *hope* it was the right thing to do," said Simon.

"I know one thing. I am going to live and act less out of fear. Prudence, for sure. I will weigh the situation and make sure there's a back-up plan. I think that will lessen fear," said Sybil.

"Logic and good common sense. You have that. It is what I like best about you."

This time it was Sybil's turn to blush. "Oh, go on. You're just saying that, Simon."

"No, honestly. You are the type of person who can think their way out of a situation. For instance, with the Snakebush. It was you who figured a way out of that one."

"I suppose," admitted Sybil. She was always shy about compliments. Recalling Simon flexing his muscles in an attempt at humour when complimented, she realized they were very much alike.

"I know you said you have to handle Wesley on your own. He needs to believe that, too. So you lead the way," said Simon. "But whatever happens with Wesley, we stand together."

CHAPTER EIGHT
Solutions

"Everything you can imagine is real."

- Pablo Picasso

Straggling into the northern compound, the last of the beleaguered refugees were greeted by worried friends, given a hearty meal and assigned tents.

Sybil and Simon linked up with Roark and made their way to Rinaldo who had already reported to headquarters. They found him with Herclan, deep in discussion over field plans.

"What would you like us to do?" Simon asked.

"We're still hunting for that last code," said Herclan. "The more bodies on that, the better."

"We're on it," replied Sybil.

They made their way to Fifth Hall to check out the cabinet. "It's that bottom drawer," said Simon, producing the key.

"What was that bright light all about?" asked Sybil.

He turned the key, carefully cracking open the last drawer. Radiant light streamed forth. "I have a good feeling about this," said Simon. "It has a familiar feel."

"It's so bright. Hard to see what it is," said Sybil. She reached in and fished around the bottom of the drawer. Her hand landed on a smooth, cool fragment of stone. The brightness dissipated when she pulled it forth.

"It looks like part of the Dragon's eye crystal!" Simon's jaw dropped as he reached for it. It had the same, cool smoothness he'd felt when he held it aloft in the moonlight at

Spoon Lake.

"This was chipped off the crystal," said Sybil. "That's how Aquadorus gained power!" The realization stunned them. If this was the last of the code, they would have to find DOU. While leaving the chaos of Seventh was a welcome prospect, they were reluctant to abandon their friends.

Roark, who had stood by silently, now broke into a jubilant tap-dance, his green eyes aglow. Sirius had been circling the room, checking out intriguing smells. He returned to sniff the crystal, recognized the scent of DOU, and gave a sharp "Woof!" He bounded around the room, leaping with joy and yapping excitedly.

"This may be the last of the code. We have to get this news to Rinaldo as soon as possible," said Simon. Replacing the key in his pocket, he added the piece of crystal and led the way through the Echo Chamber.

"Sorry for the interruption," said Sybil. "It is important."

"Come in," replied Herclan. "What is it?"

"Before going south we discovered a key when we were working in Hall Five. I kept it safe here," he said, patting his pocket.

"Didn't want rumours of its whereabouts to get around while we were on the trail," added Sybil.

"A key?" asked Rinaldo.

"Yes, we just checked it out," said Sybil. "We found a piece of DOU's eye crystal. We think it is the last of the missing link, the means to Aquadorus's power. It may provide energy for the Duplicating Chambers."

"It needs to be returned to DOU," said Simon.

"So, once the dragon has gained full control, this will all be restored as it was before?" asked Rinaldo.

"We hope," said Sybil.

Simon had come to realize that hope played a huge part in life. To hear about it again set his heart soaring. If that were true, would his family in Fifth be restored? His heartbeat did a flip-flop, faltered and jolted to life, sending a rich coursing of hope through his arteries.

Sybil, aware of his excitement, grabbed his arm and stayed his urgency. There was much to do before leaving for Fifth. How did the Duplicating Chambers work? Did each person need to go back through in order to be restored? Or would the dragon's mysterious power break some sort of spell? It was baffling. Thinking about her first encounter with the Leanori Truids, she had wondered why Gerardo and Gergenon had been so at ease with her and the Hetopians. Were they actually Aquadrians? The rest of the commune had seemed distrustful. Maybe this was all orchestrated to get them both to Seventh!

"Come, Simon. We need to think about this." Her dad's default answer to anything baffling rose in her naturally.

Roark decided to stay behind and listen to field plans. His father, Profrak, had come north with them to lead the Opeggee escort, see to safety, and relay information back to the rookery.

Once outside, Sybil said, "Maybe we should test this out before we find DOU. That crystal must have the power to transform. Once we check the crystal fragment with each colour-coded file maybe we can find a clue as to how this actually works."

"That could take a very long time," replied Simon.

"Okay, the top drawer had red files. We thought maybe the colours correspond to different species or perhaps dimensions."

"Why colour code? Are some files for animals, while others are human?"

"You mean, like taking on traits of the species?" Sybil thought about it for a while. "So, let's say, the Namors Guardia have a keen sense of smell, sharp-nosed you could say. Who do you know has a good sniffer?" she laughed, giving Sirius a playful tussle.

Simon enlarged on the theory. "Suppose they sent bloodhounds through the Duplicating Chamber. Voila! Some very hideous, sharp-nosed guards are produced!"

"Too weird, you think?" asked Sybil. But the thought stuck with her. After mulling it over, she said, "You may have hit on something there, Simon. Let's explore that idea a little more."

"What about the Leanori Truids at the underwater city? Farmers, just as the Leanorians were." The thought made his stomach lurch. Had they been transformed and sent to other underwater settlements? "We may be on the right track, Sybil."

"We know this is happening here in Seventh. Rinaldo confirmed that some of the halls used existing life forms to mutate species, as in the Aquadrians. They are becoming fully aquatic. But Rinaldo has human features, too. So maybe there is cross dimensional infiltration. Those who did not take well to transformation were unable to undergo these changes."

"Maybe one has to be willing to do that. The will has a lot of power," said Simon. "No one is just going to lie down and let things happen. So unless they agree to it…" He left the thought hanging.

"The halls can create new life forms? Like bloodhounds to Namors? This is some scary stuff!" said Sybil.

"Over-the-top outrageous. That's too insane!"

"Well, let's say, for the sake of argument, we are right. It might mean all those files we went through…hmm. What a job that would be; sorting everyone out individually."

"Can't help but think about the colour-coded files again. If they pertain to species or even different realms, they could be sent through en masse. We've never been inside the actual Duplicator. The capacity could be enormous," said Simon.

"How do we manage that? Those loyal to Aquadorus are not going in without a fight."

"Difficult for sure. Maybe impossible."

"Remember how the guards reacted to DOU's beam in the pit that night? They dropped their weapons and stood in awe," said Sybil.

"Yes, until the commander yelled at them to pick up their weapons. Does DOU need to come back or will the fragment of crystal have the same effect?"

"We could try it with Dimondus. Even though he confessed about the key, that scoundrel is still loyal to Aquadorus through and through."

"If it can change him, then we are on the right track," said Simon.

"We don't want to injure him. Let's catch a rat crab first and send it through."

"No, too risky. We might end up with something much worse. Imagine a rat crab with a nastier attitude."

"You're right. But who or what will Dimondus become?" asked Sybil.

"I think he will just go back to being Aquadrian, before Aquadorus set this whole thing in motion."

"If this works and the process is completed, we can destroy these halls. Roark would like that!"

"He sure loves the sound of vulcan pellets exploding," laughed Simon.

"But why was Dimondus looking for the key to that cabinet? If he looks at the crystal he will have an attitude change."

"Maybe that crystal is needed to operate the Duplicator

somehow."

"This is getting complicated. On one hand it might change people's attitude, on the other, it may hold power to generate reversals."

"Let's take a look at the Duplicator," said Simon.

She switched on the illuminator and entered the mirror maze.

"This is a huge maze. It's as large as the one at the lake bottom settlement," said Sybil, recalling that she'd counted 175 footsteps along the outside wall. She had been right to question Namors Guardia involvement in the courtyard that night.

Sirius, who was tagging along between them, looked at his reflections and began to bark loudly. Missing his dog friends, he trotted over to the nearest dog. When his cold, wet nose investigated the glassy surface, his enthusiasm faded.

"We'll be home soon," said Simon, giving him a reassuring pat. When they reached the Duplicating Chamber, they hesitated. "Look for an outlet. This is hall number Five. It must be the main generator. If we can find how this crystal fits, we know we are right."

They searched the walls and even reached under the outer edge of the Duplicator, but found nothing.

Sirius, nosing around the floor, came to an uneven surface in the corner near the Duplicator and whined.

"What is it, boy?" asked Sybil. "Did you find something?"

Simon ran his hand over the spot Sirius had discovered. "Looks the same as the rest of the floor, but feel here. There's an impression."

Sybil touched the surface and felt the indentation. "Try the crystal. See if it fits."

Simon reached into his pocket, drew forth the piece of crystal and set it in place. The interior of the Chamber lit up and the Duplicator began to hum.

"Wowsers! This is unbelievable!" said Simon.

"We might have it figured out," said Sybil. She switched off the illuminator and looked around the room. "The Duplicator in Fifth at the lake bottom city could be connected to power in the Seventh."

"Or, there is another piece of crystal in Fifth."

"Now, all we need to do is compare colour codes. Didn't Rinaldo say they had only one code to crack? I think we just did that," said Simon.

"No, it isn't the code. Like we said before, it's the energy supply to the Chamber. The crystal is the source of energy."

"Okay then, Rinaldo must mean that their scientists have figured out the DNA codes.

"Let's go find him," said Sybil. They unplugged the crystal and the room went dark.

"Where's your illuminator, Sybil?"

Fumbling for the light that hung on her belt, she lit up the chamber again. Looking around, they realized Sirius was missing.

"Where is he?" said Sybil. "Sirius!"

"He's gone into the Duplicator!" cried Simon, horrified.

"Hurry, follow me."

"We can't go in there."

"It's not powered up, Simon. You have the crystal in your pocket."

"Oh! Right. Still, what's on the other side?"

"We have to find Sirius," said Sybil. Grabbing his hand, she plunged through the Duplicator field wall. A vast panorama extended before them—an exotic oasis of sand and sun. "Sirius, where are you?"

"It's no wonder they don't mind going through transformation," said Simon. "I could lay on this beach without a care in the world."

"Well, we have a care. Follow those dog tracks. We need to find him."

They set off over a sand dune and ran after the disappearing tracks in the distance.

"Crikey! He sure is fast," said Simon."

"And stubborn, when he gets something into his head. What if we can't find him?"

"You have the BanquoeBag. Try that. He always responds to food."

She hauled out his favorite dried beef sticks, but he did not respond to their calls. "Power up. We need to fly."

Following his trail, they skimmed the sandy surface. He was nowhere in sight.

"He can't just disappear like that. Something or someone has got him," said Simon.

The sound of waves in the distance drew them on. They picked up his tracks again. "Simon, he's heading toward the ocean! This is where they are set free when they become fully aquatic."

"Over there to the right, is that Sirius?" He was running in the surf and biting at the foam of cresting waves.

"Sirius, come here!" He was having too much fun to hear or obey. Catching up to him, Simon grabbed his ruff and scolded, "Sirius, you can't keep running off like this."

"If he hadn't, would we have discovered this?" asked Sybil. "He has a mind of his own but it has led us in wondrous ways."

"You're right. He does have a mind of his own. I just don't like to follow it sometimes."

"Now that we know more about how things work, let's go back," she said, forming the mind net and hauling Sirius aboard.

Safely out of the Duplicating Chamber, they went to the cabinet that housed the colour-coded files. "Rinaldo says their scientists have these codes cracked. We have to let command know," said Simon.

Defence preparations were in full swing at command centre. When they caught Rinaldo's attention he came over to speak with them, anxious to hear if they had learned anything new. Following their revelations, a meeting with the scientists was called. When asked to turn over the crystal, Simon glanced at Sybil and made a decision.

"This crystal does not leave our possession," he telepathed.

She nodded. "*Under no circumstances! We must return it to DOU.*"

"Who can we trust?"

"No one. We keep control. When it is used, we have to be present at all times."

"This piece of crystal belongs to DOU. We were entrusted with finding the dragon's eye crystal, so it stays with us," said Simon.

One of the scientists protested. "But you know nothing about it, how it works, how it should be used."

"That doesn't matter. We know enough. You can use it to set the codes in place to do the work. But it stays with us," Sybil echoed Simon's last words.

Rinaldo intervened. "Sybil and Simon are responsible for the crystal. It stays with them." He eyed the scientist who had challenged them. One could never be too careful.

Outside, he approached Simon and told him to guard the crystal well. "I know that man Brutanus. He was influential in the scientific community. Bears watching."

"No worries, Rinaldo. We can handle it," said Simon. "See you later."

Walking past the last hall, Sybil said, "I could sure use a ramble in the forest away from all this craziness."

"Let's head out for a bit," agreed Simon. When they had distanced themselves from the settlement, he handed her the piece of crystal. "They know I am carrying it. Might be better if you keep it safe."

She accepted the crystal and tucked it in her pocket, secured the flap over it and tugged down her tunic. "Maybe it is better if neither of us carries it."

"What are you suggesting? We stash it out here in the forest?"

"Maybe, but I don't feel safe doing that either."

"Nothing is safe these days. We carry it with us and watch out for each other."

"That man Brutanus; Rinaldo said he was a prominent scientist. Someone had to design these halls and set up the scientific protocol," said Sybil.

"Could be many more involved. Builders, contractors."

"These are dangerous times. We must take care, trust no one."

"Not even Rinaldo?" asked Simon.

"I suppose he is the one person we can trust," said Sybil. "And, Dr. Teselwode."

After their walk, Rinaldo came looking for them. "We have a plan in motion. Brutanus is anxious to give it a trial. He's pretty agitated."

"Why is that?" asked Sybil.

"He wants the crystal now and doesn't wish to wait upon you. He will try to gain control of it."

"Well, he's out of luck. To make it easier for them, we will be available at all times and we go together. Neither one of us will be alone with the crystal."

"I, too, will be there," reassured Rinaldo. "You have my

protection. I'll have my trusted advisors posted discretely. You will be safe."

Arriving at Hall Five, they gained access to the Duplicating Chamber. The room was crowded because everyone from the scientific community had turned out for the first experiment. Herclan, Hermaine, and Calazone were also on hand.

"Do you have the crystal with you?" asked Brutanus. He fidgeted and stamped his feet, impatient to get on with the experiment.

"Yes, I have it," replied Sybil, holding it out for all to see.

Dimondus, who was standing in the centre of the room trembling with fear, lifted his head when he heard her voice. He glared at her, hatred oozing from his pores. It was all her fault, and that brother of hers.

"Okay, go ahead," said Brutanus.

Sybil stepped forward and placed the crystal in the space on the floor near the Duplicator. The room lit up and people extinguished the torches they were carrying.

"Brutanus, who was holding the DNA code for Dimondus's species, stepped toward the Duplicator and held the holograph over the top of the crystal. The genetic sequencing lined up against universal order. To reverse the changes he flipped the holograph over so that it sequenced according to universal law.

"Looks like all is in order; we can proceed. Step in," said Brutanus, pressing him toward the energy field.

Dimondus shuffled forward, trembling. His lip quivered in protest, but he knew better than to resist. He stepped through the energy field and disappeared.

"It will take only a few minutes to reverse his sequence," said Brutanus. "He was a human before. He should come out as human."

"A human! Dimondus was a human?" said Simon.

"This is some scary stuff!" replied Sybil. *"Where do you suppose he came from? Can't be Seventh!"*

"Likely from Fifth," said Simon.

"You mean, a Leanori Truid or Graenwolven?"

"Very possible. There is connection to Fifth and they have all but disappeared."

"Totally insane! Aquadorus is insane."

Those assembled held their breath as Dimondus re-emerged, fully human. He was a youthful lad, not much older than Sybil and Simon. His face was glowing with health and he was in good humour.

"W-what happened?" he asked, looking at the crowd of people in the Chamber. The glassy sheen in his eyes held a dazed confusion as he checked his hands. He lifted his trembling fingers and traced both sides of his jawline. "Where h-have I been?" he laughed shakily.

The crowd in the room gasped. It was more than they could have hoped for. A complete reversal.

Brutanus snorted. "Hah, we have it! We can do mass processing!"

Herclan stepped in. "Good! We'll get started straight away. Rinaldo, Hermaine, Calazone, bring all those who belong to the human files first. They were eager to undergo their own transformation, but they would have to wait.

Reversion went on all afternoon until they agreed to quit for the evening. Sybil retrieved the crystal and tucked it in her pocket. After dinner she handed it to Simon. "Best we keep alternating who carries it."

"Excellent idea. Look at all these humans amongst us. Almost feels like home."

"Let's go find Dimondus and see what he has to say," said Sybil, threading her way through the crowd. "It's strange to see so many humans and Aquadrian folk together. We must have looked very odd to these people."

"Yes, they used to call me 'Nogillers,' " said Simon. "When I was living here."

Up ahead, Dimondus was engaged in easy banter with a number of other humans. Curious Aquadrians had gathered around, plying them with questions. Simon and Sybil ambled over.

"How are you feeling, Dimondus?" asked Simon.

"Hard to explain. There's a lightness I never had before, as though a weight has dropped away."

"Do you remember anything from Aquadrian times?" asked Sybil.

"Not really. It's all very hazy. Fragments maybe. More like feelings, not memories."

"How about before? Where you came from, who you were or I should say, *are*, I guess," said Simon. He wanted to know more of what happened in Leanoria. Maybe Dimondus would have knowledge of his family.

"At the moment, I am scrambled. It might take some time."

Sybil posed a question that was utmost in everyone's mind. "How long before we can return?" She longed for Hetopia and home. Her problems in Third seemed insignificant. School and her trouble with Wesley Peters paled in comparison. That bully! He needs to have a reversal. If only it were that easy.

Later that day, while they were making their way toward the mess tents, Dr. Teselwode caught up with them. "There you are! I was dreadfully worried when you didn't return that day for our dinner engagement."

"Dr. Teselwode!" said Sybil. "Sorry we couldn't get word

to you. Thank you for letting Herclan know. He sent out a regiment and they met up with Rinaldo."

"Yes, I know. Heard all about it when they came into camp. That Rinaldo is a very determined man. Insisted on returning south immediately. He was terribly concerned about those who were left behind."

"We made it to safety at the cliff top rookery. Sure happy to see Rinaldo when he got back. Had no idea whether he made it through safely."

"Why don't we sit together for dinner and you can tell me all about it," suggested Dr. Teselwode.

After collecting their trays of food they settled in a quiet corner of the mess tent.

"Adelaide is meeting me here shortly. Sure was happy to see her. I hope you don't mind having dinner with the two of us."

"Not at all. We ran into her in the south," replied Simon.

"Yes, she told me all about it. I was very concerned for her welfare when she struck out on her own. She didn't dare come back to the city."

"Those were pretty grim days. We left just in time before the flooding began."

"That was a very decent thing you did; rescuing her from that sulphur pit in the cave."

"It was nothing, really. You do that for people," said Sybil.

"All the same, it is very admirable."

"Thank you, Dr. Teselwode. You have done some very admirable things yourself," said Sybil.

"Just my job, honestly. Can't imagine doing anything else."

"There you are," said Adelaide, setting her tray beside Dr. Teselwode. He moved over to make room for her.

"Hi, Adelaide," he greeted her with affection. "I asked Simon and Sybil to join us."

"Wonderful. I was hoping we'd have a chance to meet and talk. You have been so busy with the reversals going on. Isn't it exciting?"

"Yes," said Sybil. "It will take time to get it all done. But this first day has been a good beginning."

"Tell us what happened in the city after we left," said Simon, looking at Dr. Teselwode.

"I joined a group, about the time Dimondus was hauled before Aquadorus to account for your disappearance. We hiked north as fast as we could. A lot of people joined us along the way. I am not too sure what went on in the city."

Simon nodded. "Thought I would like to have seen what happened to Dimondus, but now that he has gone through reversal—the poor guy."

"I heard many were lost in the flood," said the doctor. His tired face sagged with sadness. "Such a waste of life."

Sybil thought about the last time she had used that phrase. 'Such a waste.' They were passing a war memorial at the Keith Wilson intersection on Vedder Road in Third dimension. It was the morning of her Grade 8 field trip. The thought of war always distressed her, and now she was in the middle of one. She was beginning to understand the concepts at work. Power, ego, greed, fear. Still, something must trigger all those feelings. Inadequacy, ineptness, fear? Maybe it only boiled down to fear. I must remember to talk to Simon about this.

"What are you thinking, Sybil?" asked Adelaide. She had been studying the young girl, watching emotions ripple across her face.

"Oh, I was just thinking about what Dr. Teselwode said. 'Such a waste of life.' "

"Had we stood up to events in the city earlier, perhaps we'd have had a different outcome," said the doctor.

"Yes," said Adelaide. "I am as much, if not more, to blame.

I let my bitterness get in the way." She looked at Simon, lines of regret deeply etched across her face. "I can say from my own experience; I chose the wrong path."

"Now, Adelaide," said the doctor. "It is time to forgive yourself." He had befriended her over the years, checking in on her regularly during his rounds in the city.

"I left Ninth and escaped through Fifth." She felt the need to confess. "I was sure no one there cared a lick for me. I was difficult to be around, that I admit. It took me a long time to accept the loss of Benni. Having more children never deadened the pain of that loss."

"How many children did you have?" asked Sybil.

"Anna was my first, Benni came second. About a year after Benni died, I had twins Jules and Oliver. Another son Ambrose came two years later, followed by a daughter Mary. We had six altogether."

"That is a nice number," said Sybil, thinking of herself and Simon. Just the two of them, and she had been an only child for her first 13 years. It was a lonely existence at times.

"It doesn't matter how many children you have. When one is lost, it stuns you." She held up her right hand, touched each finger and said, "Which one would you miss the most?"

Putting it that way, Sybil could better understand. But there was no way of ever knowing fully what that was like. She caught Adelaide's eyes and held her gaze, sending her a warmth of compassion.

That evening, as they settled for the night, Sybil shared her concern. "What if someone comes for the crystal tonight?"

"Do you want to sleep first while I keep watch?"

"No, I can watch first. You sleep." She stood near the corner of hall number one. They had set up camp in the very same spot as the night they had followed Dimondus and

Sladus to the dragon pit.

"If anyone tries, Sirius will give them *serious* trouble," Simon chuckled at his pun.

"Oh, brother," Sybil groaned, rolling her eyes. "Give me a break. That one's getting old."

Simon grinned as he turned over for some shut-eye.

It was nearing two bells when a commotion along the path erupted. A clash of metal hitting metal and loud voices broke the stillness of the night. Sirius set up a frenzy of barking.

Simon woke instantly. "What's going on, Sybil? You okay?"

"Yes. It sounds like there's a fracas on the trail near the halls."

After a few moments, quiet prevailed. Simon and Sybil held their breath, prepared to disappear into the night. Poking his head around the corner of the hall, Rinaldo called out softly, "All's well."

"What's going on?" asked Sybil.

"We caught Brutanus. He was on his way here, no doubt trying to steal the crystal. Nothing to worry about. We're going to put him through the Duplicator tomorrow, see what comes of him. That should fix him up," he laughed. "It sure improved Dimondus's outlook on life."

"That *was* an improvement," Simon agreed. "But who would have thought he was a human? And so young at that!"

"We may be in for a lot of surprises," said Rinaldo. "It's late now, try to rest."

"Thank you, Rinaldo," said Sybil. "What about you? You can't keep pushing yourself. Those long marches north and south. Now you're on night duty."

"I'm all right. Had a good sleep earlier. I'll leave you until tomorrow, but we'll keep watch every night. Who knows what else will come your way."

Faithful to his word, Rinaldo kept watch, alternating with

his trusted friends while reversions were under way.

CHAPTER NINE
Reunion

"I have never let my schooling interfere with my education."

- Mark Twain

Aquadorus had used mutation to exploit the greenish cast of Aquadrian skin. Given the choice to remain Aquadrian or to complete full aquatic transition, most chose to revert to their previous form. Since there were few of Aquadorus's supporters who had come north, a very small percentage did not re-emerge. Enthralled by sand and tide, they went on to life at sea, fully aquatic. Gradually, the old order in Seventh was returning.

Simon and Sybil stood watching on the final day while Herclan, Hermaine, Calazone and Rinaldo prepared themselves for reversal. Together, Herclan, Hermaine and Calazone stepped through the energy field, while Rinaldo held the correct holographic DNA code in place. They re-emerged as original Aquadrians, plainly recognizable, but changed.

Returning to their original form was a powerful experience. All three stepped back into their former existence, a bit shaken but otherwise complete.

Rinaldo, the last to transition, looked at Simon and Sybil for a very long time before he said, "Here goes…"

Herclan held the holograph in place while Rinaldo stepped through the energy field. He re-emerged in human form, a bit dazed but totally aware of who he was. It was one of the smoother transitions.

For Simon, it was a total shock. He lost consciousness, slumping to the floor with a thump. The man who was Rinaldo, rushed to his side.

"Simon," he called out. "Is it really you?"

Bewildered by this reaction, Sybil knelt to tend to her brother. "Simon, are you okay?" She shook his shoulders. "Wake up, Simon."

"He's out cold," said the man. "It was too much of a shock. I had no idea!"

"We have to do something," said Sybil.

"Nothing to be done except wait. He'll come around in a few minutes."

Sybil leaned toward the man. "What happened?"

"He did not expect…I did not expect to meet him here."

"What do you mean? Who are you?"

"I am Karl Dugall, his pa on the farm. Claire entrusted us with his care. He became our third son."

Sybil nearly joined Simon on the floor. No words came to her, for her tongue cleaved to the roof of her mouth. She had not believed that her promise made to Simon, to help find his family in Fifth, would actually happen.

Eventually, she managed to attempt a feeble response. "How did you get here?"

The answer had to wait because Simon began to moan. Consciousness seeped into his awareness and he opened his eyes. A concerned image floated before him. He blinked and rubbed his eyes, restoring his blurry vision. Rolling onto his side, he slowly pushed himself into sitting position.

"Pa, is it you?" Simon was overwhelmed. "Really you?"

"Simon…" He gently pulled him into a comforting embrace. Simon let himself be held in the arms of the man who had reared him, taught him to show respect for all living things, to stand fast in the face of uncertainty and to persist beyond defeat.

After a moment, he pulled Simon to his feet. "Stand, son. We walk out of here together." He put his arm around Simon and stepped into the mirror maze, out of Hall Five, out of that hell-hole in which he had been trapped.

Simon turned to his pa. "I almost gave up hope. Thought I'd never find you. If it hadn't been for…" he turned and gave Sybil a grateful smile. "I want you to meet my sister. This is Sybil, from Third."

"Glad to meet you, Sybil. Claire would be so proud," said Karl, smiling broadly at the two of them. "Come, let us find a place to talk."

Simon and Sybil led the way to where they had set up camp. They found a comfortable spot and sat facing each other, their backs resting against trees. Simon's need for answers spilled over. "What happened to everyone after we were taken from the farm?"

"Things are still a little hazy, Simon. Please, let me adjust for a while. First, tell me what happened to you. Where have you been all this time?"

Simon recounted his story, telling him of the two years he had spent in the dungeon at Leanoria under the harsh conditions of the Namors Guardia. He spoke of his despair, his loneliness, his fear. He told him of his rescue by Sybil and the Hetopians. But he decided to wait for a more opportune time to tell him of life in Third with his family. Pa had been an influential and revered part of his life in Fifth. He did not want to negate that or hurt him.

"Do you remember what happened after they took me from you at Leanoria?" Simon wanted to understand.

"Same as for everyone else, I suspect. When our family was rounded up off the farm, we were first taken to Leanoria. That much you know. When they separated us, the very thought of you…alone." His voice broke. "I could not bear it. Thinking of what they would do to you."

"I was terrified," said Simon. "What would happen to you, m-my family?" At the thought of it he choked on his words. "W-we must find everyone."

"We will," said pa. "You and I will make sure of that."

"And Sybil," said Simon.

"Yes. Sybil, too." He appraised her face. It was comely and serene. There was a joyful smile illuminating the passion that inspired her determination.

"So, what happened after they took Simon from you?" Sybil wanted to hear the full story.

He glanced at Simon. "We were taken through a tunnel, a long walk. All five of us: me, your ma, Elsie, Peter and Davie."

"That's the tunnel to the lake bottom settlement. That's how I found Simon."

"We were taken to a room where many other families were held. After that, the order of things is still unclear." He paused for a moment trying to recollect. "I think we were examined by some doctor or someone acting in that capacity. From there we were taken to a large hall. The noise of it still rings in my ears."

"The Echo Chamber," said Simon.

"Yes, exactly like the hall we just left. It had the mirror maze too."

"At least we have broken the silencing code. The crystal must hold the key to that, too." She held it up for him to see. As she turned it, light reflected off the facets, illuminating Pa's face.

"Beautiful! What is it?"

"It is a piece of DOU's eye crystal. The Dragon of the Universe," said Simon.

"It is the energy source that Aquadorus of Seventh stole to

build all of this." They filled him in, recounting the history of Aquadorus's battle with DOU and his rise to power.

"You were here for your first four years? Before you came to live with our family?" Karl was flabbergasted.

"Yes, and later I was rescued by Sybil, just as the Book of Wisdom foretold, I was taken to recover in Hetopia. That is a western civilization in Fifth dimension, a long way from where our farm was."

"Incredible!"

"From there we went to Third."

He left that thought mull a bit, prompting Pa to ask, "What is Third like?" He was curious about Simon's other family, for he had always known of them.

"Sybil and I are twins, as you know. I met my family in Third. Lived there a short while until we realized we had been called for something larger. We came back to Fifth and here we are."

"Finding you was always Simon's goal. I promised to help him," said Sybil. "And now we must look for the rest of your family."

"Thank you. Without your help none of this would have happened."

"They have to be here in Seventh," said Sybil. "Those people living at the lake bottom city at Leanoria are cloned, which means that hall must have the capacity to clone and transform."

"So, we were sent here to Aquadria to mutate and when the time was right would have been sent through Fifth Hall, the final transformation. From there we would've been set free on the high seas."

"Must admit, the panorama of sand and ocean is very appealing," said Simon.

"Certainly is beautiful on the other side. A siren's call. I can see the allure it held for some," added Sybil.

"You've seen it?" asked Pa.

"Yes, our dog Sirius ran off while we were exploring inside."

"Pretty brave of you."

"Had no choice. He ran through the Duplicator field wall. Once we figured out the crystal provided the power, it was safe enough to enter," said Sybil.

"A lot of us did not want that. And I suspect many of us were incapable of fully transitioning."

"So, is that why this sort of thing is doomed to fail?" asked Sybil. "Forcing people against their will does not work. The will has power in itself."

"The right to decide. Everyone has the right to choose for themselves," said Pa.

"Many ways to live," said Simon. He certainly had had a lot of different experiences lately. Where did he finally want to settle in his life?

Dusting twigs from her clothing, Sybil stood up. "Now that we have caught up a bit, I think it is time to go looking. Your family is out there somewhere."

"Shall we split up or stay together?" asked Simon.

"Stay together." Pa was reluctant to let Simon out of his sight. "I don't want to take the risk of losing you in these crowds."

They searched for the rest of the afternoon and all the next day. Simon was becoming frustrated. *"Let's take to the air,"* he telepathed.

"Might alarm your pa."

"He has to know sometime. I'll explain it to him before we go."

"Okay, if you think he's ready for it."

"Pa, the Hetopians have taught us many things. They are an unusual civilization. We have learned time travel and alternate travel methods. Sybil and I want to step up the search. We're going to take to the air."

"Take to the air. What do you mean? Fly like a bird?" Pa looked at him as though he were daft.

"Nothing to it and we'll cover more ground in short order."

"Well, I suppose," he said, scratching his head. "Let me see this."

Lifting off, they gave a short demonstration, surprising all surrounding them. Humans and Aquadrians, after making their final choice, had no knowledge of this capability. They gaped in disbelief and awe.

"We'll check in with you from time to time."

"Why don't you go to the main mess tent and have a bite to eat, Pa. We can easily find you there."

"Okay, that's fine by me. I am tired and hungry. I'll wait."

"I don't know who to look for," said Sybil.

"It has been well over two years since I saw them last. I'd know Ma, but the kids will have changed. Still, I think I would recognize them."

They made a general pass over the multitudes but had no luck. "Could be anywhere and probably not even together," said Simon.

"Very likely, since everyone has gone through in random groupings," said Sybil.

After searching all that day, Simon became despondent. "Let's check in with Pa." His hope of ever finding them was waning. What if they chose another path? Maybe sand and surf…the thought stalled.

When they entered the mess tent, Simon let out a whoop. "It's Ma! They must have found each other here." He rushed forward, welcomed by Josie's bear hug.

"Simon! Thank the Stars you are safe! Pa told me

everything that happened since we saw you last."

"We need to find Elsie, Peter and Davie now," said Sybil.

"You must be Sybil. I am Josie." She gave her a warm hug. "So glad to finally meet. Claire would be so proud of you two!"

"Hope we can end this soon. Aquadorus needs to be brought under control. Holding command over these halls is crucial. With northern forces in charge; I hope it won't be long," said Simon.

"We should get back to the search," said Sybil, lifting off. They made numerous passes over the crowds. People stared up at them in shock.

"Let's get the crowds to help us," suggested Sybil. "Tell them to spread the word. Ask them to inquire about Elsie, Peter and Davie Dugall. Tell them to report to the mess tent. Their ma and pa are waiting for them."

"You're a genius," said Simon. He swooped over the crowds, delivering the message. By that evening they had covered the majority of the area and decided to return to the mess tent, hoping the strategy had been successful.

When they arrived, they saw two out of three had made it to the tent. Elsie and Peter had changed a lot in the intervening time and Simon had to look twice to make sure. Davie, the youngest, was still missing.

"The best plan is to stay here for the night," decided Pa. "In case Davie makes it back. We don't want him to come here and not find us."

Simon nodded. "Let's have dinner and bed down near the entries. Sybil and I will take the far one."

"And we'll stay near this entrance," said Pa.

The search resumed early the following morning.

"He must be afraid," said Simon. "All alone." He recalled

his own loneliness in prison at Leanoria. Simon was determined this should be the day to find Davie. He had to be somewhere in the crowd.

By late afternoon, after an exhaustive search, their hopes faded. "I hate to go back without him. How do we tell Ma and Pa?"

"We've covered the area many times. He isn't in the crowd," said Sybil. "Let's regroup. Maybe someone will come up with an idea."

Back at the mess tent the family waited in hope. Sirius, who had stayed behind, nudged Ma's knee, sensing her distress. The dogs on her farm had always held a special place in her heart. She had taken to the bloodhound immediately.

"We looked everywhere. Covered the area many times. I doubt he's in the crowd or he would have turned up by now."

"Where is he?" Josie's worried face held a sadness devoid of hope. She stroked Sirius's head as he nuzzled her thigh.

Simon watched the hound comfort his ma and a thought began to form.

"If only we had something of Davie's. Sirius could track him."

Ma's face brightened. "Simon, I do have something." She drew forth a leather pouch she kept secured around her neck. "I have always kept a lock of hair from each of my children. I have yours here, too."

"You do?" Simon was touched. What a stroke of luck that Ma, in all her sentimental ways, had managed to preserve the pouch.

She searched among the locks and drew forth a reddish-golden curl. "This is Davie's. He was always the fair one in our family. He took after the Dugalls." She handed it to Simon.

"Come here, Sirius." Holding the curl to his nose he commanded, "Find Davie. Go on, you can do it. Find Davie."

Sirius bayed and set off. Weaving through the crowds, he located the scent he was looking for. It was a meandering path, long and convoluted. Eventually it led toward the halls, visiting each one.

"He must have been curious about these halls. To go back and visit them? Why would he do that?" asked Simon.

When Sirius approached Fifth Hall he bayed loudly and entered.

"Davie's gone back in?" asked Sybil.

"Or Sirius is picking up the scent from when he left," said Simon. "Check it out, boy."

They made their way through the Echo Chamber. The silence was eerie, for the power of the crystal, no longer engaged, rendered it ineffective. Once through the mirror maze, Sirius followed the track to the Duplicator field wall that separated the two worlds.

"Has he gone back in, or is this his trail coming out?" asked Sybil.

"Go on, Sirius. Lead the way," said Simon. Following him through the deactivated field wall, Sirius again picked up his track.

"He's headed out to sea!" cried Sybil.

"He's chosen the ocean?" Simon was scared and confused. "How could he?"

"Let's just see where this goes first," said Sybil. "Maybe he was only curious. Sand and surf has its beauty. It's restful and refreshing."

"What if he wanted this?"

"If he has chosen this—what did your pa say? Everyone has the right to choose for themselves."

"He's only a kid."

"True, but he can still determine what he likes for himself."

"He doesn't have a full experience. How is he to know?

There are so many ways to live. Wouldn't it be better to experience more before you decide?"

"You would think," said Sybil. "But, it is what it is now."

Sirius surged ahead toward the surf pounding the shore. He was happy to be back at the seaside. Plunging into the waves he began to dog paddle. He headed out to sea, determined to retrieve an object on which he was fixated. He latched on and hauled it to shore buoying the form to the top of the cresting waves. A head of reddish-golden hair broke the surface.

"Help me, Sybil! It's Davie!" Simon dove into the water, followed by Sybil. They tugged at Davie, floated him to shore and carried him onto the sand.

Rolling him onto his back, Sybil began resuscitation, just as she had been taught in First Aid class at Explorers Club. She felt for the carotid pulse, locating a faint irregular thread that disappeared under her fingertips. She tilted his head back and pulled his jaw forward to open his airway. Then she blew a breath of air into his lungs, followed by a second. "Simon, push here on his sternum." She showed him the proper compressions. "Breathe, Davie. Come on."

Conflicting thoughts hurtled through her mind. She was told current practice required no rescue breathing. But that made no sense to her so she continued giving him air, alternating turns when they tired. Davie's chest heaved with each breath and chest compression until finally he coughed, bringing up water. When he began breathing on his own, and his pulse grew in strength under her fingertips, they rolled him on his side in recovery position.

"Davie! It's me Simon. Can you hear me?"

Davie's eyelashes quivered and briefly fluttered open. Sirius's snuffling nose nudged his cheek and his long, pink tongue massaged his face, willing life back into him.

"Okay, Sirius. We know you're happy. Now let me see

Davie."

Lying on his side, Davie spluttered, "B-burns." His voice came in gasps between fits of coughing. He took in sips of air, fighting the pain as his chest revolted against the natural rhythm of his diaphragm. "Ch-chest…burns." He continued heaving and coughing, clearing mucous that clogged his airway until his breathing began to ease.

"You'll be okay, Davie," reassured Simon. "Can you try sitting up?" Simon and Sybil lifted him to sitting position where he sat for a long time in a confused state. He drew in deep breaths, huffing and coughing, coaxing the salty brine from his lungs.

"That's it, Davie. You'll be fine," said Simon.

Davie turned toward the voice and a slow dawning of recognition lit his face. "S-simon! That you?"

"Yes, Davie. It's me."

"H-how, how?"

"Long story. Right now we have to get you out of here. Can you stand up?"

"I think so," replied Davie, pushing himself to his knees. Simon put his arm around his waist and hoisted him to standing position.

"What are you doing here, Davie?"

"I was curious. Went inside and saw the sand. Never saw the ocean before."

"So you decided to play in it?"

"Yeah," grinned Davie, sheepishly. "Dumb idea, wasn't it?"

"Not a good one, with the power of ocean currents. You must have been caught in an undertow," said Sybil.

"Last I remember, it felt like someone was pulling on my feet. Sucked me right under. Had to fight hard to come back up for air."

"Not like our swimming hole or the lake back home," said

Simon.

"Sure lucky we found you when we did!" said Sybil.

"Thanks to Sirius," said Simon. Sirius sat next to Davie, panting. He pressed his head against Davie's thigh and nuzzled his outstretched hand.

"Is this your dog?"

"Yeah, we came by him at Leanoria. Been together mostly since then."

"He's one awesome dog," said Davie.

"Yeah, he pulled you to shore," said Simon, running his hand along the wet fur of his back.

Davie bent over and hugged Sirius around his neck. "Thank you, boy."

"Let's get out of here," said Sybil. "Your ma and pa are terribly worried."

"Yeah, let's go."

"You have chosen, then?" asked Simon.

The long walk back across the sand gave Davie time to think. "Of course. I belong to my family on the farm. Sand and surf doesn't beat that."

"Of course not," agreed Simon, thinking about his own families. He had two, but in his mind there was no longer a division. Even if they lived in separate worlds he had the best of both.

Simon threw his arm around Davie's shoulders steering him toward the mess tent. "Sure glad to have you back, buddy!"

"I was so scared when they separated us in Leanoria. After that I don't remember much. It isn't very clear."

Elsie and Peter saw them coming and ran to meet Davie, shouting his name in joyful reunion. Josie and Karl joined them, folding their youngest son in their arms as tears of relief coursed down their cheeks.

"Where were you, Davie?" cried Ma.

"Sorry, Ma. I did a stupid thing. When I couldn't find anyone I just wandered around. I passed by those halls so many times. I got curious about that one we came out of and went back in to have a look."

"Davie Dugall! Why did you do that?" scolded Pa.

"I know, I know. I shouldn't have done it, but I did."

"He was in the water when Sirius found him. Just in time, too. Another minute he'd have been gone," said Simon.

Ma gave Sirius a hug and said, "Davie Dugall. Whatever possessed you?"

"Don't know, Ma. Never saw the ocean before. It was beautiful."

"And dangerous," added Pa. "No more wandering alone while we're here, okay?"

"Yes, Pa. I promise."

Pa turned to look at the big hound sitting quietly next to Davie. "Sirius, you are one heroic hound."

"He deserves a special treat tonight," said Davie, running his hand down his back.

"Give him one right now," said Sybil, handing a dried beef stick to Davie. Sirius took it gently from Davie's hand, lay down at his side and began to chew.

They sat at dinner trading stories. When the last table guests had left, they retired from the mess hall and walked to where Sybil and Simon were camped. After the long, oppressive exile, it was good to be a family once more.

CHAPTER TEN
Final Thrust

"It takes courage to grow up and become who you really are."

- E.E. Cummings

A general assembly was called. Now that all transitions had taken place, there was much to decide. Who was in command? What was the best approach for defence?

Before final reversals, Herclan, Hermaine, Calazone and Rinaldo had held them together as a defensive unit. Now, it fell to them to organize squadrons consisting of humans and Aquadrians. Allowed to choose freely, they presented a unified front.

While transitioning was taking place, daily practice and tactical maneuvers strengthened their defensive position. Frequent patrols of the countryside kept northern forces at bay. Growing more daring under their leadership they made short offensive forays. Southern forces were captured and given the right to choose. Further transitions swelled the northern ranks.

Those assembled owed a lot to these four men. Herclan, Calazone and Hermaine, all Aquadrians, had been best of friends and they chose to remain in Aquadria to defend their way of life. Rinaldo, once again Simon's pa, was welcomed as senior commander that he was. His natural leadership was unchanged, for he had played a crucial role in Aquadria.

It was decided that Aquadorus would be exiled to sea, where he belonged. It had been his choice from the outset. Once the crystal fragment was restored to DOU, Aquadorus's reign of terror would end. He had usurped the power of the crystal to serve his lust for fame and glory.

Dimondus, a blameless human, had been corrupted. Restored to his full potential, he became an adept and proficient commander, ready to serve. His transition was the most dramatic of all. A sense of justice rose to the surface and he vowed to defend northern forces, restoring his honour. Simon and Sybil were astonished by the changes in him. Clearly, the crystal had redemptive qualities, none more apparent than in Dimondus.

When it was estimated that the balance had tipped in their favour, the final assault was laid out in command centre. Since the efficiency of mixed forces was proven time and again, it was decided the thrust should be fully integrated.

Profrak, who played a large part in advising, assured them of Opeggee air support. He assembled his forces and gave instructions, leading the way in reconnaissance.

"Roark, go south. Take all young commanders and fortify our arsenal of vulcan sacs. Advise your mother of our plans and reassure her. All is under control in the north. It won't be long before I am home with her."

"Yes, sir!" Roark immediately marshalled the forces under his leadership. Simon and Sybil chose to serve with Roark. Their co-ordinated efforts provided a strategic advantage to the troops below.

After flying south with his force and leaving them to begin work on vulcan sac detail, Roark sent out a bulletin, his cheerful message drifting over the rookery.

"Mother Meerak. We are all safe. Simon, Sybil and Sirius are here with me. Will be arriving shortly."

"Thank the Universal Stars!" she replied. Keeping the home fires burning alongside the other women in defense of the youngest Opeggees was a heavy responsibility. Her worried face relaxed in a sigh of relief when they landed at her doorstep.

"How is your father? What is happening up north?" She could barely restrain herself.

"All is going well," replied Roark. "Father has sent me south to fortify our vulcan sac reserves and to bring you news."

"Thank that darling man," Meerak sniffed back a sudden moisture that had leaked into her beak. Her two green eyes blinked back tears of relief, while her purple eye kept watchful vigil.

"We have managed final transitions for all those in the north and a lot of southern forces have been captured. They've lost heart. Given the option, most have chosen their original Aquadrian status," said Sybil.

"It shouldn't take long to mop up the rest of them," added Simon. "Aquadorus's days are numbered."

"That scoundrel has caused enough grief," said Meerak. "We will have a huge celebration once this is over. There will be a grand feast. Aquadrians and Opeggees united. I never thought I would live to see the day I'd say that."

"The reign of Aquadorus has taught us much, Mother." Roark's maturity had recognized the futility of war. Still, there were always those in a crowd whose desire led people in devious ways.

"The march south will begin as soon as we return with our vulcan sacs," said Roark. "We will lead the advance thrust, providing surveillance and airborne Intelligence."

Sirius let out a "Woof." Meerak brushed her soft, blue wing across the top of his head and he turned to lick her wingtip.

"Sirius has been a great help, hasn't he?" said Meerak, stroking his velvety fur.

"He certainly has," said Simon, recounting the details of their search for Davie. "If it hadn't been for Sirius we would not have saved him. Or Adelaide, for that matter."

"How is Adelaide?" asked Meerak, concerned for her welfare. "After all she has been through."

"We haven't had much chance to be with her. She seems content to help with the children. On the journey north she kept them cheerful and quiet when danger was close. She has a way with children. Same as Roark."

"He does amuse them, doesn't he?" laughed Meerak. "Always has been a playful fellow."

On the way north with vulcan sac reinforcements, they observed a squadron of Aquadorians in one of the mountain passes, well south of the northern boundary.

"What should we do?" asked Sybil.

"We have two options," said Simon. "Send word to Profrak. He will alert the rest of the force and meet them head on, or we can deter them with a peppering of vulcan pellets and drive them back."

"Vulcan pellets!" cried Roark. He'd seen this method work wonders.

"Send the alarm north at the same time," said Sybil.

"I'll do that," said a young Opeggee, as he flew off.

"Ready, everyone? Charge!"

The Opeggees dive-bombed and dropped pellets, blocking their advance. A few attempted to hunker down and return arrow fire, but the overwhelming assault of volcanic lava pellets drove them south. They had routed the advance.

Proceeding north they met with the main body of troops. Herclan, Hermaine, Calazone and Pa led divisions marching in ordered file.

"We've turned them back on Caliper Pass," said Simon. "They were no match for your vulcan pellets."

"Turned tail and ran," chuckled Roark. "Gets them every time."

Northern forces pursued them as far south as the flood plain. Halting to rest, they set up camp bivouacking on Plynthe Plateau, a high plain overlooking the city of Aquadria.

"We'll have to find a way to drain the city," Herclan said. He shook his head, disgusted by the wasteland before him.

"How are we going to do that?" asked Pa.

"Capture Aquadorus's forces. Offer them amnesty. They are still very adept in water. They will be able to reverse flow through the pools."

"By now they must see they are losing ground. Their days are numbered," replied Pa.

"The flooding stopped, so it's my guess there was a malfunction. Our forces have to make sure that intake valve is operating and reverse the flow at the pumping station. Hermaine and Calazone, take your best troops and form a task force for this mission. You will encounter loyalists working on this problem."

Scouting west of the submerged city, Simon and Sybil came upon a small encampment hunkered down in the forest.

"It looks like they've been cut off from the main contingent," said Sybil. "Head count around fifty."

"Perhaps," said Roark. "Or maybe they're ready to join northern forces."

"How do we find that out?" asked Simon.

"Show ourselves," suggested Roark. His daring personality

sometimes led him into situations. But he had a hunch about their hang-dog look.

"Okay, so what do we do?" asked Sybil.

"Fly in closer. I will brandish a vulcan pellet and challenge them," said Roark.

"We'll be right beside you," said Simon. "Ready now, go ahead, Roark."

"Surrender!" said Roark. Swooping in on the small group, he surprised them. They threw up their hands in alarm. As part of the force that had been turned back on Caliper Pass, they were no match for vulcan pellets.

"You will be granted amnesty by northern forces. Join us. We will escort you safely to our side."

A spokesman stepped forward. "I am Aldon. How do we know we can trust you?"

"I haven't dropped any vulcan pellets, have I?" said Roark. "You have Herclan's word."

"I knew of him in the city. He's a good man," replied the spokesperson.

"He will treat you fairly. And you will have a final choice," said Sybil.

"What do you mean?"

"When this is over. If you still choose to become fully aquatic, you may make your final transformation."

"Herclan would do that?"

"Yes," assured Simon.

"He must want something in return."

"Yes. To return things to the old order we need to drain the flooding. Are you still proficient in water?" asked Sybil.

This was an offer they could not refuse, for they had lost confidence in southern command. The way things had gone with Aquadorus was very troubling. They no longer trusted him.

He turned to those around him. "Are you willing to do this? This means we still have a choice."

The majority of them decided outright to join northern forces. A few holdouts needed time to think. If they were called to help drain the city, it was not without danger. After some discussion, they were convinced it seemed the best option. Joining back up with their regiments held no appeal. They would be sent north to fight again by ruthless commanders who didn't give a lick about their safety. The allure of sand and surf was tempting, but they had not bargained on civil war.

Arriving at Herclan's field command, Simon and Sybil quickly introduced the spokesperson Aldon.

"There are about fifty people here," said Simon. "They are willing to work with us. It is our best chance for draining this swamp." He chuckled at his own clever allusion. It best characterized conditions under Aquadorus.

"Hermaine and Calazone have gone east to the pumping station, to where the main valve regulates water intake. If we can coordinate our efforts, reverse the valve pump and open the pool intakes at the same time, it will create a massive, multi-pronged suction. The main switch that operates the pool valves is located at the palace. Aquadorus had control of that at his fingertips—ah flippertips," laughed Herclan. "I wonder where that maniac is now."

"Maybe at the pumping station," said Simon. "He hasn't made his final transformation either. Has to keep one foot in both camps to maintain control."

"Who among you has the greatest swimming ability, Aldon?" asked Herclan.

Thinking it over, he replied, "I guess that would be me." He had taken part in the city games each year and won the sea horse races many times. "Dovera is pretty fast, too."

"Simon, Sybil, catch up with Calazone and Hermaine's troops. Tell them of our plan to open the pool drains. When their forces are in place, one of you can let us know."

"Will do," said Simon and Sybil.

"Roark, you stay here with us. When we get the all clear, you fly to the palace. The turrets are still protruding. You should be able to see Aldon and Dovera."

"We'll be watching for you," assured Aldon. "When you are ready, we'll flip that switch."

"Hah," said Roark. *"We can use Telepath."*

"That would save a lot of time. It has to be coordinated precisely. Reversing the valve before the pools are open could damage the drainage outlets," said Sybil.

"Not only that, the force of the suction would prevent them from opening," added Simon.

"Best I go with Aldon and Dovera now," said Roark. Sybil or Simon can catch up with me directly instead of coming here first."

"Makes good sense," said Herclan. "I'll know by the water level if things have gone smoothly."

"We're on our way," said Sybil, as they lifted off.

Aldon and Dovera slipped into the water, alternating between powerful swimming strokes they had mastered at a very early age. They swam underwater for most of the way. Roark kept watch from above as they made steady progress toward the palace turrets in the distance.

"There's Hermaine, over on the right," said Simon. "And Calazone is approaching from the left."

"Smart maneuver," said Sybil. "They will outflank the pumping station. If Aquadorus is there, he won't suspect."

"One of us should take a look," suggested Simon.

"Go ahead, Simon. I will make contact with Calazone and make sure nothing threatens his advance."

"Keep in touch," he switched to Telepath.

"Right. Roark, are you receiving us?" said Sybil.

"Loud and clear. Keep on testing as we go."

"Where are you?"

"We are about halfway there. How about you? Getting close?"

"As soon as Calazone and Hermaine are in position we'll synchronize the signal. It needs precise timing."

"Could take some time. Depends on what they run into at the pumping station. Aquadorus will put up a fight," said Roark.

"Once we tell them of Herclan's plan, Hermaine and Calazone will remain on standby until you are in position."

Sybil caught up with Calazone, and when Simon returned they stopped to listen to his report.

"Aquadorus has a couple of guards on the control shed at the pumping station. Sentries are posted along the main trail west. He has a small squadron on standby in a clearing east of the compound and another on the north side."

"That means he's not expecting anything from the south. Therein lies his nemesis. He's too sure of his southern flank. Hermaine has the advantage of surprise," said Calazone. "I will outflank the north side and subdue that threat."

"Okay, I am off to Hermaine with the news," said Sybil. Simon will stay here with you. We will coordinate between you."

"We have a good chance of making this work," replied Calazone.

After Sybil delivered the news to Hermaine, he confidently moved into position to make the final approach.

"Hermaine is ready. Let me know when Calazone has control on the north side and we'll converge on the pumping station together," said

Sybil.

"Calazone is moving out now. I will fly point and alert him of any changes."

On the final approach, Simon noted the small northern group had relaxed their guard. They were sprawled lazily on the ground. He withdrew the crystal and flashed the force below, illuminating them with understanding brilliance. They rose to their feet and stood in awe of the beauty reigning down on them.

Kept in abeyance until Calazone's troops were upon the clearing, he tucked the crystal safely away and dropped in beside him.

"Surrender peacefully and you will be given amnesty. You are free to choose your way of life," said Calazone.

"Choose? What do you mean?" asked one of the Aquadorians. It was a foreign concept. There had been no choice under Aquadorus's rule.

"It means, if you join northern forces you are free to choose your way of life—where you want to live. Our scientists have cracked the codes. This crystal is the key. It holds the power to reversing mutations. You can go on to full Aquatic stature or choose to be as you were before. Remain Aquadrians or other life force. Your choice."

A spokesperson turned to the crowd. "Who among you wants to take up this man's offer?"

Not one dissenting voice was raised. They were war-weary and Aquadorus had not come through on his promises. They'd had enough of the political upheaval in Aquadria.

"What about Aquadorus?" asked one of the men. Fear still haunted his eyes.

"He is surrounded. We are in position. Join us and we will close the pincer. We have only the trails east and west of the pumping station left to deal with," said Simon.

"Doesn't surprise me. Most of his army has deserted," said the man.

"Yes, they are fleeing north in droves and making their final choice. You, too, can have your freedom."

"Then, we surrender and join you."

A number of them who had known Calazone in the city, fell in beside him and clapped his back. "We are ready."

"They surrendered without resistance. Calazone is moving out now," said Simon.

"Let me know when they are close." It was almost too easy, thought Sybil. I guess these folks have had enough of Aquadorus and his ill-fated promises.

"They're in position, Sybil," advised Simon.

Converging on the compound, Hermaine subdued one guard while Calazone took care of the other.

Bursting through the door, they surprised Aquadorus and a mechanical engineer in the act of putting the final bolt in place. The valve was repaired and he was ready to open the sluices.

"Not so fast, Aquadorus!" commanded Hermaine. He pinned the engineer to the wall, while Calazone subdued Aquadorus with lashing, binding his hands in front of him. He offered no resistance.

"Traitors!" Aquadorus roared. "I'll see to you." His blustering did not scare either of them. "You will pay for this."

"No, it is you who will pay," said Calazone. "You have turned a peaceful Aquadrian nation into ruin. You will be escorted west and will surrender to Herclan."

"That ignoramus! He's not fit to rule. I will never surrender to him!"

"You're coming with us," replied Hermaine.

Having proceeded east on the pumping station trail to offer

amnesty to the troops located there, Calazone returned. Sybil and Simon stood next to him, studying the tyrant who had struck terror in their lives. Aquadorus glowered back, his eyes black with hatred.

"I should never have given you the run of the city. And you," he looked at Simon. "You *are* that baby from all those years ago. Adelaide of the Ninth. Hummph! Nasty woman. Couldn't trust her either. I suppose it is that mother-heart of hers. Too soft."

"We have work to do," said Calazone. "Drain this swamp!"

He entered the shed and stood waiting to open the valve pump. "Let me know when they are in position," he called.

"We'll take care of that," said Sybil and Simon. "Wait for the all clear signal."

Simon flew south a short distance and prepared to relay the message.

"Roark, are you there? Aquadorus has been taken. He is no longer a threat."

"Thank my lucky wing feathers for that," said Roark. *"Aldon and Dovera have located the main switch. We're waiting for your signal."*

Simon relayed the message to Sybil. *"They are in place at the palace. Let me know when Calazone is set to open the valve."*

"Are you ready, Calazone?" asked Hermaine, standing at the doorway of the pumping shed.

"Standing by. Let them know and we'll do it on the count of three.

"We're ready. Calazone said to do it on the count of three."

"On the count, now. One, two, three. Switch!" cried Calazone.

The order was relayed simultaneously and the pumps went to work, reversing the flow. Great eddies over the city pools indicated that water was being pumped out of the city through a massive pipeline to the sea.

"We're finished here," said Calazone. "I will post a squad to guard this until all has returned to normal." A group of twenty Aquadrians volunteered to stay behind. Among them were former city engineers who would be able to resolve pumping issues or technical problems.

"Form up," ordered Hermaine.

"Fall in," said Calazone.

Their troops lined up on either side of Aquadorus. He marched between the two columns in a subdued cloud of anger and belligerence. Along the way they took in others who had lost faith in Aquadorus. It was the most peaceful surrender in history. The oppressive regime could not subdue the will of the common people. When given choice, people would rather live in peace and harmony.

When they reached Herclan, shouts of triumph filled the air as crowds roared their approval.

True to his word, Herclan gave Aquadorus Oceanus the choice everyone else had. He was free to undergo his final transition. On the appointed day, Sybil and Simon were in attendance.

Simon produced the crystal, brandishing it in front of Aquadorus's face. He was incapable of recognizing the beauty it held and turned away.

Seeing the negative effect it had, Simon quickly set it in place and the room lit up. The Duplicator powered up.

"What do you have to say for yourself?" asked Herclan. "Is there anything you wish to say to the Aquadrian people?"

"No, but I have something to say to you! I won't live under your command. You are unfit."

Aquadorus scowled, promptly stepped through the energy field and made his way to the shore. He was in his kingdom now. A balmy resort of sand, sun and sea. Try as he might, he had not succeeded in converting everyone to his way. He had no use for those who would not join him.

"Good riddance," was his last retort before he made his final transition. He entered the surf and swam out to sea.

Back on the other side of the energy field, Herclan was not so sure this was the end. He voiced his reticence. "What if Aquadorus changes his mind? Is it possible to access another reversal from the other side?"

"We can't do anything about this hall or the others until we have completed all changes in Fifth," said Sybil, understanding that she and Simon would have to coordinate that. How to do so was still a mystery. For all they knew, the Namors Guardia in Fifth were still as powerful as before they left. And what about the Leanorians at the lake bottom city? Gergenon and Gerardo, how did they fit in with Aquadorus's mad-man schemes?

Life in the Aquadrian city slowly returned to normal. Clean-up following the flood was dealt with in a spirit of co-operation. The Opeggees brought their expertise to bear in the only way they knew how. Hospitality was brought to the Aquadrians. Young wing commanders ferried food and refreshments while the work was going on. Opeggees became widely known for generously sharing all they had. On the final day of clean-up when all was restored, Meerak planned a lavish festival of celebration. It was held in the main square occupied by the largest pool. Young Aquadrians and Opeggees played games in the streets while adults loaded their plates and found groupings to sit with. They shared stories, promoting understanding by relating the best of their cultures.

When all was cleared away, the entertainment committee called them to attention. Herclan jumped onto the rim of the largest city pool, a symbolic gesture of triumph over

Aquadorus's oppression.

"We have suffered greatly. But today marks a new era. In a spirit of congeniality we work together in peace. It is a long time coming. We must thank our Opeggee friends for working with us to rid ourselves of tyranny and for providing valuable support throughout clean-up. In a new way, we come together in peace and prosperity. Let us commence the entertainment portion of this festival. Our youngest Aquadrians have prepared a song to honour Opeggees, recognizing their true community spirit."

A young Aquadrian appeared in the centre of the square atop Sirius. It was little Carpetia. She was very smitten with the bloodhound. As the spokesperson for the group, her tiny voice rang out across the square to all who had stopped to listen. No voice was too small, for in this new Aquadria, everyone must be heard.

"Now, we thing you a thong," lisped Carpetia. "It ith for Opeggeeth everywhere, thpeciawy Woarkie." She beckoned with her tiny hand. "Come, Woarkie. Lead Thiriuth. Now we thing."

The crowd cheered their approval as the parade circled the square, sending up a choir of children's voices.

"Can you believe the changes we've seen since we first arrived?" asked Sybil.

"You would never know Opeggee chicks were once hunted by Aquadrians."

"I suspect it was only those who chose to make their final transition. They are no longer part of this Aquadria."

"Are you thinking what I am thinking?" asked Simon.

"Yes, it is time to leave. We have a lot of work to do in Fifth. But how are we going to do that?"

"One of us needs to stay behind to provide energy from

the crystal. That hall cannot be left untended."

"It is impossible to do everything alone in Fifth. We need each other," said Sybil.

"The only other way I can see, is to trust Roark with the crystal. The Opeggees have nothing to gain. Herclan will back him if things go wrong."

"It is best to keep the crystal's whereabouts secret," replied Sybil.

They found Roark, who had grown tired of the crowds, soaring above the rookery enjoying a carefree afternoon. His home was safe. He had earned much respect for his actions in the turmoil that had threatened to destroy his family, his people and the good citizens of Aquadria.

"There you are, Roark," called Simon.

"Hello, you two. What a grand day I am having."

"We have something important to ask of you," said Sybil.

Roark caught a note of concern and paid closer attention. He had come to know these two friends well. His loyalty to Simon and Sybil went without question.

"What is on your mind?"

"This isn't finished until we return to Fifth and deal with Leanoria. What role do Gergenon and Gerardo play in Aquadorus's scheme? We have to check that out. One of us alone can't do that. But someone needs to stay here to set the crystal in place."

"How did the Duplicating Chamber operate in Fifth?" asked Roark.

"We think it is connected to the power here in Fifth Hall," replied Simon.

"Does that make sense?" asked Roark. "Herclan has complete control of Aquadria. Why leave the crystal here?"

"Do you think they operated with their own crystal in Leanoria?" asked Simon. He was reluctant to leave the crystal behind and was glad Roark saw it that way.

"That would explain their ability to circumvent the encrypted Echo Chamber. We always wondered how they communicated between themselves," said Sybil.

"You may be right. They must have their own crystal. That means we have to find it."

"Maybe not. It could operate off the crystal we have."

"Let's call a family meeting. Everyone must be ready to go early tomorrow morning. We'll use the ozone portal and return to Icelandia at Graenwolven Palace. The Hetopians may be waiting there for us."

"What about Adelaide?"

"We'll ask her to come with us. It has been a long time since we spoke with her about that," replied Simon.

CHAPTER ELEVEN
Restoration

"Knowing yourself is the beginning of all wisdom."

–Aristotle

Sybil and Simon found Adelaide in the nursery unit.

"Hello, Adelaide. We've been looking for you," said Simon.

"I like working here with the youngsters," she replied. "They have a curious approach to things."

"You do have a special way with them," said Sybil. "They love having you around."

"We plan on leaving for Fifth tomorrow. Will you come with us?" asked Simon.

Adelaide lowered her head, deep in thought. It was a long time before she answered. "I don't know. I am not sure I would be welcome. Why would anyone want to see me after what I've done?"

"I am pretty sure our grandmother would," said Sybil.

"Least of all, your grandmother," Adelaide shook her head.

"Wouldn't you like to know for sure?" asked Simon. "If you don't try, you will always wonder."

"I'm not sure what I should do."

"You belong in Ninth, Adelaide. That is your rightful place," encouraged Sybil.

"Do you really think?" She turned to look at Sybil, a flicker of hope lighting her eyes. "Is it possible?"

"Come with us. We will explain what has happened in Seventh," said Simon.

"Yes, it is possible," said Sybil. "We know Grandmother. It will be all right."

"I truly believe your change-of-heart has already registered with the universe. What we send out has an effect on all," said Simon.

"And it has a way of coming back to us. I believe that to be true, Adelaide. We already understand each other. Isn't that an indication of more to come?" said Sybil.

"Yes, I suppose. I never thought about it in that way. I would like to come back. That is not the issue. I am mortified by my behaviour; by my betrayal."

Simon could see this was an obstacle. He decided to let it be. "If you change your mind we are leaving on the seventh bell."

"I will give it more thought," replied Adelaide.

"Then, this is goodbye," said Sybil. She gave her a gentle hug and felt the softness of her shoulders, the shoulders that bore the pain of loss so long ago.

Simon crossed the space between them and gathered her in his arms. She was a frail woman, worn down by the cares of life. He would give anything to lift that weight from her. Things unfold as they are meant to. Of that he was sure. He understood her role in what had happened and was at peace with it.

"So long, Adelaide. We will see you again, I am sure."

"Thank you," she whispered softly and turned away so they wouldn't see the tears that welled.

Finding their family back at camp, they explained what they intended to do.

"You think it is safe to go back to Fifth?" asked Pa.

"We can't stay here forever. If we want our lives back, things need to be taken care of in Fifth."

"That's what I like about you two. You don't procrastinate," said Pa.

"We just want to go home," replied Sybil. "Aquadria is an interesting place now and I will miss our friends here, but I miss my family."

Simon could hear the longing. He understood. It had been much of his life experience—missing people. He had learned to live with it. A warm feeling flooded through him. He was determined to spend as much time in Fifth with his family as he could. He would continue to live in Third and get to know his family there, too. Telomeres be darned. He would not fear aging. It was a fair trade. The Hetopian Sanctuary would offset many of those concerns.

The following morning, after saying farewell to the Aquadrians and Opeggees, they made their departure. Using the ozone portal, they carried the family and Sirius, landing in Fifth."

"That was awesome!" said Davie.

"Totally cool," said Peter.

It shook Karl and Josie, leaving them wondering if this was how they first got to Seventh.

Lifting the knocker and letting it drop, they waited patiently.

The door opened to the surprised face of Icelandia. "Sybil! Simon! You're here. We had no idea what happened to you. You left without a word. We have nearly given up on you."

"It *has* been a very long time, Icelandia. So much has happened," said Sybil.

"Well, don't stand out there getting cold. Please come in. And bring your friends with you."

As soon as they made their way to the parlour, Simon began introductions. “Icelandia, this is my family. I’d like you to meet Karl and Josie Dugall, Elsie, Peter and Davie. They are the family I lived with—friends of Claire’s. That was when your mother Frestoria was still here.”

“Yes, that is how I knew of you.” She stifled her curiosity in favour of manners and welcomed them to her home.

“Please, come sit for a while before the brazier. Warm yourselves while I arrange for refreshments.” She left the room and returned shortly with hot tea and cakes.

Her desire to know could not be suppressed any longer and she blurted, “Tell me.” Her breath came in excited rasps. “Where have you been? What is happening?”

“We don’t know where to begin,” said Sybil, whisking a tendril of hair from her face.

“It is rather complicated and we still don’t have all the answers,” said Simon. “What we can say for sure is that Aquadorus is no longer in power.”

“The Seventh was in the midst of civil war when we returned,” said Sybil. “Sirius must have sensed Roark was in trouble.” She patted his head. “That day when we were about to leave for Third, he took off and wouldn’t come back. We had to follow him.”

“You’ve been in Seventh all this time?” asked Icelandia. “How did you get back?”

“Through the ozone portal, the same way we left,” replied Sybil.

“Who is Roark?”

“Oh Roark!” Simon’s face broadened into a fond grin. “He’s our good buddy, an Opeggee in Seventh.”

“An Opeggee?”

“Lovely race. Very welcoming folk. Would give you the shirt off their backs—if they had them.” He laughed suddenly at the thought of trying to explain an Opeggee to Icelandia.

"Simon, let me explain," interrupted Sybil.

"An Opeggee is…" she stopped. "How did Roark say it? A one purple-eye, two green-eyed people eater." She laughed when she said it because it sounded so…well, so unusual.

"A people eater?" said Icelandia in alarm.

"Well, no, they don't eat people. Roark says there is misconception, prejudice. Things get distorted." She conjured up Roark's beautiful Opeggee face. "He is one of the best. And his family are wonderful hosts. So open and giving."

"Sounds like you two have had quite an adventure."

"Adventure? You could definitely call it that," said Simon. "Best of all, we found my family." Simon playfully high-fived Davie. "Lucky we found you when we did. Right, buddy?"

"Yup," Davie responded with a grin and reached for another cake.

"So, how did Aquadorus fall out of power? How is this connected to Fifth?"

"He unleashed the flood after we came here with DOU," said Simon. "But there was a malfunction. Folks who supported Aquadorus were well along the way to becoming fully Aquatic. In fact, some even converted spontaneously. At least, that is what we assume happened, because there were Aquatic life forms in the water when we flew over on our way to the rookery. Those who dissented fled north and gained control of the Duplicating Halls. Hall Five was used for the final transition. Scientists cracked the codes and we found the key to the cabinet that held the holographs for change."

Sybil brought forth the fragment of DOU crystal. "This generates the energy that powers the Duplicators." It sparkled brilliantly in the cosy parlour as she held it out for all to see.

"The underwater city at Leanoria must have another fragment of the crystal. Rather than trying to find it, we hope this one will work in Fifth. Two 'Fifth' halls. Not a coincidence, right?" asked Simon.

Josie and Karl beamed when they heard the rationale. "I like what I'm hearing," said Ma. "Maybe we can all get back to normal here, just as in Aquadria."

Elsie, who had been listening quietly, finally spoke up. "If anyone can do it, you two can."

"Thank you," said Simon. He wasn't sure how Elsie was taking Sybil's appearance in his life. She hadn't said much since they were reunited. He was grateful for the comment. It indicated acceptance.

"We'll do our best," said Sybil. She had knowledge of the lake bottom settlement, knew Gergenon and Gerardo. And Simon had the most experience with the Namors Guardia.

A gong rang out announcing visitors at the door. "Excuse me a moment," said Icelandia, exiting the room.

A commotion in the foyer, accompanied by excited barking, got Simon and Sybil to their feet.

"It's Longille and Maerwyn!" cried Simon, as they rushed out of the room. Sirius was ahead of them, cavorting around the front hall with a furry companion he had not seen in a very long time.

"Sybil! Simon! Thank the Fifth. You are here. You are safe," said Maerwyn. "You never said goodbye."

"We had no idea," said Longille. "Haven't heard word of you since DOU left. What happened?"

"Long story. We'll tell you in a minute, okay?" said Simon, stooping to greet the hound. "Where's your other dog?"

"She stayed behind," said Longille. "Turns out she was a female. She's had pups! I named her Sadie."

"Pups! You named her Sadie," echoed Sybil. Her face beamed with delight. "How many did she have?"

"She's had four of the furry little bundles," laughed

Longille. "They create all manner of mayhem in the apartments."

"Awesome," said Simon. "Can we give one of them to Roark? He was very keen on Sirius."

"Yes, he was sad the day Sirius left. Wished he could have a hound one day," agreed Sybil.

"He can gladly have one," said Longille. "Caring for four rambunctious pups is wearing me out."

"Oh, come now, Longille," teased Maerwyn. "It is you who wears them out. You should see him down on the floor wrestling with them."

"Yes, I start it, but *they* don't give up," he grinned, sheepishly. "They are already learning to fetch balls and stay when I tell them to."

"That's what comes of all the attention, Longille. They learn to co-operate with you," said Simon.

"Three of the pups are already spoken for. Turns out, bloodhounds are much in demand at the castle these days. Even Ebihinin has asked to have one. Roark may have the last one."

"So, do you think Sirius is now a father?" asked Simon.

"By the markings, I would say it is a positive supposition," replied Longille, grinning proudly.

"How soon before they can be weaned from the mother?" asked Sybil.

"We've already begun that process," said Maerwyn.

"I've Googled information on it. Suggested age is about eight weeks," said Longille. "They'll be ready soon."

"Have you named them?" asked Simon.

"No, I will leave that up to those who will give them a good home."

"What name did you choose for your dog, Maerwyn?" asked Sybil.

"Thought you'd never ask. Take a guess."

"That could go on forever. Tell us his name, Maerwyn."

"What else could it be? They are companions in the night sky," he hinted.

"Orion!" Sybil and Simon were both familiar with the night sky. It was one of their favourite constellations.

"Great name for him," said Sybil. "He's always with Sirius and he likes to hunt, always chasing birds."

"Never catches any," said Maerwyn. "He just likes to flush them out of the draws in the countryside."

"He's rather a big old boy," agreed Longille. "Galumphs along happily. Wouldn't harm a feather."

"Okay, enough about dogs. Tell us what happened to you," said Maerwyn. "You had us all worried. Might be a plan to let someone know where you're going."

"We didn't have much choice," said Simon. "You know how Sirius is when he sets his mind on something."

"Wouldn't come back for bones or jerky," said Sybil. "That boy has a mind of his own."

"Good thing," said Simon. "He's warned us, saved us, lead us out of danger. Wouldn't have him any other way."

"He saved Simon's brother, too."

Simon and Sybil sat on the settee in the hall and explained. The Hetopians would not think of refreshments that were offered until they'd heard the whole story.

"Amazing!" said Maerwyn, grinning from ear to ear.

"What's to be done now?" asked Longille.

"We have to come up with a plan," said Sybil flatly. She was not keen on entering enemy territory again. Memories of the hideous Namors Guardia flooded her inner sight.

That evening, when everyone was settled in their rooms, Sybil and Simon called upon the Hetopians. "We want your opinion on the best way to go with this," said Simon.

"It might mean having to re-enter the castle and accessing the underwater city through the tunnel," said Sybil. The thought of it made her stomach lurch. Bile rose in her throat and her stomach heaved. Taking a deep breath, she held it back. If we can get to the Duplicating Chamber and set the crystal in place…"

"You and Simon can do it. We know you can. Take Sirius with you," interrupted Longille.

"No point in waiting, I guess," said Sybil.

"Longille and I will come, too," said Maerwyn.

The gong indicating more visitors sounded in the palace. Shortly thereafter, a gentle knock was heard on their door.

Sybil rose to answer and opened the door to Claire.

"Grandmother! You are here!" Her heart soared. "Claire, we should have known you would come."

"Of course, my dears," she said, sweeping her arms around both her and Simon who had bounded over to greet her.

"This is a surprise!" said Simon. "How did you know we were here?"

"Ninth has a way of knowing things, feeling things. You can develop this. Fifth is growing more adept and some Thirds—like you."

"Yes," said Sybil. She remembered the days when she fought against it. Back then it was spooky. Now it was more of an asset and she was glad of it. Her mom had been right.

Claire sat and listened, letting Simon and Sybil recount the story once again. Her eyebrows lifted when she learned about Adelaide.

"Adelaide?" asked Claire. Her old friend had survived. Maybe there was still a chance to meet on common ground.

"She has made many changes in her life. We asked her to come back with us. She wants to return but is ashamed of her betrayal. She doesn't think she will be welcomed by anyone in Fifth or Ninth."

"Nonsense, forgiveness is the key," said Claire. "She may have forgiven Friederich and me, but she needs to forgive herself."

"That's what Dr. Teselwode told her," replied Sybil.

"Who is Dr. Teselwode?" asked Claire.

"He saved my life." Sybil told her about her brush with the deadly Crimson Snakebush in Seventh.

"Sounds like a kindly old gentleman. You have managed to make friends wherever you go."

"There were a lot of helpful people," said Simon. "Good friends."

"What's the plan, then?" asked Claire, getting to the point.

"We will access the underwater city through the tunnel and try to power up the Duplicating Chamber. Beyond that…"

"You will need to subdue the Namors first," suggested Longille. "We could help with that."

"If the crystal has the same effect it had on the guards at the dragon pit, it shouldn't be too much of a problem."

"When?" The question was short, but Claire had waited a long time and she was anxious to have it finished.

"Tomorrow night. We will land near the lake just as before, then make our way to the barn."

The old familiar dock on Lenore Lake had become an integral part of the journey. Entries, exits, tragedies, all symbolizing the flow of their lives. Once landed, they made their way toward the barn some distance to the south-east. This time it felt like home. Claire, Longille, Maerwyn, Simon, Sybil and the hounds were meeting on common ground. It had taken cross-dimensional effort to bring them to this point.

"Once we gain entry to the castle and have the Namors

Guardia under control we can access the tunnel leading to the lake bottom settlement," said Sybil.

"They won't expect us," said Simon. "It feels good to take back some of my life here."

Outside the castle wall, Simon pried open the window and motioned everyone through. Sybil held the crystal up before them as they made their way.

Proceeding with caution toward the cell block, murmuring voices grew more distinct as they approached.

"All is lost," said a guttural voice. "Aquadria has fallen and Aquadorus has been banished to sea."

"We're on our own now," agreed his companion. "Useless to resist."

"What about Gergenon and Gerardo?"

"They have no control over us now," replied the other. "Nothing to fear from 'em."

"You talked to Commander SzGrog bout 'em?"

"Uh-huh, he figures they'll try to escape. We are ordered to surrender. Nothing left in Aquadria to fight for."

"S'pose it's the best option."

"Can't say I mind at all," confided the other one.

Emboldened by the conversation unfolding, Sybil rounded the doorway and entered the room, surprising the two guards. They stood up, blinking in the dazzling light of the crystal. At one time she would have recoiled with revulsion at their terrifying appearance. Hearing them speak now about their fear had shown her a different side to them.

"You're ready to surrender?"

"Nothing more to do here. Aquadria is finished." The Namors Guardia nodded in unison and remained silent, glad to be relieved of their irksome duties.

"Come with us, then" said Simon.

Scouring the castle, more Namors were encountered as they made their way toward headquarters. Those who had retired in dorms for the night were roused from sleep.

Following rigid military training they lined up in neat, orderly columns. Holding up the crystal for all to see, Sybil and Simon led the way through the tunnel to the lake bottom settlement. Claire and Sirius walked beside them. Longille, Maerwyn and Orion brought up the rear. Nearing the exit where the tunnel met the Duplicating Chamber, they encountered two more Namors Guardia.

One turned to Simon and said, "What do you want?"

"We are here to reclaim our lives," said Simon.

"And hopefully yours," added Sybil.

Ascending the stairs leading to the entry of the Duplicating Chamber, Sybil held onto her belief, hoping the crystal was interchangeable. The entourage had swelled to a large group that filled the room, flowed out into the hall and down the stairs to the tunnel.

"Before we can do anything else we need to find that cabinet," said Sybil. "We must have those codes."

She handed the crystal to Longille. His face glowed with pleasure. To hold a fragment of DOU's crystal was to hold the power for change. Goodwill, compassion and understanding sat in the palm of his hand. It was the key to peace. His Hetopian heart expanded and sent it out tenfold. Maerwyn sensed the change and reached for the crystal, allowing his hand to envelope Longille's. Energy flowed through them simultaneously.

Sybil and Simon left the chamber and located the business section where she had sat long ago upon arrival at the underwater city. Searching through rooms, they found the cabinet they were looking for. Locating the key on the bottom they pried it off and opened the top drawer. Colour-coded files were lined up in neat rows.

Pulling forth red files, they searched for information and discovered human DNA codes. When they came to a file marked *Other Life Forms*, information on Namors Guardia DNA was found.

"This is it, Sybil. Let's get it done."

Arriving back at the Duplicating Chamber, Sybil said, "We'll send the Namors Guardia through in groups of ten."

The room grew quiet. All waited in anxious silence. After a few minutes ten bloodhounds re-emerged, rather subdued and dazed.

"We were right about that," said Simon, pleased by the sight of so many bloodhounds milling about.

Sirius and Orion approached the new-comers and sniffed noses. Their tails began to wag and they whimpered softly.

Soon, the whole room was swarming with bloodhounds. They wandered into the hall as the genus reversal was completed.

"We'll take them to the tunnel for now until you sort this out," said Maerwyn, leading the way.

The code search for Gerardo and Gergenon continued. When Aquadorus's DNA code was discovered in the green files, they opened a corresponding holograph and found Gergenon and Gerardo under a C list, designating them as clones. They were recreated Aquadrians who had taken on a clone form. Aquadrians were in charge of the operation at Leanoria.

"Does this Fifth Hall act as a portal?" asked Simon.

"How else would they send conversions to Aquadria?" replied Sybil. "Too inconvenient to use the ozone portal."

They exited the business section through the Echo Chamber. Sirius padded along dutifully. He followed Sybil who threaded her way through quiet streets and lanes, past slumbering huts of Leanori, until she came to Gergenon's and Gerardo's sleeping quarters. Knocking on their doors, she called out, "Gerardo, Gergenon, wake up."

There was no answer. She knocked again, but all was silent.

Simon lifted the latch and looked into Gergenon's hut. It was empty. Gerardo was also gone.

"They're trying to escape!" cried Sybil. "Hurry, they must be headed toward the Duplicator." Her leg muscles kicked into overdrive as she sped through empty laneways with Simon hot on her heels. Sirius loped on ahead, baying an alarm. Slumbering Leanori emerged from their beds, shouting in confusion. The streets erupted in chaos as they milled about, impeding their progress.

"Let us through," shouted Sybil, elbowing her way past. Fearful of the loudly baying creature, Leanori Truids scattered in all directions.

"Good boy," shouted Simon. "Find 'em." Urged onward, Sirius picked up the pace.

As they approached the administration building and entered the Echo Chamber, a cacophony of encrypting echoes resounded off the walls.

"Simon, we left it powered up!" shouted Sybil, her frantic echoes reverberating in her ears.

Easing Sirius through the confusion, Simon steered him into the mirror maze. Their reflections multiplied, splintering infinitely in the brightly lit corridors.

"We've got this," said Sybil. It was she who had counted the steps forward, backward, left and right, that first time long ago when Gerardo and Gergenon boldly took them through the mirror maze to show them the Duplicator. It had been a confounding experience. Since then, the strange had become commonplace. Life held twisted turns of fate and Sybil's ability to embrace the extraordinary had grown with each new challenge.

Emerging into the Duplicating Chamber, Sybil said. "If we are right, this must also be a portal to Seventh."

"They must have already gone through. Now what do we do?" said Simon.

"But how will they operate Fifth Hall in Seventh?"

"Bollywocks!" shouted Simon. "We didn't check that drawer for a crystal fragment!"

"Chances are, they had it on them anyway. Don't suppose they'd leave it in the drawer, especially after Aquadria fell," said Sybil.

"Of all the stupid things to do. We should have unplugged the crystal. Now what?"

"We go after them," replied Sybil.

"But we don't know how this thing works," said Simon, his Spidey sense raising the hair on his neck. "What happens if we go through? Should we test it and find out exactly where it leads?"

"I don't think it would be a very good idea, do you?"

"I believe Gerardo and Gergenon have gone on to Hall Five and it does lead out to sea."

"Right, but are you willing to take that chance?"

"Let's go back to the business section," said Simon. "Maybe we can find out more. Since this is the only Duplicating Chamber in Fifth, it may be very different from the one in Seventh."

Following Simon, Sybil said, "There's still a chance. We forgot to check the bottom drawer of that file cabinet. The fragment of DOU crystal could still be there."

"How could we be so careless?" asked Simon. "Not to look for it first."

"Well, you must admit," replied Sybil. "Gaining control of

the Namors Guardia was a high priority." She hurried to the file cabinet. "If the cabinets are the same, it should be in the bottom drawer."

"This cabinet is different than Seventh's Fifth Hall," said Simon.

"How so?"

"It has an extra drawer."

"You're right. There's a sixth one."

Simon joined her on his knees as she tugged the bottom drawer open. Expecting dazzling light to pour forth, they were crestfallen. The drawer was empty.

"Oh no!" Her voice squeezed past the stricture in her throat, an unrecognizable, high-pitched squeal. "They must have it with them!"

"Maybe we have the wrong cabinet," suggested Simon. He looked around the room and realised they did, indeed, have the right cabinet. The crystal fragment was missing.

Sybil's spirit, which had been riding the highway to success, skidded to a stop. "Uh-oh. We messed up."

"If Gergenon and Gerardo have that crystal they can power up Fifth Hall in Aquadria."

"Bollywocks! We *are* in big trouble. We have to go back," said Sybil.

"We would have had to go back anyway to send them through Fifth Hall. If they are on the loose in Aquadria with the DOU fragment…" He shuddered.

"Let's fess up. Tell Claire what we've done."

As they approached her in the tunnel where she was assisting with the bloodhounds, Claire looked up, saw the tension on their faces and asked, "What is it?"

"Claire, Longille, Maerwyn, can we have a word with you, please." Sybil began hesitantly. "Ah, we did something…"

"Yeah," said Simon. "We messed up. We left the

Duplicating Chamber powered up and the DOU crystal fragment they used to operate it is missing."

"And what's worse, we think either Gerardo or Gergenon have carried it with them when they left for Aquadria," added Simon.

"It was a bad oversight. Maybe we should have left the crystal with Herclan in Aquadria, but we didn't know if we could find the one they used here. The way this has gone, we were right to bring the crystal with us," said Simon.

"Don't be too hard on yourselves," Claire said gently. "You can go back and make sure they get to where they are going. Find that crystal and bring it back."

"If they have not *already* gone through Fifth Hall. What if they take it out to sea with them? Aquadria is in trouble. If Aquadorus gets wind of it he could rise to power again." The scenarios spun out of control.

Simon's thoughts returned to the idea of entering the Duplicating Chamber. "That extra drawer. We should check it out," he said, leading the way back to the business section.

"It's this fifth drawer. We haven't looked inside," he said. Dropping to his knees, he tugged on the handle and it slid open easily.

"What are we looking for?" asked Sybil.

"I don't exactly know. Maybe directions that allow us to use it as a portal."

"Check that purple file," suggested Sybil.

Simon pulled it forth and opened it. A holograph shimmered before them, showing vistas to other worlds.

"This is it!" cried Simon. He jumped up, replaced the holograph in the file folder and tucked it under his arm. "Let's go."

"Are you sure?" asked Sybil. "How did Gergenon and Gerardo use it as a portal without this file?"

"Don't know; duplicate file? Maybe they had their own escape plan."

"I don't know," said Sybil, caution holding her back.

"See for yourself. This can only mean one thing. Has to be it. We're running out of time. If we want to catch them we must take that chance."

"All right," said Sybil. "How do we use it?"

"It says right here. To use as portal, power up with crystal, and place the holograph over it. It will change automatically."

"That makes me feel a whole lot better. Before we go, we'll let Claire and the Hetopians know. Claire will have to operate this hall in Fifth. We can't take the crystal with us."

When all was in place, Simon held Sybil's hand and they stepped through the energy field. Picking up speed, they went through a series of light fields and re-emerged in Seventh outside Fifth Hall.

"Hurry, Simon." Noise assaulted their ears as they crossed the Echo Chamber. It was powered up! Once past the mirror maze, they came upon Gerardo and Gergenon in the middle of a heated argument, preparing to make their final transition.

"You stay behind while I go on ahead," said Gerardo. "One of us must stay to operate the Duplicator. I will find Aquadorus and come back for you."

"That could take a very long time. What do you expect me to do in the meantime?"

"Send anyone through who wants to come. And if they don't—force them through. Imagine! Giving people a choice."

"Why me? You stay behind and do that," grumbled Gergenon.

"You know I've always been the better swimmer," said Gerardo. "Once I am transitioned, I need to find Aquadorus. You must stay behind to operate the Duplicator. And you will lead the counter offensive."

"With what? There aren't enough of us left."

"You have to stay!" shouted Gerardo, running out of patience.

Gergenon gave in. "Oh, all right. Go first. But hurry up. I don't want to be here long. Who knows what these Aquadrians will do."

Gerardo slipped through the energy field and left. Gergenon fussed and fumed impatiently.

Sybil dashed across the room while Simon confronted Gergenon. "We have you now!"

Gergenon attempted to slip past him to grab the DOU crystal, but Sybil was too fast. She snatched the crystal and the room went dark.

"Hold him, Simon." She quickly switched on her illuminator and confronted Gergenon. "What do you two mean, 'Imagine, giving people a choice?' Society thrives on choice."

"Aquadorus forced others against their will. That is precisely why Aquadria ended in civil war," said Simon.

"He had them cowering in fear," replied Gergenon. "A great ruler. Leave it to the weak-minded and things go to pot."

"Fear cannot hold us forever," countered Sybil. "Aquadrians rose above it."

"It was those nasty blue feather-brains. They caused the unrest. They should be relegated to stock pots, every last one of them."

"Enough!" said Simon. "You have no idea what you are talking about. The Opeggees are kind, welcoming people. They are peaceful folk, if left alone."

"Threaten anyone's safety and they will defend themselves," said Sybil.

"They're scum, just like you and this foundling brother of yours. We had him safely in our clutches at the dungeon in

Leanoria. Waiting for you to come along."

"Waiting for me? You knew all along I would come?"

"Well, of course. The Book of Wisdom foretold that. Aquadorus knew you would come one day."

"Why did you let me go about daily life in the lake bottom city?"

"You needed to reunite and seal the power before we could use you!" said Gergenon. "Thought you would never go looking for him."

"We got away on you, though," said Simon. "You never bargained on that, did you?"

"Must admit, we underestimated you. We failed at our end. Aquadorus was in a rage over that."

"We got away on *him*," said Simon. "He underestimated us, too. Or maybe our strength became too much for him."

"So, after the dragon escaped he decided to begin the flood. Never counted on equipment malfunctioning," said Sybil

"No, that wasn't the only failure. With you two united, the power of the crystals grew too strong."

Simon glanced at Sybil. *"Had we not discovered the crystal at Spoon Lake, taken it into our safe-keeping…if the south had got their hands on it…"*

A cold chill juddered through Sybil. They let me find Simon. But they hadn't counted on us escaping. Figured the hounds would set up a ruckus. Her heart skipped a beat. She returned Simon's look. *"If it hadn't been for Sirius, that beautiful dog-soul, this could have ended badly."*

Simon had gone pale. His lip curled in disgust as he glared at Gergenon.

Sybil felt the edges of his anger and stayed his arm as he raised it in contempt. His desire to lash out at the arrogant bid for power, the blatant disregard for others, was overwhelming.

"Retaliation only magnifies disorder. Allow it to be. It will die of its own accord."

"How do you figure that?" asked Simon.

"Just look at the pathetic man. He's got the eyes of a zealot. Blind to others. Blind to his own true nature."

Simon began to relax under the light pressure of her hand on his arm. *"I am beginning to see that. He holds no power over us unless we allow it."*

"Precisely. Let's turn him loose. His desire is to go seaward. Go ahead, offer him the choice. See what he has to say."

Simon nodded, understanding Sybil's line of thought. If Gergenon experienced the power of choice, maybe he would come to understand.

"Okay, Gergenon. It comes to this. You have two choices. You can stay here and live in peace with us, free to come and go as you please, or you can choose to go on with your friend Gerardo. Go seaward and join Aquadorus on the high seas. Which will it be?"

Gergenon was baffled, unprepared for choice. He stood gaping, his eyes roving from Simon to Sybil and back again to Simon. "Is this some sort of trick? You're not going to lock me up here?"

"No, you are free to stay, as long as you live in peace with the rest of us. If you do otherwise, you will still have the choice to go seaward. What do you have to lose?"

His eyes darted about in disbelief. Still suspecting a trick, he retorted, "I'm not living with the likes of you and those feather-brains. And those Aquadrians who rolled over—weak-livered lot." His hard heart solidified. "I choose the high seas."

"No use in waiting any longer. You have chosen well. It suits your temperament. May you find happiness in your choice," said Sybil. She powered up the Duplicator and Simon nudged him forward. "Live in peace, Gergenon."

He snorted, turned his back on them and entered the energy field toward his destiny. He would join Aquadorus and Gerardo as they began the subjugation of others swimming beside them.

Returning to Fifth through the activated portal, they found Claire anxiously waiting for them. "Did you find it?"

Two wide grins told her she had nothing to be concerned about. It was a long time coming and the end of this saga was looming before her. The lost fragments, usurped by the greed of Aquadorus, had twisted that energy for personal gain. DOU power was universal, meant to serve all. It was time to restore full power to Ninth.

"Now, for the rest of the clones," said Sybil, re-entering the mirror maze.

The streets of the underwater city were frantic as Leanori Truids milled about in confusion.

"You told me about clones, but I had no idea!" said Simon, his eyes roving over the crowd of look-alikes. Had I not seen this, I would never have believed it."

"Who are they all?" asked Sybil. A stirring of compassion for lost individuality aroused a strong desire to get on with their transitions.

She approached a group of young women huddled together in mistrust, her hands extended in peace. "Please, you have nothing to fear. Let us help you." She scanned their faces, looking for some sort of recognition and came to rest on one who eyed her curiously.

"I remember you," said the young woman. "You are that girl who stayed here a long time ago!"

"Yes," said another, her brow knitting together in concentration "You are…your name was…"

"Sybil," volunteered the first to speak. "That was your name. Right?"

"Right, I was here. My name is Sybil. I worked alongside you on the farms and tended aquariums with you."

"I am Greeta #253." A smile slowly enlivened her face and her blue eyes lit with the pleasant memory of this enchanting girl.

"Right, I remember. It was fun to work beside you. Visiting made the task of weeding so much easier."

Simon slowly approached so as not to alarm the trust unfolding between them.

"This is my brother Simon," said Sybil. "We are here to help."

"Gergenon and Gerardo are gone," said Simon, "They no longer have any power over you."

"We have come to liberate you. It is time to restore Leanoria," reassured Sybil.

She held the crystal fragment up for all to see. "This crystal has the power to change. Those of you who wish to follow Gergenon and Gerardo to Aquadria may do so. Those who want to resume your former lives here may choose reversal."

Leanori Truids began to congregate around them as word spread. At the administration building it was discovered that the Leanori clones belonged to the human genus file. A holograph was held up for all to see.

"You must make the choice before you enter. We will do this in large groups. If you wish to go on to Aquadria, step forward." No one in the room moved.

"Once you enter the Chamber, you will have made your choice. Be certain this is what you want," said Simon. Still no one moved.

"Very well, proceed," said Sybil, and the first group of young women entered the Duplicating Chamber.

Simon held the reversed holograph over the crystal in the floor and they re-emerged as young Leanorian women who once had inhabited the area. Thereafter, large groups entered the energy force, emerging a few minutes later, some as Leanorians; others as Graenwolven from the north. They were shown the way through the tunnel and set free to rebuild their lives. Many Graenwolven travelled north together, convening at the Ice Palace looking for direction and companionship under the organizing abilities of Icelandia. Partisans, who provided support during her lonely confinement within the palace, set up shelters and supplied returning citizens with food and warm clothing. They joined the efforts to rebuild their society in a spirit of co-operation and gratitude.

CHAPTER TWELVE
Homeward

"I can't change the direction of the wind, but I can adjust my sails to always reach my destination."

–Jimmy Dean

At village centre, Leanorian town folk who had been freed from the lake bottom settlement, gathered in groups, still shaken and dazed. Simon, Sybil and Claire wove their way through the crowds, stopping to chat and reassure.

"How many have already been sent through to Aquadria and set free on the high seas?" said Sybil. "Those who have undergone reversal in Seventh need to re-populate Fifth."

"The Duplicator portal is the easiest way to bring people home," said Simon. "Its capacity and ease of travel beats the ozone portal."

"You have to hand it to Aquadorus. He may be a madman, but what he built here is ingenious. Who could think up such a system?" Sybil shook her head in wonder.

"Seventh is unusual. Life forms have fluidity. It's as though mutation comes readily to them. That lovely Aquadrian skin shade lent itself well to Aquadorus's love of water," said Simon.

"He must have had a brilliant core of scientists and engineers," said Sybil. "Energy was easily repurposed."

Listening quietly to their conversation Claire added, "By using DOU energy transformation took on unusual properties. It accelerated rapidly."

"We have to decide the right time to return the crystals to DOU," said Sybil. "Too soon and we will not have accomplished the full return to normal."

"What is normal?" asked Simon.

"That might be hard to distinguish," conceded Sybil. "Maybe it's best to allow things to progress on their own. What do you think, Claire?"

"If we summon DOU, restore crystal power fully, perhaps it will trigger the path to normal."

"Then that's what we should do," said Sybil.

Longille and Maerwyn arrived with Orion. Sirius had been dogging along beside them, happily reunited with his furry pal. He bounded over to Simon and wriggled with pleasure, shaking water everywhere.

"Hey, Sirius. What have you been up to?" said Simon.

"He and Orion have been romping in the meadows outside town limits. A rain cloud just dumped a good soaking on us."

"That's a good sign," said Sybil, retreating a step as Sirius gave a vigorous shake, showering her with water. "This dry, old, dusty place needs a good freshening up."

"What's up, Simon, Sybil? You look a bit edgy." Longille had grown very fond of them and was sensitive to their needs.

"We have to return to Seventh," said Simon. "We must find a way to repopulate Fifth's citizens. "But before we do, how long until we can bring a pup for Roark?"

"Last time we spoke of this, they were nearly ready. I don't see why it can't be done now. I am on my way. Won't take long before I'm back with him," he said, lifting off.

Turning to Claire, Sybil continued their discussion. "DOU

must restore the crystals and claim full power."

Before they could utter another word, the rush of DOU's wings parted the air above and circled the town, bathing the crowds in a brilliant glow. The astonished Leanorians turned skyward. DOU's beauty illuminated their faces and reflected back as peaceful coexistence. Before the invasion by Seventh, Leanorians had been known as a peace-loving society, an agrarian culture that lived in harmony with the land. The appearance of DOU reminded them of their true nature.

Swooping low, DOU alighted next to Sybil and Simon.

"Greetings, DOU," said Claire.

Simon and Sybil held the crystal pieces aloft.

"I see you have recovered the missing fragments," said DOU.

"Rightfully yours, DOU," they replied, dipping their heads in respect.

The crystals began to glow and shimmer, sending warmth radiating through their palms until their fingertips tingled. The dragon's eye crystal rose up out of DOU's eye flap and hung suspended in mid-air. The fragments vibrated with energy, left their hands and rejoined the crystal. With a powerful flash the crystal generated full power and settled back into DOU's eye flap. The crowd fell to the ground, prostrate. As they stood up, one by one, clarity returned and growing awareness began to restore their senses.

"I will return to Seventh," said DOU. "We need to reclaim all those who have crossed over."

"Crossed over?" asked Sybil.

"Those who were forced to serve on the high seas shall be restored to their rightful existence."

"Does that mean you will enter Fifth Hall there?" asked Simon.

"Precisely. I could not do that until now. With full

restoration of the crystal I will set people free."

Longille, arriving back, was astonished by the scene before him. "DOU! You have returned."

"Yes, Longille. And what have you there?" asked the dragon, focusing a beam on the furry creature tucked securely under his arm.

"It is one of Sadie's pups. He will be living with Roark."

"Ah, yes. Roark is one fine fellow. I am looking forward to seeing the Opeggees again."

DOU's crystal glowed with pleasure and the pup wriggled in response.

"Let me see the little one," smiled DOU.

Longille held the pup for all to see. Sitting him upright in his arms, his little face sagged in characteristic jowliness, common to bloodhounds. His sad puppy eyes looked out from under droopy lids.

"Furry little creature, how beautiful you are!" DOU brushed the pup's head with wing-tip softness. The pup squirmed with delight and made little whimpering sounds.

"He seems to know you," said Sybil.

"Love touches all creatures," replied DOU. "*That* is easily recognized."

Something familiar about the radiance beaming off the crystal jogged Sybil's memory. She'd seen that pure, radiant light at the Wellness Flow in Hetopia. Could it be DOU energy flowing downward through those falls? And at the Wellness Sanctuary, was it the radiance coming off everyone's faces? Yes, it was DOU radiance, DOU energy with its power to change. How could that be if the crystal had been lost? There must be a reservoir in Fifth. Or better still, maybe it cycled, flowing in an eternal stream.

It was beginning to fit together. She was coming to have a deeper understanding of the driving force in the universe.

Elusive as it was, there were moments seeping through. It was there, in this loving interaction with the pup. There, anytime one person helped another and forgave hurt in fractured friendships. There, when someone stood with you during events that seemed to conspire against.

Living was not easy nor was it perfect, but it was life. It had beauty when compassion created harmony. Live and let live. How many times had her mother spoken of this? She thought it an old cliché. Now she was not so sure. Cliché or not, people brushed the old sayings aside in arrogant pride. She was seeing it in action and accepted it for what it was—truth.

Her thoughts turned toward Third. She missed the comfort of her parents and the familiar routine of home. She even missed school with all its intrigues and hardships. Could she make a difference in school? Wesley Peters and Alex were still roaming those halls waiting for her. It would take a lot of courage to confront those bullies. They had no right to treat her and Simon as they did. What was driving their anger? She resolved to speak to Claire and Adelaide when the opportunity was right. Those two had had their differences. But it was relegated to the past and new understanding was being forged.

DOU made the first move. "It is time, my friends. Shall we?"

"Thank you, Longille, for bringing this little pup. He is a darling one. Roark will love him!" said Simon.

"Gladly. He needs a good home and Roark appears to be just the person. Oh, how I wish we could meet the Opeggees. They sound a wonderful lot," said Longille.

"You believe you are in mortal danger in Seventh. Why is that?" asked DOU.

"We have always believed that," said Maerwyn, who had joined the conversation.

Maerwyn and Longille looked to DOU. There was a

strange gleam emanating from the crystal. It held a gentle, nudging undercurrent.

"What are you trying to tell us, DOU?"

"Think about it," replied DOU. The experience intensified. "The *knowing* must come from somewhere."

Sybil and Simon watched while the Hetopians grappled with DOU's wisdom. Their faces became animated as they slowly recognized the limitations of their former belief.

"Beliefs can be limiting!" They both replied at once.

"Have your beliefs limited you?" DOU's gentleness had nudged them in a direction they were prepared to go.

"Yes," said Maerwyn, recalling his brush with the northern ozone portal.

"Beliefs *and* fear," added Longille. He grinned at DOU. "You mean to say we have always believed Seventh was our downfall, when it was fear that stopped us? Hetopians have always believed this."

DOU flashed an understanding beam. "Could be. Are you prepared to find out?"

"Fear," said Sybil. She and Simon had known a lot of fear, both individually and together. "It is constricting."

"Take back your power. Be prepared to stand and face your fear. Courage is hard won. It requires knowledge of the unknown. How can you fear something if you don't know it?"

Simon and Sybil nodded simultaneously.

Sybil thought about the Great Hall and the red veil. How was that supposed to give you courage? Clearly, it was what you were led to believe. Hetopian beliefs about Seventh dimension overrode beliefs in the Great Hall. Interesting!

DOU looked at Longille. "Bring the pup to Seventh yourself. What is stopping you?" The nudge had grown to a challenge. "Face that belief."

"When?" asked Longille, hesitating a moment. "Right now?

With you?"

"Of course. It is always good to be among friends when facing fear."

"How will we go?" asked Maerwyn.

"We will use the Duplicator portal. I have full power now. No need for a crystal fragment. We will all go together."

Sybil and Simon's excitement at returning to Seventh for final restoration was contagious. Claire, along with Maerwyn, Longille and the hounds joined them as they stepped through the energy field in the Duplicating Chamber. Landing in Seventh outside of Fifth Hall, they remarked on the ease of passage.

"That portal has special properties," said DOU. "It has been generated by DOU energy. Now it is time to make all things right. Once this is finished, I shall close this portal forever. I will close down the ozone portal, too. It has grown too large."

Simon and Sybil held their breath and exchanged glances.

"But don't worry. I shall leave a small portal open there. We can still visit. Seventh will be accessed in the usual way."

Their breath rushed out in relief upon learning Seventh dimension was not totally closed to them. The Opeggees were so much a part of their lives. They need not have feared. Walls of division had no place in DOU's world.

After passing through the Echo Chamber and the mirror maze, Simon and Sybil entered the Duplicating Chamber in Seventh with DOU. The crystal radiated glory and the interior blazed with DOU energy as they approached the energy field.

"Let us enter," said DOU. Stepping through the energy field, they were drawn forward across an expanse of soft, silky sand, dry as talc. It stretched on and on, eventually becoming a compacted wet surface where wave action had created corrugated sand art interspersed with sea weed and shells. They walked far out to meet the pounding, frothy confection of ocean waves. The haze of sea spray blown on the wind misted their faces, a curative brine from whence sea life flourished and evolved.

Nearing the shoreline, DOU lifted off and soared over the churning surf. The crystal shone far out to sea, a beacon of hope drawing all home. Wave after wave of Sevenths and Fifths left the pounding surf. Swimming to shore, they emerged out of the salty brine, morphing before their very eyes as DOU energy transformed them. Standing upright, they trudged along the sand, drawn toward the portal that would bring them home.

The multitudes thronged, milling about until DOU unleashed full power, sending them through the energy field, through the portal to Aquadria in Seventh.

DOU waited patiently for the last of the homeward bound, gathering stragglers who had been last to hear the call, passed along in watery communication one to the other. Not one was left behind, depleting the force and power of Aquadorus. Rejection of tyranny, no matter where its black heart beats, calls for solidarity of like-minded folk working together. The power of one, multiplied.

The liberated crowds burgeoned to capacity in the Aquadrian countryside. Sevenths were free to rejoin their community. Under DOU's direction, the task of reversing the portal and accessing Fifth fell to Sybil and Simon. They began the process of transporting the tide of humanity from Seventh, home to Fifth. Families lost long ago, regrouped, waiting desperately for loved ones as they emerged in full restoration. Released from oppression, freed from the shell of forced identity, they came home to the truest self. A self that emerges under freedom and choice.

When the final group went through, DOU said, "We must visit the Opeggees before we leave."

Flying south to the rookery, DOU, Claire, Simon, Sybil and the Hetopians made their approach, landing in front of Roark's home. Longille held the pup, excited by his first encounter with Opeggees.

Meerak emerged from her dwelling, wings extended in perpetual welcome. Her open and loving heart did not understand the concept of inhospitality.

"DOU!" she curtsied. "How wonderful. Sybil! Simon! Please introduce your friends." She gave Claire a delighted smile and gazed at the Hetopians in rapture, enthralled by their overpowering physique, their snowy locks and captivating eyes.

The Hetopians gestured in a grand way, conveying their delight at the profound beauty of the Opeggee race. For, they were uniquely endowed with the heavenly shade of open skies from whence they emerged. Born of the heavens they were, or so it seemed. Their grace and ease, soaring on the winds of the stratosphere, instilled awe. Even DOU, though a capable aeronautic, admired their aerial abilities.

"Meerak, meet our grandmother Claire of Ninth," Sybil began introductions.

"Pleased beyond doubt," said Meerak, performing an elegant curtsy.

"Thank you for your kind hospitality," said Claire. "Sybil and Simon have told me so much about you. My deepest gratitude for making them welcome when they first arrived."

"T'was nothing, nothing at all. We love having visitors."

Following introductions and exchange of pleasantries, they were led to an outdoor lounging area, for DOU was of such proportions it would have been impossible to navigate the ninety-degree angle of the entrance to Meerak's home.

Presently, Meerak's eldest appeared with nettle tea and seaweed crisps.

"Would you care for a cup of tea?" asked Meerak, smiling.

Claire smiled in return. "Yes, that would be lovely." She accepted the cup, sipping the cool, delicate flavour.

"Refreshing," smiled Longille.

"Very pleasant, indeed," Maerwyn nodded, intrigued by the new taste.

"Not at the moment, thank you," said DOU, refraining from all sustenance, for dragons did not drink tea. "It is a most delightful afternoon."

"Where is Roark?" asked Simon. He was disappointed his friend was nowhere in sight.

"Said he was going aloft to ride the air currents a while. He is sorely pressed," said Meerak. "There's a restlessness about him. I suspect he is missing you and Sybil."

"I will try sending him a telepath," said Simon, as he lifted off. He flew to the top most prominence of the cliff.

"Roark! Are you anywhere near home, buddy?" It took several bulletins before Simon received an ecstatic message in return.

"Simon! Is that you?" Roark's excitement rippled through the stratosphere. *"I will be right there."*

"I'm on the cliff top waiting for you."

Two minutes later, Roark swooped in, landed beside Simon and enfolded him in a blue-winged embrace. "How I have missed you. Good to see you, my friend!"

"And you, Roark. It has been too long. Come, everyone is gathered near your parents' home."

Before long, Simon was introducing Roark to Claire and the Hetopians, while Roark bowed and dipped his greetings.

Longille called Simon aside and handed him the pup. "You must give him to Roark. It will mean more if the pup comes from you."

Simon held the pup to one side as he approached Roark. "We have something for you, Roark." He held out the pup and watched as Roark's green eyes grew round and blinked in surprise. He quickly turned his head, examining the creature in Simon's arms with his purple eye. Yes, it was a hound like Sirius, only smaller! He popped his suction cups and tap-danced a jig of happiness. His moroseness of the past days evaporated under the spell of the furry pup wriggling in Simon's arms. The pup, who had sensed Roark's eager playfulness, squirmed to be let down. Simon set him free and he raced around the blue-feathered figure, excited by the sound of popping suction cups.

"He's mine? Are you sure? Really mine?" Roark spun pirouettes and flapped his wings with joy. A shower of blue rained over the pup. He snapped at the downy feathers, sending them aloft to ride the updraft across the Aquadrian countryside.

"Yes, buddy. It turns out one of the hounds was a female. Sadie gave birth to four puppies. Longille brought him from Hetopia in Fifth."

"Oh, thank you, thank you so much!" He bent down and stroked his soft fur. The puppy sidled up to him and licked his red toes. "You look just like Sirius. Same markings."

"No doubt he's the father," said Sybil, enjoying her friend's happiness.

After the excitement had settled, Claire drew Meerak to one side. "Is Adelaide here?"

"Yes, she is in the nursery hall at the moment. She spends a lot of time there. Loves to work with the younger Opeggees."

"I would like to visit with her."

"Oh? Do you already know Adelaide?" asked Meerak. While she was never one to pry or gossip, her curiosity was aroused.

"Yes, we were friends from long ago. Would it be all right if I wander over that way to see her?"

"Of course, dear. Just follow this path around that grove of trees over there," she gestured with her wing tip. "You can't miss it."

Claire strolled down the path, wondering how her old friend would receive her. As she approached, she saw Adelaide in the distance playing a game with a number of young Opeggees. She looked tired or perhaps the sadness about her eyes gave that impression. Although the years had taken their toll, she still recognised the woman she once knew and loved so well.

"Adelaide, old friend. I see you have not changed. Still enjoy youngsters as much as ever."

Adelaide looked up, startled. She caught Claire's gaze and held it a moment, then looked away. Her hands fluttered in a nervous gesture.

"Claire, I did not expect you," she said, looking at the ground in embarrassment.

"I have wondered about you all these years. Do you think it is possible…could we start over?" Claire's gentle voice disarmed her.

She had expected retaliation and recriminations. Instead, she was hearing a softness. Her voice held hope, offered a second chance.

"Oh, Claire…" She lifted her eyes to her friend's face, saw kindness in her eyes and a welcoming smile curving her lips. "Is it possible you can ever forgive me for what I have done?"

"It was forgiven long ago," said Claire gently. "No need to ever mention it again."

"But I need to tell you how deeply sorry I am. I was bitter for so long. It took me a very long time to resolve that. I was such a fool."

"You should have come back to Ninth, Adelaide. We could have worked things out."

"I didn't think I would be welcome there, or anywhere, after what I had done. Taking Simon from you was the lowest, an unforgivable deed. I have lived every day in regret for a long time now." Tears had gathered in the corners of her eyes. One slipped its fleshy canal and flowed down her left cheek.

Claire reached over and brushed it away with a tenderness that warmed her starving heart.

"Come home with me—home to Ninth. There's no need to stay here."

"Do you think I can? Will anyone want me?" Her hesitancy touched Claire's forgiving heart.

"Of course. You will be received cordially. For those who question, I will explain. Please, come home."

"What about my work at the nursery? Meerak has welcomed me; so kind of her to give me a place here. And I would miss the youngsters so. The Opeggees have plenty of them. Aren't they just darlings?" She smiled fondly as she watched them prance in circles, imitating Roark who often kept them amused and entertained.

"We must resolve things before we can move on, Adelaide," said Claire, touching her shoulder lightly. "You will manage the next step. We will do it together."

"The next step. I had forgotten about that," sighed Adelaide. She thought for a long while, then brightened. "I do believe you are right. We are ready for the next step."

"Good. Thank you, old friend. I knew you would be. Shall we go?"

"Please, I must say goodbye to the little ones. And I must tell those in charge that I will not be returning. It is time to go home." She felt relief, as though she had laid down a heavy burden, one that she had carried for a very long time.

Claire stood and waited while Adelaide finished her goodbyes, grateful this had gone well. Having Claire back in Ninth would be a pleasure. The rift had grieved her to the core.

Walking along the path toward Meerak's home, Adelaide said, "I wish we could have those years back. I have missed you, oh so much."

"We have a lot of catching up to do," agreed Claire. "But first let us get back to Fifth. We can sort things out there."

DOU looked up as they approached the yard. "You are Adelaide," said the dragon. DOU flashed her an understanding sparkle that landed on her face. It illuminated her eyes, lighting a fire within—a burning desire to be home in Ninth.

"Yes," Adelaide said, at a loss for words. A brief silence lingered. Then she managed to say, "How can anyone forgive what I have done?"

"Everyone has something to work on, Adelaide," said DOU, understanding this was not easy for her. "Don't let it wear on you any further."

"Let us put the past behind us," said Claire, patting her shoulder gently. "We must live in the present and the future will take care of itself."

Adelaide hesitated, turning Claire's words over in her mind. "I never thought of it that way before. If only it were that easy."

"Let it all go," said DOU. "There is no control over the past, is there?"

"No, no control at all," said Adelaide. All the bargaining, the wishes she had made back then, when her son Benni had died in the electrical storm, were useless. Struck by lightning. Who could control that? Claire and Friederich had no control over that. No one had.

"And the future? Any control of that?" asked DOU.

All who were present contemplated the wisdom of what the dragon was saying. Many times they had railed against the past, agonizing over what should have been done, wishing to change things; to no avail.

"So, how does hope for the future come into this?" asked Simon. It was the thing with which he wrestled most. "If there's no control over the future, what is the point of hope?"

"Ahhh, what do we have control over?" asked DOU.

Sybil and Simon looked at each other. "Now!" The answer burst upon them with the speed of fireworks.

"You have the future in your hands at present," said DOU. "You can influence the future right here and now."

"So, what I decide now affects my future," said Sybil. Her mind was humming with possibilities.

"Hope is fed by our actions in the present," said Simon. He finally got it.

"Yes, something like that," replied DOU, smiling broadly. Sparkles of hope danced off the crystal. Beaming into the universe, it fell back on the crowd as a shower of infinite possibilities.

"Not every decision we make works out, though," said Sybil.

"No, sometimes the universe has other means. Things just happen. But the present is always with you, right?" said DOU.

"Yes," said Simon. He exchanged glances with Sybil. They had made decisions through this whole wild journey. Any one of them could have had a different outcome.

"We can act in the present moment as it comes," said Sybil. How would that have changed the storm at the lake? She pondered the reality of that. Everyone was making decisions that day. Claire, Friederich, and the boys who were so anxious to be out fishing on the lake. No ifs or shoulds, only numerous decisions made; all interrelated, to end in catastrophe.

"Live with reality in the present. No blame on anyone. It happened, therefore it is," said Sybil.

"Yes," said the dragon. "What may seem like a bad decision ending in tragedy sometimes emerges as a priceless gem in the future. Adelaide's decisions may actually have worked out very well."

Baffled by DOU's comment, Adelaide asked, "How? What do you mean?"

"If Simon had not lived in Seventh, would he have been able to act intelligently in Seventh when he went back?"

The thought struck Simon with force. "Aquadria could very well have been a different kettle of fish!"

Laughter rolled out of DOU with the force of an explosion. The unintended pun ignited the whole group and the force of the concussion swept through the Opeggee settlement. Other Opeggees ambled over, curiously hanging around the periphery, mindful of intruding. They could not help themselves. Belly laughs erupted everywhere. It was contagious and Opeggees were gregarious by nature, joining in readily. They loved to be together and found every excuse to do so. Laughter was the glue of their community.

"C-come j-oin u-s, p-please," chortled Meerak in between breaths, words cascading over each other. Her merriment was uncontainable.

"Oh my, my, my," the dragon said at last. "I haven't laughed like this in eons. You are hilarious, Simon."

No sooner had one person got their laughter under control, another would snort and it would begin again, round after round of guffaws and giggles. Opeggee tears were flowing freely, green eyes and purple, all weeping mirth.

"Okay, enough now," said Profrak. "My innards are killing me." And, he would promptly go off on another round. He could not stop himself. Roark joined his father in the circle and they began an energetic dance, one they had worked up for the fall festival.

"We shall feast tonight!" cried Meerak, and she rushed in to join the dance, her free-form swaying with delight, her blue finery elegantly twirling and weaving in and out of the circle. Soon, all present were dancing, abandoning themselves to exuberant merriment dissolving the tensions of the past years.

When the group finally came to a semblance of propriety, they were spent. "You shall stay the night with us," said Meerak.

Profrak would hear of no protests. "We will set up shelters out here," he indicated, sweeping his large wing over the yard.

"See those trees. We will anchor vines between them and to the ground, and lay fronds over the top. It will ward off any night chill."

Everyone pitched in, constructing a cosy shelter. Opeggees were resourceful people, utilising things at hand to make do. Nothing was wasted and everything was repurposed for another use.

"We could learn a lot from this," said Simon. He was intrigued by the tying techniques they had mastered using their powerful beaks. Two, working in co-operation, had developed a strong knot that supported the weight of the tree fronds.

Meerak was in charge of dinner preparations. Claire and Adelaide pitched in, following her directions. Sybil and Simon shared Hetopian rations, laying them out on rock table surfaces surrounding Meerak and Profrak's home.

"We shall make the most of this evening. Who knows when we will meet again," Meerak said. There was an undercurrent of sadness and a lonely chill overcame her as she realized how much she would miss her new friends.

After dinner, Roark asked Sybil and Simon to take a stroll. Sirius ambled along with the pup running beside him, his little legs working overtime to keep up.

"Have you chosen a name for your pup?" asked Sybil.

"I have been thinking a lot about that," said Roark. "It has to be something special and grand."

"How about Quasar?" Simon suggested. "Or Pulsar?"

"Why not Pluto?" added Sybil.

"Yeah, I like Pluto!" Roark grinned. "Has a comical ring."

"Used to be known as a planet in Third," said Sybil. "Until that powerful telescope aboard a space craft was launched. Now they call it a dwarf planet. It's only about the size of our Earth moon. But there are hold-outs. Some still think it deserves planet status."

"How do you know all that?" asked Simon.

"I read about it on my iPad. New Horizons space craft travelled there in 2015. Pluto is in the Kuiper Belt."

"What's a kuiperbelt?" asked Roark.

"A lot of rock and debris orbiting together with Pluto."

"Hah! I got'ta read up on that," said Simon. This new information piqued his interest. He loved the night sky and spent hours observing nature. Science came naturally to him.

"Okay, so Pluto, it is," said Roark. "He *is* comical, don't you think?"

As though the pup understood Roark's words, he nipped at Sirius's tail, tugging it mercilessly until Sirius let out a loud "Yipe!"

The pup let go and Sirius nosed him as though to say "Enough of that." He turned and ran, initiating a game of chase, Pluto trailing behind. Wheeling in a wide circle, Sirius turned and bore down on him, leaping over his head. Pluto spun around and chased after him. The play went on until the pup tired. He was no match for Sirius. He plopped down on the grass at Roark's feet, panting, his little pink tongue lolling out.

"We're sure going to miss you, Roark," said Sybil. "Tomorrow is our last day here."

"We'll come visit again. It may not be as easy because the northern portal will be altered. But we can chance time-travel every now and then," added Simon.

"Tomorrow we'll be back in Fifth," said Sybil.

"Aren't we stopping to see Herclan, Hermaine and Calazone?"

"Never really thought about it. Has DOU mentioned a stop? Doubt we'll have time."

"You're right. We should get back to see what is happening in Leanoria."

"Leave that decision to DOU. Though, I sure would like to see the Aquadrians before we leave," said Sybil.

The following morning after farewells, the party of mixed dimensions lifted off. Instead of heading north to the Duplicator portal, DOU veered south. Intuitively aware of their desire, the dragon said, "Thought we'd pay the Aquadrians a little visit before we start for home."

"Oh, could we?" Sybil could not believe DOU would know her very wish.

"Thank you," said Simon. "We have made many friends there. At least, before they went through reversal."

"You will know them, rest assured. Their essential spirit shines through."

Before long they were landing at the palace gate. It stood open and welcoming, a drastic difference to conditions under Aquadorus. The courtyard was thronging with citizens, some lounging, others conducting open air markets. Reading circles, enjoying the latest poetry offered by thriving writers in the city, gathered in the square. Artists, skillfully applying paint to canvas, were offering portraiture and creating beautiful landscapes. Scheduled afternoon performances by local dance troupes entertained daily. The arts were thriving, nourishing the beauty of individual expression. Dimondus, who was engaged in theatre, raced over to greet Sybil and Simon. He was a tall, strapping youth exuding charm and self-assurance.

"We heard you were in Seventh and I hoped you would come to see us before you leave."

"Thanks to DOU, we are here," said Simon.

"You have decided to stay in Aquadria instead of going back to Fifth, have you?" asked Sybil.

"Yes, I quite like it here. I love the freedom theatre provides. I can find myself in all those different characters. Besides, I have made a lot of good friends here."

"What about your past?" said Sybil, intensely curious as to why he would not want to return to Fifth.

"I'm afraid that is a complete mystery to me. Not one memory from my past has surfaced. It is as though the slate has been wiped clean."

"Oh dear! Sorry to hear that," said Sybil. Her eyes caught and rested in the clear-blue skies of his orbs. An old soul rose from the depths to meet her on equal ground, revealing a sunny warmth dwelling inside. She flushed and looked away. The intensity of his gaze had stirred something deep within. It was confusing and disconcerting.

"No need to be sorry. I am content to let it be, for now. I am Dimondus."

Inner turmoil scattered any common sense she may have possessed. Dimondus was human, but knew nothing of his origins. Rising fury, directed at Aquadorus, flushed her face scarlet as she fought to keep her emotions in check. Lost identity, she thought. Another travesty of justice!

Sensing her agitation, Simon intervened and changed the subject.

"Glad to hear you are enjoying theatre, Dimondus. Maybe we can take in your play today."

"That would be great. Come back around three bells. We are playing right here in the square."

"Where is headquarters now?" Simon was anxious to learn more about what was happening politically.

"They have taken over Aquadorus's office at the top of the palace. Can we get together later? I have a rehearsal shortly."

"Of course. We'll call by on our way out."

Walking through the courtyard was surreal. So much had happened in between first arriving and the present moment. Even the sights and sounds were different. The fishy odour had dissipated, replaced by a clean, warm fragrance lingering in the afternoon air.

Arriving at the palace entrance, Simon and Sybil were greeted by two women offering a cool, refreshing drink. Declining, they were escorted to the stairs, the same ones they had climbed so many times before. Sybil and Simon spiralled upward until they were disgorged at the top. The room had transformed. Doors were no longer closed. The walled receiving area was now open to encompass the main office where Aquadorus had once bellowed and blustered.

Herclan, Hermaine and Calazone were engaged in friendly conversation over plans spread out on a large table. All the trappings of warfare: Aquadorus's weapons, shields, and mounted trophies had been destroyed. There was not a trace of him left.

Three women joined the conference, speaking animatedly and gesturing along the surface of the map.

"That's a great suggestion," said Herclan. He looked up

momentarily and grinned broadly at Simon and Sybil standing at the head of the stairway. "Come in, come in. Sybil! Simon!"

Hermaine and Calazone spun in their direction, surprise registering on their faces.

"We'd heard you were back!" said Herclan, stepping forward and extending his hand in welcome.

"Thank you for taking time to see us before you leave for Fifth," said Calazone. "I'll never forget what you did for me that day at the pool." He thumped Simon's back and grinned at Sybil.

"Didn't think we would have this pleasure for a while," said Hermaine, joining them. "That was good work in the north. You and the Opeggees. We could not have done it without your support."

"This calls for a feast tonight. We will have entertainment and dancing, food and music. It is time to celebrate!" said Herclan, rubbing his palms together.

DOU was right. They had no problem identifying any of their Aquadrian acquaintances. Gills were no longer present, flippers had vanished and their long morphing fingers were restored to dexterous appendages. The khaki skin shade had paled to green pastel, but their indomitable spirit shone through.

"Let us find the dragon," said Herclan. "We must invite DOU to our feast."

"DOU is in the courtyard, no match for that stairway," said Simon.

"We'll have to do something about that," said Hermaine. "An honoured guest needs to be received properly."

Calazone's eyes lit up. "When DOU visits next time we will have a courtyard built at the very top of this palace with open access to our offices." He had envisioned it in his mind's eye for some time. Now he had reason to press for those changes to be made.

"That will be the first item on the agenda at our next civic meeting," agreed both Herclan and Hermaine.

Descending into the foyer and out to the courtyard, all three city representatives converged on the dragon who was lounging before the dance troupe, enjoying their movement to music. Sirius, who had stayed with DOU, got up and loped over to welcome Sybil and Simon back.

"And who is this?" asked Hermaine, bending down to examine the furry creature more closely.

"This is our hound—our dog. His name is Sirius," replied Simon. "If it weren't for him, our mission to find DOU in the north might have failed."

"Well," said Herclan. "Then he, too, is our honoured guest."

Calazone was the bravest. He reached out to stroke the fur along Sirius's back. "He's so soft."

Then Hermaine ventured a pat on his back. But it was Herclan who knelt to meet Sirius on equal ground. He lifted his muzzle to look deeply into his eyes. "Thank you, Sirius. You are welcome here."

Sirius acknowledged the comment with a soft "Woof." He turned his muzzle and licked Herclan's hand, returning the greeting the only way he knew how.

"He's wonderful, isn't he?" Herclan smiled, then rose and strode toward DOU. "Greetings! We have come to invite you and our other honoured guests to an evening of celebration. Please, you must spend the night."

"It is indeed an honour. We are pleased to accept," smiled DOU. "Have you met Claire, Sybil and Simon's grandmother?"

"We are so very pleased to make your acquaintance." Hermaine, Calazone and Herclan, each in turn bowed gently and smiled.

"Pleased to know you," replied Claire. "I am aware of, and very grateful for what you have done for Simon and Sybil."

"It is our pleasure," replied Herclan. "They were instrumental in forwarding progress. The changes in Aquadria are largely due to them. They have our gratitude and respect."

"You already know Adelaide," continued DOU.

Adelaide dipped her head and smiled shyly before she said, "Good to see you all again."

"Hello, Adelaide. You have had a very bad go of it in this city," said Herclan, then went on to explain. "Dr. Teselwode was a real support for her, especially when things began to turn for the worse. He kept us informed. We were afraid for Adelaide when she disappeared from the city. Had no idea where she went or how she lived. She was wise not to say anything to anyone before she left."

"That's right, Herclan. I didn't want to get anyone into trouble, should they be questioned about me. I am looking forward to meeting up with Dr. Teselwode again. He deserves my thanks," said Adelaide.

"Seems like Dr. Teselwode deserves thanks from a lot of people, including us," said Sybil. She related the Snakebush story and how he had saved her life.

"Dr. Teselwode is a stalwart in this city. Always on hand to help people in need," said Hermaine. He had his own story to tell of the fine gentleman. "I will make sure he attends the feast tonight so you can thank him yourselves."

The rest of the afternoon passed pleasantly, sojourning in the courtyard. Simon and Sybil agreed to have their portrait done by a very good graphic artist who rendered fine charcoal likenesses. They posed together, wanting a meaningful souvenir of their days in Aquadria. In some ways they were saddened by the fact they were leaving, now that the city had been freed of tyranny. The Aquadrians were an industrious people. It had not taken long to restore the city after the floodwaters receded. Simon was positive they would return one day if the occasion presented itself. Certain they could find an excuse for that, he told Sybil later that evening what he was thinking.

A great many Aquadrians gathered that evening in the palace square, joining in the festivities. The crowds were as thick as ever, for most Aquadrians had returned from the sea. Given the choice, they'd rather live as they had before Aquadorus came to power.

Claire and Adelaide sat with DOU, content to take in the sights. Sybil and Simon circulated with the Hetopians, who were the talk of the city. The Aquadrian folk were extremely curious and impressed by the tall, rugged physique. They were mesmerized by their beguiling eyes set beneath snowy-white curls. Longille and Maerwyn felt a little overwhelmed by their curiosity, but took it all in good stride. After all, they had conquered their long-held fear of Seventh. A few stares and questions they could handle. It felt good to let go of that old fear. Aquadrians were nothing like they had imagined. They were an amiable and hardworking people, cordial and welcoming. The Hetopians felt certain they would return, maybe even set up a trade partnership.

They were making their way back to where DOU sat with Claire and Adelaide, when someone approached from behind, calling out, "Sybil, Simon. Is that you?"

Turning to see who it was, Sybil let out an excited squeal. "Dr. Teselwode! We have been watching for you. So many people in this crowd. We were afraid we'd miss you. He hadn't changed all that much, still wore his half glasses and sported whiskers. They rushed to meet him and enveloped him, two sets of arms crushing him in a hug, one he returned with equal strength.

"Let me have a look at you," he said, holding them at arm's length. "My goodness you have changed. You look older, more developed." He could not find the right word. *Mature* came to mind. But he never had a chance to say it before Adelaide joined them, excited and pleased to see him.

"Adelaide! How nice to see you here. I was worried about you after I left for Aquadria. You seemed so unhappy. How have you been?"

"Much better since I decided to return to Ninth."

"So, you are going back after all. We shall surely miss you. Promise me you will return one day."

"Indeed I will, when the time is right."

Claire wandered over. "You must be the good doctor I have heard so much about." The description of whiskers and glasses fit.

"Yes, this is Dr. Teselwode," said Simon, happy to introduce Claire to the people who had been instrumental in their survival in Seventh.

"Come and join our party," said Sybil, leading the way through the crowd to where DOU reclined, communing in silence with Sirius. Every now and then DOU stroked Sirius's velvety head and he would reply with contented throaty sounds.

"Meet Dr. Teselwode," said Simon. "This is DOU."

The dragon responded with a sparkle that landed on the doctor's face. It was a gentle kiss of gratitude, for he knew Sybil had wanted to repay the doctor's kindness and valour. Bestowing a dragon kiss was the highest honour. It meant joy would abound in one's life.

It had been done on Sybil's behalf and Dr. Teselwode recognized it for what it was. He bowed deeply, graciously accepting it with a delighted smile. "Thank you most sincerely.

I am forever indebted for your priceless gift."

After the feast and entertainment, their guests were shown to comfortable rooms in the palace sleeping quarters. A beautifully landscaped courtyard adjacent to this provided DOU shelter for the night. Sybil lay awake listening to the dragon's gentle snoring outside her window. Since her first walk into the city with Dimondus, she realised her life and the way she thought about it had changed forever. Her thoughts turned toward Third and home. That midnight swim had set her on this journey. Spoon Lake seemed a magical experience now. So many adventures, surreal in imagination, now very real and present, crowded any possibility of sleep. Her mind spun in all directions, revisiting the highlights and lows, tossing and turning until the wee hours of the morning. She finally drifted off, awaking a few hours later to a loud yawn outside her window. It was DOU.

Sybil dressed quickly and stepped though the double doors that opened into the courtyard. "Good morning, DOU."

"Good morning. You did not sleep well?" inquired the dragon, noting her puffy eyes.

"Not much. So many thoughts spinning in my head."

"What is troubling you?"

"A lot has happened since that Spoon Lake swim. How will I fit in, back in Third? School is fine, but Wesley Peters…"

"You know how this fits, don't you?" asked DOU.

"What do you mean?"

"Adelaide *Peters…*" The dragon paused meaningfully. When there was no response. DOU repeated, *"Peters…"*

"You mean…" Sybil stopped short. "You mean Adelaide is Wesley's grandmother? Generations back. Like Claire is our grandmother?"

"Yes, it seems so."

"The angst is transferred through family lines? How could

Wesley possibly know any of that?"

"He doesn't. It is encoded in DNA, or inherited tendencies perhaps."

"If Adelaide can change, then Wesley Peters has a chance, just as I always thought."

"It sometimes takes the right combination of events," said DOU. "You are a resourceful, intelligent young lady. You will discover those events. Maybe with a little help from Adelaide," hinted the dragon.

"Say, this could be interesting." Sybil brightened, thinking of the possibilities for that encounter. "I will speak to Adelaide. I know she will help."

"She does love children and her grandson will definitely come under her influence," smiled DOU. "She will know the best way. She has a lot of wisdom; wisdom that comes with experience. Valuable because it is often learned under duress."

"The best way to learn, I suspect," replied Sybil.

"Oh, we can learn from what we see happening around us. But it is our hurts and how we deal with them, learning to accept, that guides our own instinct for healing."

"You are an amazing teacher, DOU. How can I ever thank you?"

"Be happy. That is all. It makes me happy," DOU chuckled and rose from the soft bed of grass. "Time to shine. Bring beauty to our day, Sybil."

The dragon flashed her a crystal smile, showering her with sparkles of joy, sending tingles from her head to her toes. It was much like receiving a compliment or a hug from a friend, known as a 'warm fuzzy' during her kindergarten days. It would last her the day. And the memory of it would bring her back to centre when things were harder to deal with.

"Now, shall we find the others?"

"Yes, I can't wait to talk to Adelaide," said Sybil. The

possibility of helping Wesley was utmost in her mind. She had started the morning in a desolate mood. Now her spirits buoyed on the tidal possibility of change. DOU was change, DOU was truth, DOU was hope, DOU was peace, DOU was living in the now.

A hearty breakfast was hosted in the palace mess hall where Simon and Sybil had reported to Dimondus every morning during their first days in Aquadria. Their flipper polishing duties on the streets, still vivid memories, were now in the past. Still, they recalled the joy of rendering a high gloss shine.

"I wonder what happened to that old gentleman who told us about the 'foundlin' that 'distappeared' in the large city pool," said Sybil.

"Let's ask about him," suggested Simon, popping the last bit of fish crisp into his mouth. "If we hang around here in the mess hall maybe we will see him come in for breakfast."

"There's Dimondus, he just sat down. Let's go sit with him."

They picked up their trays, crossed the dining hall and stood next to him. "May we sit with you?" asked Sybil.

Thoughts of how she had tried to avoid him in the past eddied and swirled in the backwaters of her memory. Seeing Dimondus's youthful charm smiling up at her left her bewildered. So many changes in such a short space of time contributed to her disorientation.

"Hello, Sybil. I was afraid I wouldn't see you again. Couldn't find you last evening. Simon, how are you?"

"It was bedlam, that's for sure. So many people in the square. Just as crowded as the old days when we lived here," replied Simon.

"It is more crowded," said Dimondus. "Last night was only half as bad as it is in the city streets on any given day. So many have returned. But that's a good thing."

"You like crowds?" asked Simon.

"Not particularly, but there is talk of moving. Many of our residents are forming a settler's colony. We are moving to a new location."

"Where?" asked Sybil.

"East of here. Past the old growth forests, beyond the mountain ranges. It opens into a vast, broad plain. And beyond that there are rocky outcroppings. No one has gone any further than that."

"That sounds beautiful." Sybil thought of her own Rocky Mountains in British Columbia and the flat Prairie provinces where her people had settled long ago.

"I used to live in a region known as Centralia in Fifth dimension," said Simon. "It sounds a lot like it."

"I am beginning a new career. This moving has created a drive to know more, to explore. I am afraid I have caught the travel bug," said Dimondus.

"Wanderlust," said Sybil. "It can open a whole new world. Horizons you have never dreamed of." She thought of her own recent experiences in Fifth dimension, Hetopia, Centralia, Graenwolven Territory and in Seventh dimension. There seemed to be no end to possibilities.

Simon nodded in agreement. "Explore the world, live your dreams, Dimondus. One never knows what is around the next bend in the river."

He'd been through many different experiences in his short life. His exploration was just beginning. When he returned to Third, Simon's dreams also included pursuing new adventures. Maybe there were other dimensions still to be discovered. He felt sure Sybil would join him. They were an inseparable team.

"Thanks," said Dimondus. "We are preparing for that move now. First, a small party will establish an outpost and see to basic needs. Supplies from the city will keep us provisioned until we can build infrastructure. I leave on this expedition next week."

"So soon?" said Simon. "I almost feel like coming with you!"

"Why don't you stay for a while and help us get started on this new venture."

"Oh, don't make it any harder to resist," groaned Simon. "I'd love to stay, but we have been away a long time. Have to get back to Fifth and then to Third where we live."

"Not many Fifths have stayed in Seventh," said Sybil. "Are you sure you don't want to go back to Fifth?" She did not want to accept the fact he could not remember his past. "It might help recover your memories."

"No, I'm fine here. Too much to see and do. I don't get lonely."

"I am sorry to hear you won't be coming back to Fifth," said Simon.

"It is all right. I am used to it now. It leaves me free to explore. You're sure you two don't want to join us?"

"We have to get back. But one day we'll return and maybe take you up on this, or at least come for a visit," said Sybil.

"Well, if you change your mind, you know where to find me," encouraged Dimondus. He would love to get to know Sybil and Simon better. Wanderlust seemed to be something they had in common.

"Say, Dimondus. We wondered if you could tell us more about an old gentleman we met while we were here under Aquadorus's rule," said Sybil.

"Who is that?"

"We never did find out his name, but he was very unusual. Spoke with an accent."

Simon gave his version of the speech pattern, hoping it would jog his memory.

"That does sound familiar. Try that again." After listening carefully, Dimondus said, "That sounds like old…hmm let me see now. What was his name? Let me think on it. Nope, can't seem to recall the name. He used to live over near the big city pool. I can show you if you have time."

"That would be nice. We will make time. He was very kind and I would like to see him before we go," said Sybil.

"Are you ready?"

"Yes, thank you. We were just about to leave when we spotted you."

"Then, let's go," said Dimondus, easing his knees out from under the table. He straightened to full height and smiled down at Sybil. "You look nice this morning. Aquadrian air agrees with you, does it?"

"I guess," said Sybil absently, following him with her tray to clear their dishes. Then he headed across the room to the exit.

"Out the main entrance and turn left. You remember," said Dimondus.

It took a good hour of brisk walking to arrive at the square where the largest pool was located, the pool from which they had escaped Aquadria.

Sybil looked around in wonder. It seemed a whole lot smaller than she remembered. "Simon, this pool seems to have shrunk."

"You're right, or maybe it's just that we have grown. You know how it is after you've been away for a while."

"Could be. Even our home in Third seemed smaller when we came back from Fifth. It's all about perception."

"There are a lot of people on the street today, maybe more than on the day we left."

"We're nearly there," said Dimondus. "Just a left turn at this next street. And here we are," he announced, stopping in front of a small cottage-like building."

"Thank you for showing us the way," said Simon.

"No problem at all. Sorry, I need to be getting back. I am expected at a meeting shortly. To do with our new settlement. You are sure you won't change your mind on that?"

"Sorry, Dimondus. We promise to look you up next time we're in Seventh," replied Simon.

"Do you think you can find your way back to the palace again?"

"Sure, we've been in this area plenty of times, working the flipper polishing detail," said Sybil.

"Ah, yes. Flipper polishing. Aquadorus was big on that, wasn't he? He really had me fired up. I am ashamed to say. I am beginning to recall a bit of how I was back then. Addled, that's what I'd call myself. Just plain addled. That could be why I don't remember anything before that—from my old life."

"Don't be too hard on yourself, Dimondus. A lot of folks weren't themselves. My goodness, how could you be after all the changes forced upon you? It altered your chemistry," said Sybil.

"Well, we've all changed and are wiser for it. Follow no one else but your own truth and inner knowing," said Simon.

"We're all born with it, right?" asked Sybil.

"Yes," said Simon. "I think we all have an inner compass."

"It's our GPS," laughed Sybil.

"Then how do bullies like Aquadorus go wrong?" asked Dimondus. He was no philosopher, hadn't thought much about it really. But then, his moral compass had been usurped for a good bit of time, lead astray by Aquadorus and his machinations.

"No easy answer to that, I'm afraid to say," said Simon.

"I'd sure like to understand that," said Sybil. She was at a loss. "How do some people lose that inner GPS?"

Thinking about how a GPS worked, how co-ordinates from satellites, about 30 of them orbiting the globe could pinpoint a location, didn't really explain much. Then she thought about the process, how it pinpointed through trilateration. Three satellite spheres of radio signals picked up your GPS signal, working together to determine the intersecting point. It very accurately determines the position of your GPS location. Hmm, were there things people needed, to find themselves? She would have to think about that a whole lot more.

"I got'ta run," said Dimondus. "Sure was nice seeing you again. Please, remember what I said. If you change your mind, come back. Can always use willing hands around Aquadria."

"Goodbye, Dimondus." Simon shook his hand, giving it a last farewell squeeze. "I'll keep that in mind."

"Yes, we'll think about that offer," said Sybil. "Goodbye, Dimondus. Glad we had this chance to visit, short as it was." She gave his arm a farewell pat. To her surprise, he pulled her gently to him and hugged her.

"So long," he whispered.

Baffled by his sudden display of affection, she let herself be cradled in his arms for a moment. The clean smell of his shortly-cropped, dark hair flooded her usual reserve. When he released her, he gave her a deep unwavering look that warmed her, sending incendiary tingles up her spine, exploding in a cerebral display of fireworks. Confused and shaken, she managed to whisper back, "So long, Dimondus."

"See you then, and luck of the Seventh be with you." He turned and disappeared into the crowd, leaving her disoriented and trembling with uncertainty.

She turned to Simon. "Why would he hug me like that?"

Simon was grinning at her. "I suspect he likes and admires

you."

"Well…that kinda messes with my GPS," she scowled, unsure of how she felt. "That compass and GPS stuff we just talked about. Why do some people lose their way?" asked Sybil.

"You mean, like Aquadorus?"

"And Wesley Peters at school."

"Oh yes, I forgot about him. He's a small fry, compared to Aquadorus."

"Kettle of fish? Small fry? Simon, you crack me up," she laughed at the memory of last evening's pun.

"Okay, so I like cracking jokes. Sometimes it just comes out. Don't even intend it to be funny."

"That's what I love about you. It just comes naturally. You have a weird sense of humour."

"Thanks," said Simon. "You're pretty funny sometimes, too."

"Seriously, I was thinking about how a GPS works. The trilateration process. Three spheres of influence to find a location. What spheres of influence do we need to find ourselves?"

"Boy, you're philosophical this morning."

"No, I'm serious. What do people need?"

"Well, I know what I need," said Simon. "A good warm bed and lots of food," he grinned.

"That's it, or at least part of it. Security, food, clothing and shelter, the most basic needs. Have that and we're well on our way. I need friends and family, part of the security thing again," said Sybil. "But I guess it depends on how they treat you. No users allowed."

"Yeah, people who love us and allow us to grow, make our own decisions, with a little guidance if needed."

"That's self-determining. I couldn't do that when I was

little," said Sybil. "But I was allowed to discover things and was guided as I grew up. Now I am pretty much in charge of my daily decisions. Look at what we've had to do on our own."

"Hasn't been easy, that's for sure. Remember that blunder we made? Forgetting to power down the Duplicator before we went in search of Gergenon and Gerardo was just plain dumb."

"Yes, but Claire was very supportive. Allowed us to make a mistake and take care of it ourselves," said Sybil.

"She's a wise one. Wisdom incarnate. Well maybe not so incarnate." For, they had not decided how continuation of life in other dimensions really worked.

"So, we have basic needs met and the right to grow to self-determination. That builds character. We feel good about ourselves. Anything else?"

"When we feel good about ourselves—no put downs, we can make others feel good," said Simon.

"Ah-huh, and it needs to happen early to every generation. You know what DOU told me this morning?"

"What did DOU tell you?"

"Wesley Peters…Adelaide Peters…" She gave Simon a meaningful look.

"What?" Simon stared at her blankly.

"Wesley Peters…Adelaide Peters…" she repeated.

Simon was flummoxed. Then realization seeped into his understanding. "You mean Adelaide is his grandmother?"

"Yes, like Claire is our grandmother in generations past."

"No kidding. Well, knock me over with a feather!"

"As long as it isn't an Opeggee feather. They are too precious. Oh, I wish I had thought to bring one back with us. They are such a beautiful shade of blue. It makes me happy."

"Okay, so Wesley is related. Did some of the bitterness

alter Adelaide's chemistry? Did she pass that on inadvertently or was it how she lived with her family, her children and the next generation, all the way down to Wesley. You learn what you see."

"Maybe a bit of both. Adelaide wasn't a bully. We can't blame her. She was hurt beyond imagining. But that pain ruled her in a way that was hurtful to others," said Sybil.

"I am so glad we saw all that happening in 1910 and now finding her here. Everyone we meet is fighting a battle. We are privileged to know about this one. What if we didn't know? What about other people?"

"What about Wesley? How much do we know about his life?" said Sybil.

"Nothing. He hasn't allowed us to get that close."

"Maybe it's time we do something about that."

"Might not be easy," said Simon.

"No doubt. It will not be easy. I've tried in the past. But DOU made a suggestion. Enlist Adelaide's help."

"Do you think she would?"

"We can explain what is happening and ask. I can see she would be concerned and I doubt she would not want to help."

"We'll ask her when we get to Fifth. Now is not the right time."

They had been standing on the street in front of the cottage all that time engaged in discussion, so engrossed they had missed the door opening and closing. Now, someone peeked through a window into the street.

"Is that him?" asked Simon. "In the window."

A quick glance his way could not confirm his identity. "I don't know for sure. Let's just knock on his door."

They sidled up to the doorstep and rapped lightly. There was no answer, so they knocked a second time. This time footsteps approached and hesitated on the other side of the door.

"Who ist it?" a slightly accented voice called.

"It is Sybil and Simon.

"Who d'ya say?"

"Oh, forgot." Remembering that he had known them by different names, they replied, "It is Dominic and Sarah. We used to polish flippers here in the square," said Simon.

"I polished yours for you one day. Do you remember me?"

The door opened a crack and a grizzled, old face peered through. He was startled because he'd never had visitors come to his door before. He studied Sybil's face and a sparkle of recognition burned in his rheumy, brown eyes.

"How are you?" said Sybil. "We were back in town and wanted to see you. Do you mind if we come in for a while?"

"I suppost it'd be okay."

He hesitated, then opened the door wide. "Come in, lass. Yer name agin?"

"Well, actually it is Sybil. And this is Simon, but you may have known us by Dominic and Sarah."

"Oh ya, ta flipper polishin kids! Saw yous at breakfast up nort, long time back now."

"Yes, so much has happened since, hasn't it?"

"Yowies! That was sum problums we's had. Sure glad it got righted."

"I enjoyed polishing your flippers for you that day. We never got to see you after that. It was the day we left."

"I hert bout dat! Aqadoris sur mad!"

"It was what you said that helped us escape," said Simon.

"Me? Whut I say dat helpt you?"

"You told us about the foundling kid who disappeared. Said he went down the drain in that big city pool."

"Dat's de story, dey say."

"Well that story was true. It was actually me, when I was

about four years old."

"You? Simon. Oh ya. I member dat little kid. Dat you?"

"Yes, it is me Simon. Same kid, only bigger."

"Oh my gootness. I used to play wit you in dis street. You always lookt so lonely. No kids'd play wit you. Call't you names.

"Yes, Nogillers. That's me."

"Well, well, well. I's happy ta see ya, lad! Come sit down and I'll pour ya a cup a tea. Ya like tea?"

"Yes, we do," said Simon. "That would be very nice after that long walk over."

"Tell me, lad. How'd you git back ta dis place?"

"It is a long story. You have time?"

"Course I do. Nuttin but time dese days. You da only visitors at my door since comin' back Sout."

Simon and Sybil told him a shortened version of their adventures while he sat listening, taking it all in. His eyebrows lifted in disbelief at times. At other times he smiled encouragingly.

"You haf a busy life!" he said.

"Yes, it has been. We could not leave here without looking you up. We wanted to thank you for your kindness that last day," said Sybil.

"It was nuttin'. Just enjoyed your flipper shine and young'uns need mindin'. Glad ta talk ta ya."

"Sorry, we didn't realize it was so late. We need to be moving along. They're probably wondering where we are by now. We're leaving today."

"Tanks fer stoppin' in and if'n yer back dis way agin, come see me," said the old gentleman.

"So, we sat here and visited, and we still don't know your name," said Sybil.

"Oh ya, my name is Festus. Sorry bout dat."

"Festus, thank you for the visit and the tea. If we come back this way we'll be sure to stop."

He walked them to the door, waved goodbye and stood watching as they melted into the crowd.

The palace square was thronging with people. DOU, who was easy to spot, waved them over.

"We stopped to see an old acquaintance," explained Simon. "Sorry, we're late."

"His name is Festus. Seems a lonely old soul," added Sybil.

Claire, who had begun to worry, covered her agitation. She was secretly proud of the way they treated others. "Glad you made it back. I'm sure your kindness was appreciated."

"We on our way soon?" asked Sybil.

"Yes," said DOU. "It is getting on and we must sort things out in Fifth. But this was a very necessary trip. It is right to pay tribute to those who have helped in any way. I am indeed grateful."

Herclan, Hermaine and Calazone spotted them from across the square and headed over. "You folks heading out today?" asked Herclan.

"Yes, we must be on our way," replied DOU.

"After all you have been through, it was very good of you to pay us a visit," said Hermaine.

"It was our hope that we would have time," said Sybil. "You have been a very important part of our lives."

"And most instrumental in restoring things to order," said DOU, bowing graciously. "What can I do to repay the Aquadrians and the Opeggees? Both splendid nations."

"It was nothing, DOU. We have triumphed over tyranny, all of us working together, as it should be," said Herclan.

"Still…" DOU stopped a moment, then flashed a brilliant beam skyward. It effervesced and multiplied, spreading across the Aquadrian sky, over the Opeggee colony, and descended upon the countryside. A gentle shower of peace and joy rained down on Aquadria.

"Our deepest gratitude to all of you," said Hermaine. "We have forged a new land. Together we will work toward that peace, which is the right of all."

"We shall take our leave, then," said DOU. "Farewell, my friends." The party lifted off, circled the square in a final salute and headed northward to the Duplicating Halls.

"We must destroy those halls," said the dragon. "That is our final task here."

"We know just the person who would like to have a hand in that," said Simon. "Roark has been anxiously waiting for this day. Is it possible, DOU? Can we give that final mission to Roark?"

DOU smiled. "Already done. I made arrangements with Roark before we left."

"You did?" said Simon. "How did you know?"

"Roark and I have a special understanding," replied DOU. "Assured me he would have it ready by the time we returned."

"So, once we use the Duplicator portal to go back to Fifth, Roark will destroy those halls?" asked Sybil.

"No, I have a surprise. We will witness the destruction of the halls and return via the space-time continuum. No portal needed."

"Cool!" said Simon. "I've always wanted to do that."

DOU laughed. "You already have, Simon."

"What do you mean?"

"You have already used the space-time continuum."

"You mean time travel?" asked Sybil

"Yes, same thing. You are both very proficient in its use. Everyone here is. And we can bring the hounds with us."

"How efficient," said Simon. "I was wondering how we

would bring Sirius home to Third with us."

"Nothing to be concerned about," said DOU. "Now for the task at hand. Roark will be waiting."

"Halloo, everyone! Ready for the big show?" said Roark. "These halls have caused enough problems."

"Knowing you, Roark, it will be the best show ever," replied DOU.

"Our young wing commanders are waiting on standby. Have been working ever since you left. We have enough vulcan pellets to do the job."

"Thank you, Roark," said DOU.

"When would you like us to begin?"

"Right now. Time to get on with it." Making an exit, they took to the sky preparing to watch the show in comfort, drifting on air currents rising from the south. "Proceed when ready."

With a grand flourish of showmanship Roark cried, "Let the show begin!" He brandished the first pellet in his beak, flew over Fifth Hall and let go. Kaboom! A deafening explosion erupted and hot lava flowed. Everywhere it touched ignited fires.

"Drop!" Roark gave the order and his young commanders flew into action. More explosions followed and thick plumes of smoke rose from the wreckage. Every hall was totally engulfed in flames.

A great cheer went up from all who were gathered. Many from the Opeggee nation came out to watch. The fire blazed hot for a good part of the afternoon, finally burning low, until all that was left was a heap of smouldering rubble. Wisps of smoke continued to rise from the ashes, all that was left of the once powerful reign of Aquadorus Oceanus.

"Thank you, Roark. Thank you, young wing commanders.

You are a credit to your people."

Roark smiled and waved, accepting the dragon's tribute. "My pleasure, DOU."

"Thank you, Profrak and your most gracious people, the great Opeggee nation. We are deeply indebted for your support and for your unwavering hospitality."

The Opeggees gave a loud cheer and waved farewell to their departing guests.

CHAPTER THIRTEEN
Fifth Mop Up

"Don't let the behaviour of others destroy your inner peace."

- Dalai Lama

Under the skillful guidance of DOU, the transition was seamless, landing them outside the Duplicating Hall in the lake bottom settlement.

"Let's have a last look at the underwater city before it is destroyed," said Sybil.

"Excellent idea," said DOU. "Quite ingenious, I must admit. It is important to remember what has happened here. We must relegate it to the past but keep the memory alive, to know what people are capable of."

Claire and Adelaide were particularly interested in touring the abandoned settlement, the source of so much unrest and suffering.

"This sort of thing must never happen again," said Claire. "How could this be accomplished in the time that it was?"

"About fifty years since the first invasion," said DOU. "Aquadorus was determined."

They wandered through empty streets, past aquarium fish farms, vegetable gardens and greenhouses. "We should use the food that has been grown here," said Sybil.

"I think someone has beat us to that," said Simon.

"Seems so," added Claire, peeking into the first green house. "It's picked clean."

Every available food source had been gathered. They were returning refugees; resourceful people who had learned to survive.

"Remember our gardens in Third?" said Adelaide. "We grew a lot of food in those days."

"There were few grocery stores back then," laughed Claire.

"We always traded preserves and recipes. You made the best green tomato pickle."

"And you had the best dill pickles. Just a hint of garlic."

The two women had been silent for much of the time. Now their desire to deal with their past pressed in on them.

Adelaide linked her arm through Claire's as they strolled behind the two young people and their dog. Maerwyn and Longille brought up the rear with DOU and Orion. Each was lost in their own private thoughts as they completed the circuit and strolled back to the Duplicating Hall.

Sybil's mind wandered back to her first days at the lake bottom colony. What seemed strange back then, had taken on an aura of normalcy. Her mind had been stretched beyond the ordinary into unusual and often bizarre realms—or so she had thought. Now, it seemed those others weren't all that different. Thinking, sentient beings lived everywhere. The majority desired peace, living in co-operation with one another. To appreciate the variety meant to embrace and understand the unusual.

"Shall we walk back to Leanoria?" asked Claire. "Adelaide has not seen the tunnel."

"I'd like that. Time to leave this place forever," said Sybil.

"I will use the space-time continuum and meet you there," said DOU.

They accessed the Duplicating Hall and entered the tunnel. Sybil relived that first night she had found Simon. A lot had happened in the intervening time and the past seemed very distant. They strolled casually, committing it to memory.

When they arrived in Leanoria DOU was waiting at the castle. It was being transformed by two industrious business partners who had decided a new hotel would attract tourists.

The drought was over and newly planted gardens on town lots were sprouting under skillful, green thumbs. Trade was flourishing in street markets, as vendors offered their wares.

The town had refurbished the old prison block into a lovely new library. Shipments of books had arrived and townspeople flocked to the newly opened building, thirsty for knowledge and entertaining novels.

"Knowledge is the key," said DOU. "It unlocks the petty strongbox where ignorance lurks."

Sybil and Simon could see the wisdom in DOU's words. Their thirst for knowledge, their desire for peace and understanding, had sent them on a quest and brought them through much turmoil.

"How are we to destroy the abandoned underwater settlement and the Duplicating Hall?" asked Simon.

"Do you think we should destroy it?" asked DOU.

"Of course! Nothing good has come from there," said Sybil.

"Nothing good? Are you sure?"

"Beyond all the fish aquariums and vegetables—no!"

"How can we destroy the Duplicator and keep the underwater farming," asked Simon."

"Why destroy it? It has no power without me. It will be a reminder to resist tyranny."

"We could turn it into a war memorial," suggested Simon. "Many people would visit. We must remember these days so it doesn't happen again."

"Yes," said DOU. "Peace must always begin with us. Remembering is a good way to start."

"And that underwater farming is a novel idea," said Sybil. "People would like to see how it was done."

She had spent time working in those aquariums and gardens. Her interest in growing food was part of her heritage, passed on through the women in her family, and through the generations of men who married them.

"They're redoing the castle as a hotel. Why not create guided tours to promote tourism in Leanoria. Bring in people and generate work," added Simon.

"There are many fine cooks living here. People will develop recipes using food grown in those underwater gardens," said Sybil.

"Hey! Maybe Ma and Pa could start a restaurant," suggested Simon. "Let's go find them."

DOU smiled knowingly. Plant an idea, a hint here and there, and people rose to the occasion. It was not a surprise. Sybil and Simon had the drive and ingenuity, the will to create. They were willing to help others realize their dreams. It was in their nature. It existed in the nature of people everywhere and most especially in this town. It was evident by the work already undertaken. Leanoria would rebuild and flourish in the aftermath of Aquadorus.

Simon and Sybil hurried through the crowds searching for his parents. "Halloo, Ma," Simon called, waving to her across the street. "Wait up."

"Simon! Sybil! You're back. Are we glad to see you!" She crushed them in one of her characteristic bear hugs. Davie, Peter and Elsie who had been walking ahead of her, turned and grinned.

"Simon!" They rushed back to join in the reunion. "Great to see you both!"

"You too, Sirius," said Davie, scratching his floppy ears. It was one of the things Sirius craved and Davie had become a favourite person who was always willing to do the scratching.

"Sybil and I were just talking to DOU. We have an idea, said Simon. "You know there's going to be a hotel here, right?"

"What if the town starts promoting tourism? Why not keep the underwater gardens and aquariums? Create a war memorial at the Duplicating Chamber," said Sybil.

"Imagine the tourists. Who wouldn't want to see that? You and Pa could start a restaurant, maybe at the hotel. We could come back and work during the summer holidays," said Simon, warming to the idea.

"What about telomeres and time travel—and aging?" asked Sybil, a little surprised by his enthusiasm.

"I figure if I want to see my family here, I will have to overcome my fear of aging. Besides, a few days in the Wellness Sanctuary in Hetopia should shave off a few months. We can always use the portal at Spoon Lake. And, I figure we are in present time at both ends. What's so aging about that?"

Sybil hesitated. "I don't know…maybe in different time periods, like when we were back in 1910. But it still might be a problem."

"So what do you think, Ma? You're the greatest cook in Leanoria," said Simon, remembering his first taste of scones and raspberry preserves at her kitchen table.

"I don't know, Simon. We'd have to talk to Pa first. I can see why that would be an enjoyable venture." She had always loved cooking and entertaining guests in her home. It would be an extension of that. And they grew a lot of their own food on the farm. It was organic, too, so that would be a draw.

"Let's go find Pa," said Simon. "Where do you think he'd be?"

"Come with me. I know just the place he'll be visiting," said Ma. She was right. He was at a seed store that had recently opened, buying seeds and dreaming of the organic crops he would plant. In addition to wheat, barley and oats, he had enough seeds for a garden to supply all of Leanoria.

"Pa! How big is this garden going to be?" asked Ma, gaping at the quantity. "We won't be able to do all the work."

"We won't have to. I will hire another person if it is too much. Heavens to Fifth, people around here sure could use the work."

"Oh, Karl. You are a mastermind when it comes to business. Which brings me to another little venture I have in mind. Well, it's actually Simon's idea."

She told him about her plans for a restaurant that had begun to form. It would start as a small café with sidewalk seating. She dreamed of expanding it to become a fine dining establishment employing many people in town.

"Say, that might be a great idea," replied Karl, rubbing his chin in thought. "That is exactly what we will do, Josie. You are the best cook in the area, if I do say so myself."

"And it may generate more work for town folk. Elsie and Peter, maybe even Davie could use a summer job. And Simon says he would love to work here in the summer," said Ma.

"And Sybil will come, too. Won't you, Syb?" said Simon.

"Of course. I'd love to spend time here now that things are back to normal."

It would be a very pleasant interlude on summer break. They could visit the Hetopians and Icelandia at the same time. Roark was utmost in her mind when she thought about Fifth. Would they need to access Seventh through Fifth? Or was it possible to visit directly from Third? She must remember to ask DOU.

"There's a town meeting this evening. I have volunteered to be on council until they can elect officials. Simon and Sybil, I want you to attend with us. We can make a case for keeping the lake bottom settlement. His days in Aquadria as Rinaldo had honed his organizational skills. Although it was very seldom that he had flashbacks to those days, he had retained many of Rinaldo's traits. Or perhaps it was the other way round. He had mastered the reversal very well.

The truth of it was, Simon and Sybil missed their old friend Rinaldo. The Aquadrians who had undergone reversal still retained much of their old spirit and were easily recognised. The families from Fifth were different. Still, at times they could feel his presence, part of Pa's personality. His penchant for work and organizing came through in everything he did.

Pa had made the transition without complications. However, he was concerned about Elsie. He confided in Simon, who shared his observations. He, too, wasn't sure about his family, vigilantly watching for signs of distress. Ma was okay, that he knew. It was Elsie he was most worried about. She was a little too quiet, different from the bouncy, chatty girl she had been. She bore watching.

He caught up with her. "Hey, Elsie. What do you say we go rafting on the pond near home tomorrow? With all this rain we've had there should be a good-sized slough by now."

"I guess we could, but I'm so tired these days."

"It has been an ordeal," replied Simon. "It might take a while to get your water legs back." He tried to crack a joke but it was lost on Elsie.

Sybil sidled up to them and joined in the conversation. "Yes, Elsie. I'd love it if you showed me how to raft. I never had the chance to do that before."

Elsie brightened at this suggestion. She had not spoken much to this new sister. For certainly, if Simon was her brother that made her family by extension. "That'd be nice, if I can just get over this dreadful fatigue."

"Simon, we need to do something about this. What's in our healing

bag of tricks? What can we do to help?"

"Do we have a tonic tea? What would Claire suggest?"

"Let me think about that. If I can't come up with something, we could ask her."

"What about that nettle tea the Opeggees serve? I feel quite energetic after a cup or two of that," said Simon.

"Just the thing," said Sybil. *"It has a lot of vitamins and minerals, helps absorb iron, too."*

"Provides a lot of benefits," agreed Simon.

"Nettle tea, and let's teach her a few rounds of yoga poses. That always perk us up," replied Sybil.

"Right," said Simon. *"Thanks for showing me those moves."*

"Remember that patch of stinging nettle over by the pond, Elsie? I ran into it one summer."

"Boy, do I. Your legs were covered in a blistering rash."

"Tried washing in the pond. Didn't help much. End of rafting for that day. Ma had to apply baking soda paste when we got home."

"That helped the itch. Ma is pretty good that way."

"The reason I mention it is, I thought we could gather some nettles for tea. That might help you feel better."

"Today? Not sure I'm up to it. Too tired."

"Sybil and I will gather nettles. We can go rafting when you feel better. Tell Ma where we are going, okay?"

"Come, Sirius," said Simon. He was anxious to go exploring. When they neared the outskirts of town, they took to the air. Simon's homing instinct steered them east.

"This is it," said Simon.

"You lived *here* before? Isn't this the same farm? I think it's the same barn we came to that night."

"Is it? It was dark when we arrived and we were in such a hurry. Never thought much about it."

"It was the middle of the night and after two years with the

Namors in that cell you weren't in very good shape."

"No, I guess I wasn't." He tried to recall his rescue. "I was a little out of it, must admit. How long were we here?"

"Overnight the first time. Second time we left very early."

"Let's go to the barn. Maybe that will jog my memory."

They made their way across the yard and entered the sheltering coolness. Simon climbed the ladder to the loft.

Sybil gave Sirius a bone to chew on. "Stay here, pal. Does this place feel familiar to you?"

Simon was standing at the window when she climbed the ladder to the loft. "The house doesn't look the same as when I lived here. It's dilapidated and boarded up. Maybe the yard is familiar." He stared out of the window, rubbing his finger over a notch on the sill. "Hey! I cut this notch with my pocket knife! That day we were up here making whistles."

"You mean to say this is the same farm you lived at with the Dugalls?"

"A lot has changed. But this barn, the notch cut in the window sill. It's the same."

"You said whistles."

"Yeah, from willows bushes. In the spring."

"How do you do that?"

Cut a straight piece from the bush. The sap is running so it's easy to push the wood out of the bark. Cut a few finger holes. Shape the whistle's blowing end and fit a small piece of wood in the bark to direct the air flow. There you have it—a whistle."

"Pretty clever, Simon."

"We never had much. Had to make our own fun. Built our own kites from paper and sticks."

"Sounds like fun. Will you show me one day?"

"Sure, it's easy. We can do that in Third when we get home."

"Home feels so far away right now," said Sybil. She hadn't thought about it for a long time.

"Not long, Sybil. We'll see the family settled here first. By the looks of this place, it will take a bit of work. Pull the boards off the windows and spiff up the yard. Grass is all matted. It should take shape fast."

Sybil wandered to the north-west corner and poked around in the hay, feeling for a latch. There it was, the trapdoor where she and the Hetopians had hidden that first morning while Namors snorkel-sniffed, hunting for them in the loft.

"Yes, this *is* the same barn. Look here, Simon. The trapdoor I showed you."

"That cinches it. Wait until I tell Pa and Ma I was here with you."

"Let's go find that pond and the nettle patch," said Sybil. "I want Elsie to have that tea as soon as possible."

After descending to the barn below, they headed out the back door to where cattle once grazed. Cutting diagonally across the pasture to a stand of willows, Simon steered her along an old path to a drinking hole the cows had used.

"Not far now," said Simon. He swept aside more willows and came to the edge of a pond. "This is it," he said, excitedly. "This was my favourite place to play. In the spring we dipped for frog eggs and watched them turn to tadpoles. Once they became frogs, we set them free here again. I loved going to sleep at night to the sound of a frog chorus. Most soothing sound in the world."

An old raft, still in good shape considering the years in between, lay at the high water mark.

"I'll take you rafting one day before we leave."

"Can't wait. Looks like fun!"

"Follow me," said Simon. He headed left on a trail skirting the pond. "They're over this way."

Soon they were stopped by a heavy crop of nettles. "Take your pick," laughed Simon.

"How are we going to do this? We don't have gloves."

"I'll use my sleeve. Open the Banquoebag. We'll collect them in there."

After gathering a large amount they lifted off, arriving back at Leanoria in time to enjoy a bonfire at the sports field where a lot of people were camped. Simon's family had been given a makeshift shelter for the night.

"Pa, we just came from our farm. The house has been boarded up. But the barn still stands solid."

"We'll head out there tomorrow. I got some tools today. Just pull those boards off and we'll start living there again," he grinned.

Ma clapped her hands together. "We've been away far too long. I'm itching to get my hands in soil and grow us our own good food again."

Elsie, Peter and Davie let out a cheer. "Yaaay! Can we go rafting on the pond first thing?" asked Peter.

"The raft is still there and looks in pretty good shape," said Simon. "Oh, before I forget. We brought some nettles for tea, Ma. They will help Elsie feel better."

"Thank you, Simon, Sybil," said Ma. "I'll boil some water on the bonfire over there." She grabbed a kettle and headed across the field.

"Thank you for collecting those nettles," said Elsie. "I hope you didn't get stung."

"Nope. Know how to work with 'em now," Simon grinned.

Claire and Adelaide had joined the camp while they were away.

"Hi, Claire," said Sybil. "What have you and Adelaide been up to?"

"We walked north of town. Wanted to see what it looks like in Fifth. In Third we homesteaded over there, way back in the day."

"Those were the days. Loved every minute," said Adelaide. She had come to terms with the loss of Benni. His memories lived on in her heart and she carried them close. Every one of her children had gone. A time of separation must always come. Benni's time had come before she was prepared.

Soon everyone was enjoying a cup of hot nettle tea. The earlier arrivals returning from Seventh had made it easier for those arriving later. Shelters and essential provisions to set up housekeeping were loaned or given freely. The Dugalls were well taken care of. After dinner they wandered to the town hall where a meeting was getting underway. DOU settled outside near the side door prepared to listen to proceedings.

The meeting was called to order and a number of items were discussed. Karl let things come to a natural close before he spoke up.

"Our family has made a good suggestion," he motioned to Simon and Sybil. "With the castle being refurbished and made into a hotel, it only makes sense to attract tourists. We could use the splendid farming operation at the lake bottom to supply food for our people. Why destroy it?" Many of the townsfolk gasped, uneasy about the prospect.

"You want to leave the Chamber intact?" asked an elderly man.

Simon spoke up. "Without DOU, the Duplicating Chamber no longer has power."

"Let it become a war memorial," added Sybil. "To remind us never to let this happen again. People will come to see it."

"That farming operation will provide much needed food until this land becomes fully productive again," added Simon.

"The underwater farm and the tourist industry will provide

work for people around here," said Karl.

"Our family is going to open a restaurant. That will provide jobs," said Josie. Her reputation as a skilled cook had been well- known and many who were present nodded their heads in approval.

"Okay, this all sounds very good. But, how do we start?" asked a man sitting next to him.

"The hotel is well under way. The underwater farm is still operative. We'll form work committees. People can sign up tonight for those they want to support. I, for one, am willing to get started in the restaurant business."

He nodded at two businessmen, Ambrose Messner and Bertrand Hood who were constructing the hotel. "Maybe you'd like a nice restaurant that offers excellent meals to your guests."

"Now that was one thing we had not considered. There is a kitchen and we can design a nice dining area. It can open out onto patio seating if you choose to do that," replied Ambrose.

"Sounds just what I had in mind. Well then, we're in business," said Ma, and she stuck her hand out. The two business partners stood and shook hands with both Josie and Karl Dugall. It was the beginning of a long and amiable working relationship.

"We must get settled at our farm first," said Karl. "That won't take too long. I will spend half days here and half days there. Elsie, Peter and Davie are getting older and are hard workers. Nothing can stop us now that we have our old way of life back."

"Nothing!" agreed the four entrepreneurs. They stood beaming at each other, dreams of a good future dancing before their eyes.

Early the next morning, Josie turned to Claire. "You and

Adelaide must come stay with us on the farm. It will be more comfortable than here in this camp."

"We wouldn't want to impose on you. You have enough to worry about," said Claire.

"Nonsense! Don't you ever think such a thing. We have been friends a long time. I won't hear of it. You and Adelaide are coming with us. That's all there is to it."

"All right then, but we are working right alongside you. That farm will need extra hands to put it right after being away so long."

"Thank you," added Adelaide. "I will be only too glad to help out."

"Well then, nice to have you. And so happy to be home. That's all I can say. Can't wait to get out there."

After a communal breakfast supplied by the already established returnees, the Dugalls and their friends headed out of town, glad of the four kilometre walk. They each carried a bag of supplies on their backs.

Approaching the yard, they were disheartened by the unkempt state. Setting promptly to work, the house was readied in short order. They looked forward to spending their first night together in their home once again.

"Time for that raft ride," shouted Peter and Davie, as they ran across the yard toward the back of the barn. "Beat you there, Simon."

Simon lit out after them, while Sybil and Elsie walked at a leisurely pace. "We won't get a ride until Peter and Davie have finished anyway," laughed Elsie. "They could be hours."

When they neared the willow patch, Sybil could see how a whistle might be made from them. "Simon tells me you used to make whistles from these." She ran her hand up and down the smooth stock.

"Sure did. One year we had so many we got a pipe band

together. Didn't sound like much, but it was fun to pretend. Lots of neighbour kids joined in."

"What was Simon like when he was growing up?" The time she had missed with him weighed on Sybil and she longed to know more.

"He arrived here when he was about four. The politest little kid I ever knew. The first day we showed him our goats he was hilarious. Hadn't seen a goat before. He stuck his two fingers up over his head and followed Nanny around. They looked just like a goat's horns. Billy, that's the male goat, was not too impressed. He tried to butt Simon. Peter knew how to handle old Billy and waggled his fingers to distract him. Simon learned a little lesson that day. Don't cross paths with Billy. He was protective of the kid goats, that's all. The little kids began to follow Simon around, so I think Billy finally accepted Simon on the farm."

"Can't imagine living on a farm," said Sybil. "It sounds so freeing. To come and go, play wherever you want, do whatever you please."

"It is a lot of fun. Hard work, too. We always had chores to do before we could play."

"In the city, where I live in Third, it is convenient to be close to shops and school. There's no freedom to explore, though." Her tree house paled in comparison to wide open spaces on the Dugalls' farm.

"I guess each has its good points," said Elsie. "I wonder if it's possible for us to visit Third one day."

"I wondered about that," said Sybil. "We can ask the Hetopians. Maybe they will know."

"We were in Seventh, weren't we? So why not Third?"

"Sounds hopeful when you put it that way."

"Where are the Hetopians? Why didn't they come to the farm with us?" asked Elsie.

"I suspect they've met up with folks, got talking and decided to stay in town. They will be visiting with DOU."

"That dragon is nothing like our story books say," said Elsie. "They sure got a bad rap."

"Maybe there are dragons like that. But I have never met one. In fact this is the only dragon I know."

"I never dreamed of meeting a dragon. Pretty amazing, isn't it?" said Elsie.

"Definitely beyond *my* wildest dreams."

"Okay, boys. It's our turn," said Elsie, as they came to the edge of the pond.

"Sure, no problem," said Davie, and he steered the raft to the opposite shore."

"Not fair, Davie. You had long enough."

"Yeah, I'm only kidding," laughed Davie. He pushed hard on the long pole and propelled the raft back across the pond.

"Hop on," said Peter, handing Sybil his pole. Davie gave his pole to Elsie and the three boys prepared to push them off shore.

"Come, Sirius," said Sybil. She slapped her thigh, beckoning the hound onto the raft. Sirius made a flying leap and missed, sending water in every direction.

"Sirius! Now I'm all wet," she laughed. She brushed water off her face and brought him aboard, content to have her hound near. Rafting across the pond was more fun than she could have imagined. They stopped midway and let the water settle to a glassy sheen. She peered over the side. Blue sky, afloat with billowy, white clouds, reminded her of the Great Hall in Hetopia. How she longed to be there in the stillness of the forests breathing in the scent of the Pallid Elusive heavy on the air. She was homesick.

She picked up the pole again, changed poling directions

and they made their way to shore, landing near the boys.

"Have you had a chance, Simon?" asked Elsie. "Or did these two hog it all?"

"Oh yes. They let me go first with Sirius. I have missed this so much."

"Enough for one day," said Peter. "We'll come back tomorrow." Hard work and fresh air had created an appetite. Their stomachs were rumbling as they headed back to the farm house for a good meal.

After dinner, Sybil asked Adelaide to go for a walk with her and Simon. She wanted to talk about Wesley. Maybe there was some way they could help him, back in Third. Although she knew Adelaide would be willing to listen, she wasn't sure how to approach the subject.

They strolled through the pasture out toward the pond using the old cow path.

"This is where we were today," said Sybil. "You ever been on a raft?"

"Yes, indeed. When I was a youngster. Not much less than your age. It is the best fun, right enough."

"Nothing much beats that," replied Simon. "This was Sybil's first time. She grew up in a city in Third. No chance to do that kind of thing."

"I loved it!" said Sybil.

"What is that like? Living in a city," asked Adelaide, curious to know more about her.

"Guess I never thought much about it before. Not until I came here. I can see I missed a lot."

"Tell me about your family. What are they like?"

"My dad owns a store. *Nature's Gateway*. It's an outdoor sporting goods store. He also runs a rafting company called *White Water Rafting*. It isn't like this kind of rafting."

"What about your mom?"

"She has what they call a cottage industry. Makes jewelry, soaps, and wants to add home-grown organic herbals. It keeps her busy."

"This whole episode…" Adelaide hesitated. "Simon, you were brought to Fifth; that must have been the worst tragedy for them."

"It was," said Sybil. "It caused a lot of problems."

"Sybil and I understand now why it had to be done. My parents in Third have come to understand, too. There was no other way. Claire showed us that."

"If there were only some way I could make it up to you. For taking you to Seventh." They had been over this before and she was made to see it as part of the overall plan. But the regret still lingered in her voice.

"There is one thing, maybe," said Sybil.

"What is it, Sybil?"

"It has to do with school back in Third. There is a boy who goes to my school. He isn't very nice to me and now also to Simon. He is rather a bully. Always has been, as far back as I can remember. He came to my Kindergarten partway through the year."

"Oh," said Adelaide. "How can I help you there?"

"I'm not sure. We wanted to ask you. Maybe you will have some ideas about it."

"Who is this boy, then?"

"His name is Wesley Peters. Same age as us." She looked at Simon.

"Wesley Peters?" Adelaide looked confused. "You mean our Wesley Peters?"

"You know Wesley?" asked Sybil, surprised by the revelation.

"Yes. He would be a great-grandson. Well, three

generations back, that is. Came off my son Oliver's branch in the family tree. I'm afraid I never had much rapport with Oliver."

"Why is that?" asked Simon.

"Well, you know how it went, back in those days. With Benni's death. I kind of fell apart for a while. My bitterness probably had a part to play in that. I always blamed myself for Oliver's wildness. I guess it just festered on down the line."

"Sometimes there isn't much we can do about life's hardships. It can overwhelm us," said Sybil.

"That, it did. But I am ready to make amends. This does not have to go any further. What do you think we should do about it?"

"Not sure," said Sybil. "There must be something we can do to help Wesley. He seems so angry all the time."

"I have been to Third so that is no problem. Maybe I can have a little talk with him."

"Won't that be a bit scary for him, if you show up from the past?" asked Simon.

"Sometimes it takes a little jolt to get your attention," replied Adelaide. She knew it might require a drastic measure and was prepared to risk it. She would be there for him if he needed her.

"That would get his attention all right," said Sybil. "I would like to be there when that happens. Not to see him scared, but to help him through the first shock."

"Both of us will be there. To help him through this in any way," said Simon.

"I think we have a plan that will work," said Adelaide. "When you get back to Third I will come to you. We can find the right time to approach Wesley. He must be a frightened little boy."

"That's what I think," said Sybil. "Fear can make people

lash out. It gives them a feeling of control and power." Remembering her own fear that first night alone in her room in Hetopia, she was more understanding of what it might be like for Wesley.

Simon was amazed at Sybil's understanding. He had known fear all too often. Getting angry moved him through it sometimes. But if it lingered and festered, and boiled its way in, it could corrupt. It could become a way of life if it were allowed to rule how you dealt with things.

"I am so glad we had this chance to talk. I do want to help. There is no way I cannot. Wesley deserves some support, some answers."

"Thank you, Adelaide. It means so much to us," said Sybil. "Can't begin to tell you how grateful I feel. Life at school was hard. I think life was hard for Wesley no matter where he was."

"I am really looking forward to getting back to Third now," said Simon. "It is something we must do. It can't be left any longer."

"Is there anything you want me to tell Claire? About this, I mean," asked Adelaide. "It started between us, really. I blamed her and Friederich a long time. I am so sorry about that."

"Claire might even want to help," said Simon. "She is that way."

"Yes, your grandmother is a very special person. We have been friends for a long time. Too bad I let my anger get between us. It turned to a cold stone of bitterness rooted in my gut."

"Well, those days are over," said Sybil.

"This is one way to lay it all to rest," said Adelaide. "That's why I think we need to involve Claire."

"I can see why you would think that," said Sybil.

"Then I will tell her all about this. We will work on it

together."

"Yes, we will," said Claire. "When I saw you go out for a walk, I thought you might need me."

They turned to see Claire who had come up behind them.

"Oh, good. You are here," said Adelaide. "It seems there is a bit of a problem with one of my great-grandsons in Third. At Sybil's school. He's from Oliver's line. You remember Oliver, don't you, Claire?"

"He was one of the twins, right?"

"Yes, they were fraternal twins. I guess I did not have much time for them. Oliver was the healthy one and the other twin needed more attention. I always felt he resented me for that. My frame of mind was off in those days. I blame myself."

"Now, Adelaide. Time to forgive yourself."

"How can I? It just goes deeper and deeper. Now this with Wesley. Will it ever end?"

"Of course it will," said Claire. "That's why we are here talking about it. Planning how to end the anger, the blame, so it doesn't keep repeating."

"You are a very understanding friend, Claire. How can you be so kind after all I've done?"

"What use is it to hold a grudge? Will it make me any happier? Sure won't make you happy if I did. Look what *I* did. Just ask Simon and Sybil. You questioned me that night when we went to that hospital in Chilliwack. You wondered if I should bring Simon to Fifth."

"Well, it seems you were right about that," said Adelaide. "Look where it has brought us."

"All I am saying is, everything seems to have a purpose."

"I suppose you are right," conceded Adelaide.

They turned and walked back to Josie's warm scones and tea.

Early next morning, Longille and Maerwyn scoured the area, sending telepathic bulletins. *"Sybil and Simon. Where are you? You left without giving us directions to the Dugalls' farm."*

"It's the same farm with the old barn," replied Simon.

"No way! Really? Then we'll be there shortly."

Landing in the yard, Longille mounted the steps and knocked lightly on the screen door, calling softly, "Anyone home?"

"Come in," Josie called from the kitchen. "We just finished breakfast. Would you like a bite to eat? Wouldn't take long to whip something up."

Longille remained standing on the porch. "No thank you, Josie. We had breakfast in town before we left. We are planning to leave tomorrow. Wondered if Simon and Sybil are staying longer or if they would like to go west with us."

Elsie came to the door. "We had hoped they'd stay a bit. Haven't really discussed it. Time to move on, I suppose. She opened the screen door and peered past Longille. "Here they are now, coming up from the barn."

"Hello, Maerwyn, Longille, DOU. Did you have a pleasant stay in town last night?" said Simon.

"Slept like a dream," replied Maerwyn. "Centralian air agrees with me. And we met some very nice people."

"We are planning a trade mission back here soon. Once this settlement gets fully on its feet there will be a surplus to trade. We could use some of the grain products grown here," said Longille.

"We had thought to go back to Hetopia tomorrow," said Maerwyn. "Do you want to come with us?"

"I'd like nothing better than to go home to Third," said Sybil. "But there's so much to be done here on the farm. I think they could use our help for a few days."

"That sounds like a marvellous idea," said Longille, looking around the yard. "You're right. This is the old barn we stayed in. Remember the first morning we were here when Namors Guardia were hunting for us."

"It looks different with the house lived in and the grass cut," said Maerwyn.

"Same barn," confirmed Sybil. "A serendipitous friend to us all."

"It would seem so," replied Longille. "It has provided shelter and concealment in times of peril."

"Who would think a barn could be a safe haven?" asked Maerwyn.

"It has called us together," said Simon, his sixth sense in tune with an alternate reality. "Nothing is coincidence in my life."

Sybil thought about what he said. It was the same with her. Nothing happened by chance, it seemed. Or maybe it appeared that way after the fact. She wasn't sure. You could read all sorts of things into reality if you were so inclined. Whatever it was, she was thankful for the hayloft with the secret compartment.

"You know, I think Maerwyn and I should stay on here at the farm and help out," said Longille.

"Why, Longille, you dear man," said Josie. "That is very kind of you."

"We love that old hayloft and are prepared to spend a few more nights in it," agreed Maerwyn. "We'd be no bother at all."

"What do you mean?" Josie's grin lit up her happy face. "You think you'll be a 'bother' offering to work on our farm? Can't think how to repay you for your kind offer, except to say, I'll do the cooking."

"Then it is settled. We stay until this farm is tip-top," said Longille. He laughed heartily, aware that Simon was relieved to hear they were staying.

Pa came up from the barn and joined the crowd gathered on the verandah. "Hello, everyone. Glad you made the trip out."

"Hello, Karl. Looks like you have all been working very hard," said Longille.

"It's a lot different than the last time we were here," said Maerwyn.

"Longille and Maerwyn have offered their help. Want to stay on until the farm is put right," said Josie.

"A very kind offer. Generous, indeed," said Karl, doffing his cap and nodding his head in their direction. "Much obliged."

"DOU is taking leave today, confident that all is well in Fifth." Longille broke the news. "The Leanorians in town have already said their goodbyes."

"Yes, I must leave," said DOU, who had remained on the sidelines listening quietly to their plans.

"That is sad news, DOU. We will miss you," said Josie. "But it is understandable to want to be home again. We know very well how that feels."

"Goodbyes are not my strength. It seems I've had to say a lot of them these days."

"You can always come back to visit. It is not goodbye. See you again, friends. That's our way."

DOU smiled. "It is very pleasing to see how Fifth has managed to repopulate. So much co-operation and goodwill. How can you not succeed?" The dragon made a low bow and lifted off, hovering close to the group below. A sparkle landed on each and every one, a dragon's kiss imparting a farewell blessing. DOU circled once and waved. "See you again, friends."

The Dugalls and their guests stood for a long while, each

contemplating what DOU had said. Co-operation and goodwill were the key to success. It had been their lifestyle until the invasion. Lies, distrust, deceit, hoarding—so many alienating things had taken over. Neighbours closed their doors to strangers, even to their friends, afraid to trust. Those dreadful, fearful times were finally over.

"Now, what can we do?" asked Longille, ready to get to work.

"I was down at the cattle pen mending fences," said Pa. Would you like to help me out with that? The boys have cleaned out the pig pens and the girls were mending wire fences at the chicken run. I have arranged for some livestock to be delivered from town tomorrow."

"Did you get any goats?" asked Simon. He was very fond of them, his favourite of all farm animals.

"I sure did," grinned Pa. "The Dugall farm always has goats."

"Sounds like you have things well in hand, Karl," said Maerwyn. "How about I leave you two to the fences. The boys and I will start spading up the garden."

"Josie would sure appreciate that. She has been dying to get her hands in dirt. The seeds I bought will have a head start if you can get that done. Thank you, Maerwyn. Thanks, boys."

They headed over to a fenced-in patch overgrown with weeds. Idle tools, leaning against the fence, found their way into their capable hands and soon a large, black, loam garden bed was prepared.

Josie came out of the house with a pitcher of lemonade and a basket of seeds. "How wonderful! I thought I would be days doing that chore. Thank you, men."

"No problem at all," said Maerwyn. They stood leaning on their spades while they quaffed a glass of cold lemonade.

Josie dropped to her knees and tucked seeds into the warm

soil, giving them a pat and a promise of water from the well as soon as she had finished planting.

Longille, who had overheard, arrived at the garden spot with two five-gallon buckets brimming with water. He and the boys watered the newly planted seeds while Josie stood back looking on in satisfaction.

With everyone hauling water, they were finished about the same time Claire poked her head out the kitchen window and called them for supper.

"I wonder what they have cooked up for us tonight," said Karl.

"Claire and Adelaide have scrubbed potatoes. Popped them in the oven along with a roast. I think there is Yorkshire pudding to go with it," said Josie.

"Baked potatoes and roast beef! My favourites," grinned Karl. "Let's get washed up. I'm starving."

After many days of hard work, gentle rains began to fall on the fields they had ploughed and planted. The time had come to say goodbye.

Karl and Josie stood looking out over their land as their guests prepared to leave. "How can we ever thank you? This has been a lot of hard work and we are so grateful to all of you. Thank you, we could not have done this without your help."

Tears flowed freely, intermingled with promises of return visits. Simon turned for one last look. "See you next summer."

CHAPTER FOURTEEN
Return to Hetopia

"Be the change you wish to see in the world."

- Mahatma Gandhi

It was early afternoon when they arrived at the apartments in Hetopia where Longille and Maerwyn had taken up residence. Sadie and her pups were outside playing with a friend who had cared for them during their absence.

She rushed over to Longille, greeting him in wild abandon. The remaining three pups followed her, playfully tussling with each other.

"Hello, Sadie, old girl. Did you miss me? I sure missed you," said Longille, running his hand over her flank. "These pups of yours keeping you busy?"

Wriggling with joy, she nosed Simon and Sybil.

"Hello, mama dog," said Sybil, grinning.

Sirius briefly greeted Sadie, sniffing her nose and nudging her affectionately. Then he joined the melee, playfully romping with the pups, rolling them on their sides and enticing them to a game of chase.

"Just look at them," laughed Sybil. "They're bigger than Pluto!"

"Pluto is likely as big as they are," said Simon. "It has been a while since we left him with Roark."

They sat down beside the mass of wriggling fur that

romped and wrestled, engaging them in their playful antics. Simon lay on his back letting the pups run over him, abandoning himself to puppy madness.

Sybil sat nearby enjoying Simon's interactions with the pups. Sirius flopped beside her on the grass. "They too much for you? You tired out?" She gave him a tussle. He rolled onto his back in an act of submission and trust, wanting his belly scratched. "You are one great dog."

An affectionate rumble in his throat told her he was clearly glad to be back in Hetopia. He rolled over and fell asleep beside her.

When the reunion had come to a close, they entered the apartment, soaked in long hot baths and relaxed in the lounge. Bathing in streams while on the road in Seventh, and using galvanized tin tubs on the farm in Fifth didn't do the job adequately.

Anxious to hear what had happened on the mission, Ebihinin arrived at the private dinner they had arranged to be brought over. The story unfolded as they dined, Sybil and Simon telling her of events in Seventh leading to the downfall of Aquadorus and their return to Fifth.

Finishing up his last bite, Longille could hold back no longer. "You'll never believe this, Ebihinin. Maerwyn and I have been to Seventh!"

"Seventh!" Ebihinin's eyebrows shot up in alarm. "What!" Shocked by the revelation, she leaned forward and touched his arm. "Are you okay?"

"Yes, we are fine. Don't worry. It was DOU who challenged our assumptions. After all this time…"

"It turns out our age-old beliefs about Seventh were unfounded," interrupted Maerwyn.

"How can that be?" asked Ebihinin. "We have always known that Hetopians could not enter Seventh!"

"Our beliefs were clearly wrong," said Longille. "We've been to Seventh and back. Nothing wrong with us."

"I see that," said Ebihinin, clearly disturbed. She had been following that teaching blindly, never once questioning it. "I wonder how many other assumptions we need to question."

Ebihinin was a revered sage among the Hetopians. It was gravely concerning to have one of those ancient teachings proved otherwise. She was wise enough to see she must challenge her own beliefs.

"It's rather freeing," said Maerwyn.

"Indeed, I think I would like to visit Seventh myself," said Ebihinin. "And it has been a very long time since I've stepped foot in the Centralian region. I always enjoyed that part of Fifth."

"We have secured a trade deal with them, once they are back in full production. The grains produced there will be a most welcomed addition to Hetopia. We have river fish from the Fraezorian Flow to trade in return," said Longille.

"And timber from our forests—just enough to meet our needs. We will not deplete such a valuable part of our landscape," said Maerwyn.

"You are wise counsel. We will discuss this at next assembly," Ebihinin smiled in agreement. Hetopians governed by consensus. It took longer to reach a decision, but everyone was happier with the outcome.

Sybil looked on in silence. She had been overwhelmed by Hetopian culture when she first met them. Now, it seemed, they were as much a part of her reality as Third. Fifth, under siege was a baffling maze of deceit. Now that it was back to pre-Aquadorian times, she could relate to it. Leanorian culture was more understandable.

She had been overawed by the Hetopians, had been shown so many amazing things. To hear them question some of their own beliefs was refreshing. It meant they were more believable, subject to error like everyone else. It was not wise to blindly follow. It was a valuable insight she had gained from the Hetopians' experience.

Early next morning, after their visit to the Wellness Sanctuary, Simon and Sybil headed into the old growth forest with Sirius. The peace of the forest ran deep in their blood.

"Do you think we love the forest and nature because our people lived in the Black Forest?" asked Sybil.

"Could be a factor," replied Simon. "It's obvious the forest has a calming effect on us. If our ancestors had the same experience, just think of the chemistry it created in their bodies. It would be a physiological response. All those good endorphins—it has to have an effect on children born to them. Born in a climate of peace and tranquility."

"Just think. If those experiences became a chemical blueprint, it could be passed on through genetics," said Sybil.

"That's a very interesting concept," said Simon. "Maybe one day I will do research in that field." Science had always interested him. The study of genetics began to take shape in his mind.

"How do you think you would begin a study on that?" asked Sybil, a little surprised by the idea.

"Well, perhaps one could do some generational comparisons with pups. Not too clear on how I would do that. Or..." Simon pursued the thought. "If a baby fox was left on its own; say it lost its mother. You'd need a control group. Or maybe the wild ancestors would be the control group. If loving humans reared it in the wilderness in a forest setting and it mated with another completely different fox, exposed to the same conditions. It would take a few generations all reared the same way. Maybe we'd see changes in those foxes."

"But, you couldn't tell if the changes were due to the

peaceful forest setting or the loving affection they received from people."

"What would that matter?" If humans respond to loving kindness, so can animals."

"So now you are saying, it is a peaceful environment and loving kindness that can change a genetic blueprint?"

"Why not? It's believable and I think maybe I could prove that one day in a scientific study." Simon was very taken with the idea and dreamed of his future.

"You seem pretty sure of this theory and excited about it. Is that what you think you will study—in the future?"

"Yeah, maybe. Or meteorology. I've always had an interest in weather patterns." He shuddered at the thought of the storm that took Benni. If an accurate forecast could prevent that, it would be a very useful career.

"What do you think you'd like to study, Sybil?"

"I am interested in botany. Plants have always played a big part in my mom's life and she was beginning to teach me stuff."

"You mean, like your vegetable garden?"

"Well, that too, but no. It's more wilderness, edible and medicinal plants. She's very knowledgeable. I could go into botany or horticulture," said Sybil.

"Cool, maybe we'll end up doing the same thing together one day."

"That genetics stuff sounds pretty interesting. We could live in the forest and do both together."

"Do you think our families would want to do that?" asked Simon.

"Who? Mom and Dad?"

"No, silly. The people we marry," said Simon.

"You getting married one day?"

"Yeah, I think I would like that. Have a family maybe."

"And pass this infinity ring on?"

"Why not? It can be useful."

"I never gave it much thought, Simon. To marry? They would have to accept our quirks, and that would take a special kind of person."

"Dad did," said Simon. "Back in Third. How does he manage it?"

"Dad is pretty laid back and accepting. Though he sure had a hard time believing my story about Fifth. Took him a while before he could accept that. And when I told him about you; well, that was nearly too much for the both of them."

"I can't imagine. It does sound pretty weird all right."

"Most Thirds would think we were crazy-hats. Maybe lock us up," sighed Sybil.

"All the more reason to choose carefully, if getting married."

"No, I don't think I want the hassle of all that," said Sybil.

"What? You don't want little *Sybils* running around the garden and playing in tree houses?"

"If you put it that way—maybe. Might be fun. Just don't send twins!"

"Why not? Look at us. Pretty close in the way we think. Together we are stronger. We are unique. Wouldn't you agree?"

"Yes, I do. Don't get me wrong. I can rely on you in everything. I would not have it any other way."

"And I, you," grinned Simon. "Especially when it comes to baking chocolate chip cookies."

"That will change. When we get back to Third, the first thing I will teach you is how to bake them."

"Aw, I like it better when *you* bake them."

"Nope, that time is long gone. We do it together. Teamwork."

"Yeah, we *are* a good team."

"Getting back to the subject of twins. Think about that. If twins, say you or I had twins—maybe the gift would come out even stronger in them."

"Now that would be a genetic study worth doing," said Simon.

"Might be really hard for them. Look how much adjustment it was for us."

"We'd help them. Uncle and auntie helping each other's kids."

"Maybe we should think more on the kind of work we want to do in the future before having twins."

"Got lots of time for that. Right now I am craving those cookies," said Simon.

"That's the first thing we'll do. Bake chocolate chip cookies."

"I'm not ready to go back," said Simon. "I'd like to spend more time here with the Hetopians."

"It is a pretty cool place. That's for sure. Can't wait to go to the Wellness Sanctuary," said Sybil. Other than the forest, it was her favourite place in all of Hetopia. The energizing peace was healing. Cares and weariness flowed off her like quicksilver. Negative energy dissipated, replaced by positive.

Simon and Sybil rested, growing strong in the healing balm of the forests. They were at ease with their past, left behind in Centralia and Seventh. No more was required of them. It would be good to go back to their lives in Third. To be sure, Simon would visit his family in Leanoria as often as he could. Since the Hetopians had promised to visit them in Third, he saw no reason why his family couldn't try that. Maybe it didn't require all that much to learn. After all, they had been to Seventh.

Sirius was greatly affected by the changes. He had been to

Seventh, and away as long as Sybil and Simon. His muzzle had sprouted a few white hairs.

"I don't like the looks of that. What does it mean?" said Simon. "If Sirius is growing older after being away that long, what has it done to us?"

"You look more mature. I must admit," said Sybil. She brushed his cheek, which had become more angular. His upper torso had filled out and the shoulders were more muscular. "What about me? How do I look?"

"You fishing for a compliment?" teased Simon.

"No, silly. I want to know if I look older."

"You're still as beautiful as ever, but…" Simon played the chivalrous brother and left her real concern hanging.

"Come on, you know what I mean." He could be aggravating at times.

"Come to think of it, you do look a little older. Your facial features have changed."

"Is that good or bad?"

"Actually, I like the changes. Good or bad—I guess that depends on how long we have actually been away," said Simon.

"Life is already too short. Don't need to shave off more time. Let's head to the Wellness Sanctuary. I'm going to use it a lot to make up for lost time."

"Can time ever be lost?"

"Depends on what you mean by lost," said Sybil. "Lost as never to be recovered, like we usually think of it. Or as accomplishing something in half the time expected, as in making up for lost time. Is time a commodity or is it a way of being? If we stay in the present as in Now, just like DOU said, the past and the future have no relevance."

"Oh my, aren't we clever," teased Simon. "Still, you are right, according to DOU. Does time seem to slow down when you stay in the present?"

"I know that a school year seemed to drag when I was in grade one. A whole year was a long time," said Sybil. "And way before that, even a whole day was very long."

When they arrived back at the tree house in Third, Sybil commented on how small the space was.

"We may have grown some," said Simon.

"That doesn't make sense. You come back to exactly where you left if you get it right."

"Well, Sirius is taking up space. He's a big dog."

"No, we used to fit Hamish and Marc in here, too."

"Uh-oh, did we come back too late? How old are we? Crud! You mean we got it wrong?" asked Simon. A worried frown puckered his forehead.

"Maybe, or could be our world vision has expanded. Things always seem smaller when you've been away a long time."

"Hope you're right. Let's go find Mom. If she looks the same…"

"Sirius, you have to stay put. Stay here. We'll be back for you, okay?" said Sybil. The big hound settled down on the wood floor, prepared to wait. He'd been left before and understood.

They entered the house in a state of trepidation, the moment of truth at hand.

"Halloo, Mom," called Simon. "Where are you?"

"Upstairs. I'll be down in a minute."

"No use waiting. Let's go up," said Sybil. She led the way tiptoeing lightly. "If Mom is older we need to go back and get it right. I'm not losing a year, or who knows what, of my life."

"Mom would freak out," said Simon.

"Let me go first." Sybil tiptoed down the hall to where her mom was making her bed. She peeked around the corner.

"Go, go back, Simon. Hurry!" She shoved him down the hall. As they raced through the backyard to the tree house Sybil gave him the news. "Mom has aged. She looks a lot older. There's even some greying at her temples!"

"Oh man, I knew something like this would happen," said Simon.

"We have to concentrate, Simon. Make sure we get back to Hetopia. We were way off!" The complication sent a deep chill down her spine spilling over onto Simon. He caught the edge of her panic and stopped.

He closed his eyes. "Breathe, Sybil," he said, drawing in deep, measured breaths, returning to centre, the centre of his being in the Now. He sent a calm wave outward. Sybil caught the wave and settled into the present moment. It was, what it was. They would deal with it as they always have. They must go back and fix it.

In the tree house, the present moment expanded and they allowed time to slow. It reversed, folding back on itself. With Hetopia in mind, they focused on an image of a warm brazier in the main lounge, keeping it foremost in their consciousness. They came through the tingling mist-like sensation and emerged in Fifth.

"You're back so soon?" said Longille, startled by their appearance. "What happened? Is something wrong?"

"I'll say," said Simon.

"We went back to a later time. Mom is…she has some grey hair!" said Sybil. Her anxiety skyrocketed.

"Now, now, now, don't fret too much. It happens. We can fix that easily enough."

"You're sure?" Sybil was beginning to doubt. After all, they had been wrong about Seventh. What if they had this wrong, too?

"We'll spend more time with you in the Wellness Sanctuary," said Maerwyn. "That will put things right."

"I guess we shouldn't have been in such a hurry to get back to Third," said Sybil. "Should have taken more time."

"Now, don't 'should' yourself," said Simon.

"Right," said Longille. "We do what we do, when we do it."

"Now we must go back and spend more time on it. Time I thought we could save. More time spent then, would have saved time now," said Sybil.

"Time is an unusual concept," said Longille. He smiled at her angst.

"Remember," said Maerwyn. "When you were in such a hurry that day when you first came to Hetopia. Not linear. Think elastic."

Proceeding directly along the short cut toward the Sanctuary, the peace of the forest trail seeped into their beings, calming them as it always did. Sybil heard his comment and imagined her time as elastic, stretching out and coming back to the original position. No rush, just calm, being in the space of now.

The Sanctuary was aglow, working overtime to impart healing power. Sirius had been through the warp with them and needed the energy adjustment as badly as they did. They spent another week in Hetopia readjusting.

CHAPTER FIFTEEN
Third Adjustments

"Nothing can dim the light that shines from within."

- Maya Angelou

After long periods spent in Fifth and Seventh, resuming their lives in Third was difficult. Events were time distorted.

"This is confusing," said Sybil. "It seems a lot harder this time back."

"Is it because we've been away so long?" asked Simon.

"We had all those experiences in between. How do we fit that into present reality in Third?"

"Stretching and slowing time. I wonder how that works. Or speeding up time. Is that what happens when we enter the Plasmic Energy Force?" asked Simon.

"It's all theory. Einstein's theory of relativity has to do with gravity, and mass and energy. Mass grabs space-time, telling it how to curve."

"Whoaaa, now that *is* mind-boggling," said Simon.

"Or *mind-bending,"* said Sybil, her pun intended as humour. "I don't understand it. All sorts of theories. Like wormholes in space that could link two places in space-time. And black holes and singularities." Sybil shook her head.

"Say! What if Spoon Lake portal access is a wormhole? Is that how we end up in different dimensions?" said Simon.

"There's a thought. It's all hypothetical. If the concepts of general relativity and quantum theory are both correct, then Stephen Hawking says maybe it's necessary to take another look at how they think about black holes."

"Maybe you're on to something. Mind-bending—maybe that's all it is. What if this is all in our minds?"

"Don't get crazy on me now, Simon. You really think this is all a figment of our imagination?"

"Maybe space and time only exist because we're thinking about it. It sure would be easier to understand."

"All we know is, it works. Do we have to understand it?"

"Yeah, I know I do," said Simon. "Science needs explanations. Proof."

"Sometimes it's easier to allow it to be a mystery."

"Okay, so tell me why Hetopians have a long life span."

"Because of the Wellness Flow," said Sybil. "It helps us combat the effects of time travel so why couldn't it prolong life?"

"You think if we use it long enough *we* will live longer?"

"Nah, I doubt that. I think it agrees with their biological makeup. We're different."

"Give me scientific explanations and facts. I want to understand it."

"Even if we had all the facts, if that is even possible, there'd still be questions. I think infinity is meant to be just that—endless. So how can you ever know? Maybe knowledge is endless. There's no limit to knowledge," said Sybil.

"Maybe time travel is like our infinity rings, double-looped. Time keeps coming back on itself."

"You mean we can meet ourselves in the past? Or the future? Now that is getting too weird," said Sybil.

"All I'm saying is maybe that's how it works. To pick up where we left off we have to meet ourselves again somewhere on the space-time continuum. In the past where we left from, and later in the future," said Simon.

"I am okay with just leaving it be. As long as I get back to where I left off."

"Where's your sense of adventure?" asked Simon. "Wouldn't you like to see what you were really like as a kid? Or, maybe as you are in the future, older?"

"Isn't that just what we did? We came back in the future. Mom was older."

"Shucks! We should have found a mirror. To see what we looked like," said Simon.

"No way. I just want to know what I looked like in the past. That's why we take videos and photos. Isn't that enough?"

"Digitally it is possible to leave an imprint, the impression of who we are, frozen in time. Is it possible to leave that same impression in the energy force and encounter that *self* again?" asked Simon. "Is that how it works?"

"You mean, like a TV signal come to life? That's weird," said Sybil.

"Why not? Sound signals are relayed by cell towers. That's what you told me."

"Yes, but that is sound energy. Say, maybe you're right. If we are energy, which they now believe we are; molecularly, we are little particles. Scatter those particles and put them back together. Voila! Time travel!"

"You can scatter your particles. I think I'll hang on to mine," said Simon.

"Well, it was you who wanted proof."

"Not that kind of proof!"

"Physical proof demands physical action. No longer a theory, right?"

"Yes, if it proves to be true. But what if we're wrong and the experiment fails. Poof! Particles scattered all over the universe."

"Our particles must have come out of the universe at some time. Energy is never lost. It just transforms. Physicists in Third are finding new things all the time. At CERN, near Geneva, Switzerland, a particle, the Higgs boson was discovered and that was suspected in theory for a long time," said Sybil.

"CERN?"

"It's a lab to study particle physics. They built a hadron collider in a ginormous tunnel. The biggest and most complex machine ever built."

"Sounds complicated," said Simon.

"And very interesting. But I don't know much about it. Another mind-bender."

"Yeah, well, my particles are staying in this form," said Simon, sweeping both hands from the top of his head to his feet.

"I like you in that form, too," smiled Sybil. "No 'beam me up, Scotty' experiments in our futures."

"What is 'beam me up, Scotty'?" asked Simon.

"From the Star Trek series. We'll have to watch Mom and Dad's old videos."

"Sounds like fun."

"Our first rainy Saturday we have a date. Watching Star Trek movies while munching chocolate chip cookies."

"How do you know we haven't 'beamed me up, Scotty' already?" asked Simon. "Maybe *that* is how we time travelled."

"Doubt it. Don't ask me how. We know it happens. Let's just ride the time wave."

"You think we are ready now?" asked Simon. "Can we get back to Third at the exact time we left?"

"No way of really knowing that unless we try. I'd say we've done very well if Sirius's white muzzle hairs are any indication.

He's lost them all. And *you* have that boyish gleam in your eyes."

"You're still as beautiful as ever…in a juvenile way," Simon grinned, tweaking her chin.

"Simon, be serious." Not many had thought her beautiful and she wasn't accustomed to being told that.

"I am serious. You are beautiful, both inside and out."

Sybil smiled shyly, tucking the compliment away for the times she knew would come. Being called a freak so often had left an indelible mark. It was hard to forget. She was not looking forward to that reality in Third. Still, she had been through so much in Seventh and Fifth. It had changed her in ways she could not fathom.

On the second attempt, when they landed in the tree house, all seemed as usual. Proportionately it was the same, even with Sirius tucked in beside them.

"Do we go in cold or check it out first?" said Simon.

"I feel pretty good about this. Let's just do it."

"Okay, here goes." Simon climbed halfway down the ladder. "Lower Sirius to me. I'll take him to the bottom."

"Got him, Simon?"

"Yeah, got him. Boy, are you heavy, Sirius. Too many dried beef sticks." He wrapped one arm around his torso and clung to the rope ladder easing his way toward the bottom. Sirius leapt the remaining distance and raced around the yard.

"Come, Sirius," said Sybil, calling him to her side. "Should I go in alone while you wait here with Sirius?

"Might be best," replied Simon, holding Sirius by the ruff.

Just then, the screen door on the back porch opened and their dad came out. "Ho, Sybil, Simon. What's this? Where did that dog come from?"

Simon let go of the hound and he raced over to greet

James. "You're a friendly sort, aren't you?" said James, patting the flurry of activity at his side. "Energetic, too."

Franceska poked her head through the screen door. "What's all the commotion about? What's that dog doing here?"

Sirius trotted over to Franceska and poked his snout under her hand so that it slid to the top of his head. She began to pet him and his whole body, led by the wag of his tail, began to undulate.

"This is Sirius," said Simon. "He's been with us a long time."

"Oh," said James, his eyebrow arching in Simon's direction. "How so?"

"We found him in Fifth at the prison where Simon was held. There were two other dogs as well, but they are with the Hetopians."

"You were away?" Franceska looked incredulously at Simon, then at Sybil and back to Simon. "You've time travelled again, right?"

"Yes, Mom," said Simon. "We have, but we're here now and we are safe. Sirius is very special to us. He's helped us through some very hard times while we were away."

"It was absolutely necessary to go," said Sybil. "You said one day I would come to appreciate this *gift.*" She held her hand over the infinity ring on her left chest. You were right." She looked at her parents, sure of their support. This time it was evident in their faces.

"Can we keep Sirius?" asked Simon. "We hope he can stay."

"We hadn't counted on another family member so soon," said Franceska. "But he looks like a Huber to me or should I say Galowin. What do you think, James?"

"This family, Huber, Galowin, all the same, has been

missing something. He seems to fit right in, doesn't he?"

"That decides it," said Franceska. "Welcome home, Sirius."

"Yes!" cried Simon and Sybil. "This is the best day ever. Thank you!"

"We know you are responsible for him. That's not the problem. Where will he sleep at night? I bet he has not left your side since you met him," said Franceska.

"No, can't say that is true," said Sybil, remorse still clouding her thoughts at the memory of having left him at the rookery.

"He needs a permanent sleeping place," said James. "Is he an indoor sort or an outdoor type?"

"Both," replied Simon. "Inside at night. Loves to be with his family. He can sleep in my room if Sybil doesn't mind."

"Outdoors during the day. Loves to be out in the forest and countryside," said Sybil. "He will love our trails and rivers around here. Say, we need to take him up Mount Cheam one day."

"Yeah, where it all started," said Simon. He grinned at the thought of it. "You don't mind if Sirius sleeps in my room, do you?"

"Not as long as I get to hike with him. That is just fine by me. He snores pretty fierce some nights."

"Then we'll go out today and buy a special bed for him. It will fit nicely under your window," said Franceska.

"We'll need dog food, some chews and toys," said James. "And to be sure, we should have him checked by the vet. He'll need his shots."

"And a leash," said Franceska. "We can't let him loose on city streets when you're out walking."

Oh dear, thought Sybil. I wonder how Sirius will take to a leash and collar. Heaven forbid. He is a wilderness hound, used to roaming freely in forests with us.

"Let's go shopping. Pile in the jeep," said James.

"Can Sirius come?" asked Simon.

"Of course. We won't leave him in the yard by himself on his first day home. Someone will have to stay with him while we are in the store shopping."

"I'd be glad to do that," volunteered Franceska. "Let's go."

That evening Sirius had his first lesson on a leash. He was not pleased at first but soon settled down, especially when they let him off his tether at the dog run near Vedder River. He raced around the fenced area, sniffing other dogs, engaging them in games of chase. Simon threw a ball they had bought for him. After many retrievals he soon tired and sat panting beside him on the grass.

"Had enough, Sirius? Let's go home."

After dinner they sat in the family room chatting. Sybil and Simon recounted the latest adventures in Fifth and Seventh. Questioning eyebrows and alarmed facial expressions in response were all that came forward. James and Franceska were coming to resignation, if not acceptance, of the extraordinary lives their two unusual children led.

"We found Simon's other family in Fifth," said Sybil. "The Dugall family. Karl and Josie Dugall. They cared for Simon when he came back from Seventh."

"What do you mean, 'came back from Seventh?' " asked her mom.

"When Simon was abducted…" She didn't know how to break this news. She took a deep breath. "Remember that day at the cemetery at Lenore Lake? When we heard that voice telling us to 'find it.' Three times it said to 'find it.' "

"Yes," said her mom, hesitating, afraid of the next revelation.

"Well, I found Simon and brought him home to us. But

that wasn't what it meant. We had to go looking for the dragon's eye crystal," said Sybil. "That voice telling us to 'find it…' "

"That was Claire Huber. Your great-great grandmother," interrupted Simon. "She is the one who came for me at the hospital. She took me to Graenwolven territory."

"Her plan was to separate us until we came of age, came to our full potential. Simon was to live with a family near Leanoria. They are a wonderful, trustworthy family. After Seventh fell, we lived with them for a while and helped them get resettled on their farm."

Stunned by the news, Franceska sat immobile. Then a rush of anger surged upward, exploding in her brain.

"How dare she!" cried Franceska. "She had no right to do that to my family, to me, to us." She looked at James, sorry he had been put through this. Her own grandmother? It was beyond understanding.

"Now, Mom. Please don't blame her. There was no other choice," said Simon. "I have come to understand that."

"It was absolutely necessary. Aquadorus would have flooded Fifth. He would not have stopped there. Third was in danger as well," said Sybil, hoping it would help her mother to see how it was.

"Grandmother is a lovely, caring woman. She co-ordinated the dimensions. We were chosen to find the eye crystal and restore it to DOU," added Simon.

"Why you?" Franceska's doubt stirred a whirlwind of emotions.

"Some believe it was foretold in the Book of Wisdom," said Sybil.

"Wisdom?"

"Ancient writings known to both Fifth and Seventh," said Sybil. "Predictions, I suppose."

"This sounds like another fairy tale," said James. The travails of life, beginning with Simon's abduction, had etched permanent worry lines. The furrows deepened as he considered the wild story coming at him across the space separating them.

"Ja-ames," Franceska's voice lifted at the end of his name. He checked his disbelief and sat quietly. His wife and children *were* unusual and he didn't pretend to understand all they experienced.

"I believe you, of course I do. But I am so rooted in this reality. It is hard to let my mind entertain any other."

"That's okay," said Simon. "It *is* hard to believe. I couldn't believe it either when Sybil first told me who she was and how I fit into this family."

"If only you could meet grandmother," said Sybil.

"Maybe there is a way," said Simon. "Remember, Adelaide said she would help us with Wesley. Did we not ask Claire to be part of that?"

"She always regretted not having made herself known to you after Simon was taken. Felt her family would never forgive her. But that's not true, is it Mom?" asked Sybil.

"No, I don't think so," said Franceska. "Meeting her, if that is possible…it might be easier to understand."

"You may even be able to meet the Dugalls in Fifth. Would you like to meet them?" asked Simon.

"I can't imagine travelling to Fifth!" said Franceska. "Highly unlikely."

"Maybe they will come here," said Sybil. "We still aren't sure how that will work. We do know one thing. There is no end to possibilities."

"I am beginning to see that," said James. "My beliefs have been called into question a lot these days."

"When do you think that will happen?" asked Franceska.

"Are you okay with this, James?"

He rubbed his chin in thought. "Yes, I suppose I am. I have had my eyes opened a lot in the past few months. I can handle it." His sense of adventure was beginning to override his usual level-headed nature. "Bring it on."

CHAPTER SIXTEEN
Reckoning and Reconciliation

"Logic will get you from A to Z; imagination will get you everywhere."

–Albert Einstein

Monday morning came all too soon. Now that they were back in Third, the routine of school loomed before them. A rap on the front door announced that Hamish and Marc had arrived.

"Come in a minute. Sybil's not quite ready," said Simon.

"Nah, we'll just wait out in the yard," said Hamish.

"There's something I want to show you. Come around the side and meet me out back."

They skirted flower beds and made their way to a gate where Simon was waiting.

"Come through. I want you to meet someone." He turned and called Sirius, who came bounding across the grass to Simon. "Hey, boy, meet our friends Marc and Hamish."

"You got a dog! When did that happen?" asked Hamish.

"Just this week end," said Sybil, who had heard them at the side gate. She stepped off the back porch and joined them.

Hamish presented the back of his hand, allowing Sirius to sniff him. He was cautious around dogs ever since he'd been bitten by a stray. Sirius sensed the reticence and gave his fingers a soft lick.

"I think he likes me." Hamish's face relaxed into a grin.

"He loves people," said Sybil.

Marc ran his hand over the silky smoothness of his back. "He's so soft. Can we take him hiking with us?"

"That's kind of what we had in mind," said Simon. "He's used to running free. This yard stuff doesn't cut it for him."

"We had him at the dog run on the weekend. That's the only freedom he's had, really," said Sybil.

"Where did you get him?" asked Hamish.

"He was a rescue dog," replied Sybil, unsure of how to handle that question.

"Well, he's found a good home," said Marc. "That's for sure."

"We're taking him out to the forest after school," said Simon. "Want to come?"

"Can't," said Hamish. "Got'ta get my homework done. Been grounded for a week for missing work."

"Bummer," said Marc. "Sorry, guys. I can't go either. Have ball practice."

"Maybe on the weekend. If I get all my work done. Should be able to talk Mom into it," said Hamish.

"Let's go or we'll be late for school," said Sybil. "See you later, Sirius." She bent and hugged his torso. His big warm body bolstered her spirits. Her anxiety level had increased at the thought of facing another day at school with Wesley and Alex.

Simon gave him a pat and they headed out the gate, walking the four blocks to school.

They arrived just in time for the warning bell. "That's cutting it a bit close," said Simon.

"Good," said Sybil. "We don't have to worry about Wesley." Maybe that was the solution. Arrive just on the bell so Wesley had no time to harass her. She barely slipped the thought out when her inner voice cut that line of thinking. She would not live like that. You have faced Namors Guardia, Aquadorus and Dimondus—get a grip. Wesley Peters isn't going to run your life. Still, the old fear coursed through her.

The day at school went relatively smoothly. She suspected the meeting in the principal's office the last day they'd tangled had shut him down, at least temporarily. Wesley did not approach her or Simon, just stood off in the distance scowling.

"Wesley doesn't look too happy," observed Simon. "Looks like he lost his best friend."

"Maybe he has. Haven't seen Alex with him all day."

"Could be the two families were called in after that last incident. Maybe Alex's parents put the brakes on."

"That's a start," said Sybil, still not convinced any change was in the wind. "Let's just get through this first day back. I'll be glad to hit the hiking trail after school."

"You and me both. Sirius needs a good run."

At lunch they threaded their way through the crowds and met up with Hamish and Marc near the basketball courts.

"You any idea where you're going for that hike after school?" asked Marc. "Sure wish I could go with you."

"Sybil and I thought we'd take Sirius up Mount Thom," said Simon.

"It's the closest to our subdivision," added Sybil. "We can get there on foot. Make it to the top and back in time for dinner."

"Cool. Have fun," said Hamish. "That'll teach me to get my work done on time."

The school day drew to a close and the four friends walked home, parting in front of Sybil and Simon's house.

"Too bad Hamish and I can't come," said Marc.

"Catch you on the week end," reassured Sybil. "We'll take him out again."

Rounding the corner of their house they saw Sirius eagerly whining at the back gate. He jumped up, leaned his paws on the top of the fence and barked.

"You miss us, old boy?" asked Sybil, opening the gate. Sirius bounded through, jumped up on her with his front paws, and began licking her face. He tackled Simon, nearly bowling him off his feet.

"Ready for a run, boy? I'll get the leash," said Simon. "Sybil, tell Mom where we're going."

They entered the back door into the kitchen. Simon bounded up the stairs, changed into hiking boots and stood waiting outside.

"Mom's not home. There's a note on the table. She had to go pick up a few things. I left a note saying we were going up Mount Thom," said Sybil.

"We can run him on leash until we hit the trail. That'll tucker him out."

"Let me get my hiking boots on."

When they were ready, they set off with Sirius straining against the leash. "Here, you take over for a while. My arm is about to fall off," said Sybil.

"I got him. He's sure excited to get out there," laughed Simon.

They hit Bailey Road and were soon on the steep incline of Prest Road hill.

"He's a keener all right," said Sybil. "Good thing I remembered to bring water. I'm already thirsty."

"I miss that BanquoeBag. How will we ever manage?"

"Fifth has spoiled us. Third isn't as convenient in many ways."

"No, but it is more predictable," said Simon.

After passing through new neighbourhoods that had sprung up, they found the trail head. The peaceful forest ahead drew them in like the scent of the Pallid Elusive back in Hetopia. When they gained the sheltering trees, Simon let Sirius off leash and he bounded forward, veering off through undergrowth, nosing out intriguing scents and reappearing on the trail ahead. He ran back and forth to them, keeping contact. His hiking route was double theirs.

When they rounded the first bend, they were stopped in their tracks. Wesley Peters stood wide-legged, blocking their way.

"Step aside and let us pass. We want no trouble with you, Wesley," said Sybil.

"Trouble is what you'll get," snarled Wesley.

"Where's Alex?" asked Simon.

"He's grounded. Lost the only friend I had. All cause 'a you two that day."

"You brought that on yourself," said Sybil. "Just leave us alone."

"Nah, can't do that."

"What have I ever done to you?"

"You're such a freak show. Can't stand freaks. Ugly, too."

"Enough!" said Simon. He stepped between Sybil and Wesley. "Back off and leave. We don't need to do this."

"Yeah, we do. You think you're so special. Long lost brother. Everyone making such a big fuss."

"You know nothing about it," said Simon.

"Know enough," retorted Wesley. "Know you're going to get what's coming to ya."

"Better be careful, Wesley," said Sybil, eyeing a point beyond his back.

"Turn around and take a look," said Simon.

"Hah, I'm not falling for that ol' trick."

A deep rumble issued from Sirius's throat. He had reappeared on the trail and sensed there was trouble.

Wesley froze, petrified by the unknown menace at his back. His shoulders tightened and his eyes bulged in alarm. Sybil watched fear cloud his features. Instinctively she wanted to reach out to calm him, to tell him Sirius meant no harm. But she realized they had an advantage. To press the point home, she let him stew in his confusion.

"What do you want to do now, Wesley?" asked Simon. "Let us pass and we'll forget this ever happened."

"Have it your way," said Wesley. He stepped aside and allowed them to carry on. When he turned to see where the growl had come from, there was nothing. He heard only rustling sounds in the bush off to his left.

The thought persisted. It was a trick. Still, he figured he'd better not take any chances. He turned and headed downhill, calling back, "This ain't the end 'o things."

"How did he know we were coming up here?" asked Sybil.

"Probably overheard us telling Hamish and Marc at school."

"We have to do something about this. You think it's time to call in that favour from Adelaide?"

"Can't be looking over our shoulders wondering where he'll pop out next."

"I'm afraid he might do something to Sirius," said Sybil. "Only a matter of time before he figures out that we have a dog."

"I'm having flashbacks."

"To what?"

"Dimondus."

"Dimondus *was* as mean as Wesley. No question about that."

"But look how much he changed. Never know he was the

same person," said Simon.

"Goes to show that no one is completely bad. If Dimondus can change, anyone can."

"Think there's hope for Wesley?"

"Always felt there was. Maybe Adelaide can give him a little nudge in the right direction. Show him there's more to life than what meets the eye."

"Maybe we need to show him a few things," said Simon, chuckling at the idea forming in his head.

"What do you mean?"

"Oh, I have few tricks up my sleeve," said Simon, raising his right arm and tugging on his shirt.

"Out with it, Simon. That gleam in your eye tells me you have some mischief brewing."

"Well, not so much mischief, as truth will out."

"You mean tell him who we are?" Sybil gasped. "You can't be serious."

"Not tell him, *show* him, and I am deadly serious. Before we call Adelaide and Claire…maybe even DOU."

"DOU? You think DOU would come all this way just for our problems?"

"Maybe not for us, but for Wesley. Don't know. But it's worth a shot."

"You mean, ask DOU to see Wesley?"

"If nothing else works with Adelaide."

"That's pretty drastic, wouldn't you say?"

"Might be the only way he listens to reason. To see and feel his own value."

"Simon, I am impressed. How did I deserve such a brother?"

"Nothing special, really. I just know how I want to be treated. To feel that. It'd be a good beginning."

"Yes, I understand what you are saying."

"Well, what's so hard about that?"

"Nothing, if you aren't hardened to a way of living," replied Sybil.

"We can soften him up. Just wait and see."

"Oh, I have tried plenty of times. You saw his reaction here just now."

"Yeah, he is a hard nut all right. But shells can crack," said Simon.

"That shell is there for a reason, I guess. We just need to find the right nutcracker," laughed Sybil.

"What's so funny?"

"I just had an image of the Christmas Nutcracker chasing Wesley downhill."

"Christmas Nutcracker? What are you going on about?"

"It's from the Nutcracker Suite; a ballet of toys and Christmas frolic."

"You'll have to show me on YouTube."

"Worth watching, especially if you want to get a picture in your head of Wesley and the Nutcracker."

"Let's get to the lookout on Mount Thom. We need to be back before dinner. Mom appreciates help with it."

By the time they arrived back, daylight had faded. It had taken longer than expected. Franceska was beginning to worry.

"I realise you two have been out on your own in Fifth and Seventh, but here in Third you still need to respect our expectations."

"Sorry, Mom," said Sybil. "It took longer than we thought. Sirius really needed a run. Had a great time out there in the forest."

"I expect you to pay more attention to things, especially when it comes to time and being away in the woods."

"Yes, Mom," said Simon. "Sorry we're late. That won't happen again. We don't mean to cause you to worry."

"Okay, Simon. I just needed to make myself understood. It hasn't been easy. You two could just disappear."

Sybil heard this last comment with reservation. Mom was right. They could have run afoul in Seventh, never to be heard of again. She made a mental note to be more careful.

The following morning, Hamish had a dental appointment and Marc had early band practice, leaving Simon and Sybil to walk to school on their own.

At halfway point Wesley stepped out from behind some shrubs where he had lain in wait. He strutted toward them, his arms akimbo. One hand on each hip presented a forceful impression. Sybil stopped. Her usual response, to flee, to avoid any threat, rose to the surface. But she stood her ground, mustering forth all the determination and fortitude that had brought her through Fifth and Seventh. She drew herself up tall, placed one foot forward and balanced on her back foot. It was a non-threatening stance, yet afforded her strength and flexibility if she needed to deflect an advance. She could easily pivot or step aside. Simon stood next to her.

Wesley strolled up to them and glared. "You were lucky yesterday up on the hill. Don't expect to get away so easy next time. Better watch your back." He stuck his hand in his pocket and poked his finger at her. The gesture conjured up a menacing threat.

"You don't really mean that, Wesley," said Simon.

"You bet'cha. I always mean what I say." Wesley's bravado went on, but he sensed steel in Simon's tone. He looked at Sybil. There was something in her eyes he had not noticed before. It was strength—raw, determined strength. He stepped back just a little, enough to give Sybil the edge.

"You don't really mean *that,*" said Sybil, placing a hand in her pocket and mimicking his threat.

Wesley continued to glare at her, but he was disarmed by her reserve. There was a boldness he had not seen before. There was something else, too. Her eyes held a softness, a gaze that penetrated his blustering façade. It reached a point deep within he never knew existed. A brief warmth flickered to life, a frightening warmth, strange and foreign. As quickly as it flared, he squelched it hard.

"Better get," he resumed his threat and stepped aside. Something had changed. Things weren't right. Baffled by the subtle difference, he felt the shift and did not like it. He did not know how to respond.

All that day at school he dogged them, lingering in the background. He was in the cafeteria watching them from across the room, eyeing them with a searing, unrelenting glare. In the halls he brushed past them intentionally making contact, rudely elbowing his way past.

Sybil's cell phone buzzed a number of times. Dead silence on the other end slowly transitioned to heavy breathing, followed by silence and disconnect. She stopped answering her phone.

Texts began rolling in, two and three word utterances: 'Watching you,' 'freak show,' and the worst, 'goin' huntin'.'

Sybil was rattled. How did he get her number? Did he hack his way in? First, that menacing gesture on the way to school. Now, the allusion to hunting. Wesley clearly wanted to intimidate and he was successful at it.

When school let out Hamish and Marc met up with them for the walk home. They resisted the urge to tell their friends about what had happened on the hike the day before and the incident on their way to school. No use in alarming them. Wesley's behaviour was escalating and it was best not to involve the safety of others. Simon and Sybil were prepared to handle it themselves. They didn't want interference, nor did they want to explain Adelaide or Claire to them. What would happen there was still a mystery. Best no one else got involved.

That evening Simon and Sybil sought the comforting solace of their tree house.

"What did you have in mind with Wesley?" asked Sybil.

"Let's show him a little trick. Like lifting off a few metres."

"You mean in broad daylight?"

"No. I found out where he lives. We'll pass by his window one night."

"Like a haunting?"

"Sort of. You and I know it isn't. But he won't."

"Wouldn't that prove I was a freak? Instead of being more accepting he would shun me more."

"Perhaps, but he won't be bothering you much after that. Won't believe his own eyes. He wouldn't dare tell anyone."

"They'd think he was bonkers. Sounds like a bit of fun. But we won't let that go too far. Just give him a little shakeup, soften him up for Adelaide," said Sybil.

"Yeah, don't want to scare him too bad. Get that shell to crack just a little."

"When do you want to do this?"

"How about tonight? Supposed to be a full moon. Perfect timing."

"I'm game," she chuckled, thinking of the look on his face.

Later that night they headed out to the backyard. "See you in a bit, Mom. We're going to take Sirius for his walk before bed," said Simon.

They headed down the street with Sirius tugging at the

restraint around his neck. "We really need to take him to some obedience training," said Sybil.

"What? And train all his instinct out of him? Look how many times he has saved us. To break that natural bent in a hound would be cruel."

"Maybe all we need to do is teach him to walk without pulling."

"We can Google the best methods and work with him without interference from a trainer," suggested Simon.

"I like that idea. Let's start tomorrow after school."

"I found Wesley's place on Google Earth. Who knew he lived this close," said Simon. "He's the next neighbourhood over."

"How'd you get his address? Not sure I want to live that close!"

"Asked around at school. One guy told me he lived across the street from him."

"Imagine Wesley as a neighbour…"

"This is it. Here's his place. You ready for this?"

"Not sure," said Sybil, feeling a little guilty. She wasn't entirely convinced this was a good idea. But she had agreed and they were here now.

"You think that's his bedroom window?" asked Simon.

"Chuck a pebble at it and see what comes of it."

It took a couple of tosses before the blind moved and a face appeared in the window. It *was* Wesley.

He scowled down at them and was about to slide his window open, when Simon said, "Okay, now."

They lifted off with Sirius safely stowed in the mind net. Floating a half metre off the ground they watched his eyes grow round. Rising a little higher, they came level with the window sash. His face paled and in an instant Wesley disappeared. He dropped hard, hitting the floor with a loud crash.

"Must have knocked something over," said Simon.

They could hear shouting from inside. "Wesley Peters! What is going on? If I have to come up there, you'll be sorry. Wesley Peters, do you hear me? You answer me, boy!"

Heavy footsteps raced up the stairs and the light in Wesley's room flipped on. "Wesley Peters. Get up off that floor. You crazy boy. Look what you've done. You'll pay for this!"

"Yikes," said Sybil. "He's in trouble. Guess he landed a bit hard."

"I hope he isn't in too much trouble," said Simon. "We'd better take off."

"Or hurt! He could be hurt."

Sybil and Simon landed on the street and carried on with their dog walk.

"Do you think that was too much for him?"

"Don't know, but his Dad was pretty riled up. Maybe we shouldn't have done this," said Sybil.

"You're right. I got a bit carried away. Made me angry, the way he spoke to you on the trail yesterday."

"We'll see what happens tomorrow at school," said Sybil. "If he turns the other way, we know we got to him."

All that night Sybil felt restless. Her conscience nagged at her. Wesley's Dad sounded pretty angry. Maybe his life wasn't all that easy at home. She'd never thought about it before.

"Simon," she whispered at his door. "Can I come in?"

"Sure, I'm still awake." Sirius was sawing logs in his bed under the window. The street lamp cast pools of light across Simon's bed.

"I don't feel right about what we did to Wesley. It was harmless enough, but I never counted on his dad being so angry with him."

"Yeah, I never heard anyone yell like that before. So much rage in his voice."

"It was scary," said Sybil. "I'm sorry we did it."

"Me, too," said Simon. "I should have listened to you. Do you think Wesley will be afraid of Adelaide?"

"Depends on how she presents herself, I guess."

"I want to help," said Simon. His conscience had been bothering him. "Do you think we can help him?"

"We can try. That's all we can do. Remember, he said Alex was his only friend and we spoiled that."

"Yeah, I remember. But he spoiled that himself."

"He doesn't see it that way. Maybe he has always had blame placed on him. He might deflect blame like a heat shield. Could be automatic. It will take more than that Nutcracker I told you about. It might take the Sugar Plum Fairy," said Sybil.

"What do you mean?"

"I mean, a softer approach can be disarming.

"Of course. We have to put ourselves in his place. I said it before. How would we want to be treated?"

"We had our little revenge. Time to get serious. Claire said she was only a thought away," said Sybil.

"Right now. Let's talk to her tonight. No better time than now. Let's hold Claire close in our thoughts."

"Not here, though. Mom and Dad might hear us talking."

"Why not? Mom said she would like to meet Grandmother," said Simon.

"No, I think that is too much to handle all at once; meeting her *and* working on our problems with Wesley."

"Okay, Wesley first."

"Where do we meet? Tree house?" asked Sybil.

"Why not? Claire is up for adventure and probably has never been in one before," said Simon.

Once settled in the tree house, they focused, directing their concentration, holding Claire in their thoughts. Just as she had materialized at the lake so long ago, again her wavering reflection shimmered and came into focus until she was sitting on the floor beside them.

"How wonderful! Seeing you in your tree house at last. I have always wanted one. Had no time as a child. Where I grew up there were no trees large enough."

"You can come any time. Enjoy ours," said Sybil.

"Thank you, I will. What is it, Sybil. Simon?"

"Remember Wesley Peters? He's a distant grandson to Adelaide's son Oliver. She told you about him that day on the farm."

"Yes, Adelaide and I have discussed it. But we decided we wanted to allow you to work things out on your own. There are complications with his family."

"Yeah, we sort of know," said Simon. "We pulled a little prank on him tonight. It did not go well. Poor Wesley. He blacked out."

"To make matters worse, his dad went roaring upstairs shouting at the top of his lungs. It was dreadful. Scary!"

"We left in a hurry. Don't actually know what happened after that," said Simon.

"We feel it is time to step in. Adelaide said it got pretty messy. She's been keeping her eye on the situation," said Claire.

"We didn't mean any harm," said Simon. "I am sorry we ever thought up such a thing."

"I know. Scaring him won't help, I'm afraid. That poor boy has already known a lot of fear in his life." Claire's compassionate nature made it easy to see other viewpoints.

"Need a kinder way," said Sybil.

"We can be part of that," said Simon.

"Of course. It will be a team approach. Adelaide is in favour of this. Wesley needs friends and it is our hope that you and Sybil can help with that terrible void in his life."

"I've tried over the years," said Sybil. "But he has resisted anything I have ever said or done."

"Perhaps I am partly to blame for that. Adelaide and I. That old problem we had long ago. It tainted our family lines."

"You mean like the Hatfield and McCoy feud?" asked Sybil.

"I know nothing about that," replied Claire.

"It was a family feud in the southern USA. Started sometime in the 1860s. Not many know about it today. Heard Dad and Mom talking about it. Unbelievable. Thought they were talking about a movie. Sure enough, when I Googled it, there's all kinds of information on it. There even *was* a movie made."

"Family feuds. Adelaide and I can attest to that. Hopefully we can end this here and now."

"I'm all for that," said Sybil, breathing easier. She hated nastiness, hated her fearful life at school. All she wanted was peace.

"Why can't Wesley just leave me alone?" asked Sybil.

"What is driving his need to pick on people? Especially you?" asked Simon. He touched Sybil's arm gently.

"Like I said. The past might be felt well into the future," replied Claire.

"So we have to deal with it in the present," said Simon.

"We must make it right, now," added Sybil.

"Adelaide is on her way—ah, there you are, dear. Thank you for coming."

"Hello, Claire. Sybil, Simon. I'll do anything to help."

"Thank you, Adelaide," said Sybil. "We are worried about Wesley. Did something we shouldn't have."

"Yes, I am aware of it. Wesley's father is a bit of a hothead."

"Poor Wesley. Hard to live with that."

"What do you think should be done?" asked Adelaide.

"I think Simon and I need to talk to him again when he is alone," said Sybil. "We'll try to find a good time."

"Will he be able to see you, Adelaide?" asked Simon.

"I can make myself known," replied Adelaide. "If it's necessary."

"We'd like to try first. It would be nice if you were on hand, just in case we need help," said Sybil.

"It may take a little more persuasion," agreed Adelaide. "I'll be there if you need me."

"I'd like to try the forest trail again," said Simon. "It has a healing atmosphere."

"Do you know anything about Wesley?" asked Sybil. "He has never told us anything about himself."

"Not much," replied Adelaide. "I was in his room after the big row. Stuff was broken. It got a little physical, caused a lot of trouble. He's grounded for a week. Let out for school only."

"Might be hard to find him alone," said Sybil.

"That forest trail may have to wait," said Simon.

"Well, I'm not waiting," replied Sybil. "Tomorrow at school, I will be the one following him. He can't avoid me."

"What are you going to do?" asked Simon.

"He's going to know I care. Somehow, I will let him know."

"Good luck," said Simon flatly. "What else is in his room?"

"Posters, mostly space posters, sports equipment, clothes all over the floor," said Adelaide. "But the biggest thing was that telescope. It was broken along with a lamp."

"A telescope?" Sybil was immediately interested. "That

could be expensive."

"I heard his dad yelling about paying for it. Must have meant the telescope. How's he going to pay for that?" said Simon.

"It really is our fault. We'll pay for it." Sybil already had ideas surfacing. She would find a summer job helping out on a farm or picking berries in the Fraser Valley. While they were in school, she suggested they could work at a local fast food restaurant on weekends. And there was always the restaurant in Fifth over summer holidays. For that matter they could make use of time travel and work double time.

"I have nearly $200 in my bank account. How much money do you have saved, Simon?"

"Not sure off hand. Less than that probably."

"We can Google the cost of a good telescope," said Sybil.

"A very kind thing to do," said Claire.

"Not really," said Sybil. "We caused the problem in the first place."

"He must like astronomy," said Simon. "Would be pretty upset that it's broken."

"He lives with his dad. No other brothers or sisters," said Adelaide.

"Must be lonely." Sybil remembered the days before Simon.

"We'll leave it up to you and Simon for now. But we'll check in with you soon," said Adelaide. She turned to Claire, who nodded in agreement.

"You will find a way." Claire smiled and they were gone.

When they arrived at school the following morning Wesley was nowhere around. She watched for him at the morning break, but he had not come to school.

"Crikey! I hope he wasn't hurt," said Simon.

"Not like him to be away. He never misses school."

All that week Wesley did not attend classes. As often as she had wished him to be away in the past, she now hoped he would show up.

The following Monday, Wesley made an appearance. There was slight bruising on his forehead, the blueness now turning a sickly yellow.

Sybil walked over to him immediately. "Hi, Wesley. I hope you are okay."

While his face registered a blank expression, she could tell there was a nervous edge. His eyes darted about. She willed him to look at her and slowly his eyes came to rest in hers. There was a long silence while he grappled with emotions that threatened to overwhelm him. The intensity of her eyes burrowed to his core, creating that soft warmth he was afraid to acknowledge.

When he could no longer stand it, he growled, "Stay away from me." He turned and stocked off down the hall, glad to be away from her piercing eyes.

All that day Sybil remained close to him. She stood down the hall watching him fumble with his locker. He furtively kept her in his peripheral vision. She made a point to catch up with him on the block changes between classes. Once, in a gentle voice, she asked him, "Are you okay, Wesley?"

"Yeah." He mumbled a quick response, caught off guard by her boldness. He had been the one who had always initiated an interaction, intimidating her. And no one had ever asked him if he was okay, at least not that he could remember. This was new territory for him.

After school, Simon and Sybil waited for him just off school property. He did not show. When they arrived home they Googled the cost of telescopes and realized a good one would cost them a fair bit of money.

"We have to make some money fast." Simon's remorse was beginning to weigh heavily on him. "That was a total foul up. I wasn't thinking."

"Well, it's done and I am as much to blame," said Sybil. "I am going to apply for a job with a local greenhouse, potting plants after school. They'll need help with the Christmas rush."

"Maybe they will hire both of us," said Simon. "Let's do up our resumes and drop them off."

The following week they were interviewed and hired to work three hours after school, two days a week and full time on Saturdays. It would cut into their studies and leisure time, but they were determined to make it work.

Avoiding Sybil was not easy. She showed up wherever Wesley happened to be, greeting him politely and inviting him to join in group activities on the playground. He had no idea how to handle the situation and did his best to steer clear of her. He walked the other way if he saw her coming and refused her invitations when he was confronted by her unexpectedly.

CHAPTER SEVENTEEN
'Nutcracker Sweet'

"Everyone you meet is fighting a battle you know nothing about.

Be kind always."

- Unknown

At school, Simon joined the *Nutcracker Sweet* project, as they called it. They made a point of greeting him when he entered the schoolyard. At first he ignored their greetings, looking the other way and breaking into a trot to escape them. They let him get ahead but trailed him, maintaining normal speed. Wesley resisted these overtures at first. Consistency and sincerity began to break down the barriers he had built around himself. One day he let them walk beside him while they headed to their lockers. He ignored them silently but kept pace with their even strides.

After this silent routine had gone on for a few weeks, they invited him to sit with them at lunch. He looked shocked and wasn't sure how to answer.

"We'll meet you in the lunch room when the bell goes," said Sybil.

They were surprised when he showed up, making his way hesitantly toward them through the noisy crowd. Sybil waved him over and moved aside so he could sit next to her. "How's your day going, Wesley?"

“Okay, I guess. Liked the science block this morning.” He sat down and pulled a sandwich from his bag. When he’d finished it, he pulled out a juice box, gulping it noisily, slurping on the straw to get the last drops.

“Want to share one of these?” she asked, holding out her chocolate chip cookies.

“Gee, thanks,” he replied, biting into the moist chewy goodness. “Mmm…good! You bake ’em?”

“Simon and I did.”

“Yeah, she used to do them by herself, but insisted I learn how to bake.”

“Would you show me? Dad and I don’t bake. Have nothing but store bought since Mom’s gone.”

Listening carefully to this last comment, they let it slide by. No one had ever mentioned his mother. The thickness in his voice revealed a hesitant undercurrent of emotion.

“Come on, let’s go find a ball for a game of soccer on the back field,” suggested Simon. He stood up and headed outside, leaving Sybil and Wesley trailing behind.

“There’s Hamish and Marc,” said Sybil, when they caught up. “They already have a ball.”

“Hamish, wait up,” called Simon, loping across the field.

“Want ’a play?” asked Hamish.

“Sure,” they replied.

Sybil slid in beside him. “Hey there, Hamish. Last one to the field forfeits throw in.” She sped across the field under the high voltage wires buzzing overhead.

Soon a group of classmates had gathered and teams were formed.

“He can’t play,” said Hamish, scowling at Wesley. He’d had too many altercations with him in the past and wanted to avoid further trouble.

“Yeah, he’s playing today,” said Simon. “We asked him to

come."

Hamish looked at Simon as though he were an alien from space. Then he thought better of it, shrugged and said, "Okay." But his look conveyed the message 'don't say I didn't warn you.'

The game was going well until Hamish skidded into Wesley, knocking his feet out from under him.

"You jerk! You did that on purpose!" shouted Wesley. He jumped to his feet and glared at Hamish. "You idiot!"

Sybil intervened, laying her hand on his arm. "Stop, Wesley. It was an accident. Hamish didn't mean to knock you over. I saw it. His shoe slipped on the grass."

"No, he meant it. Doesn't like me. I know it."

"No, Wesley. Honest. I wouldn't lie. I saw it."

He stopped, unsure of what he was hearing. His breath came in short angry bursts.

"Breathe, Wes. Take a deep breath." The anger searing his brain began to drain away with each inhalation until he was again in control of himself.

"You sure 'bout that?"

"Yes, I know Hamish. He wouldn't do that on purpose. Look, he's tried to get up. He's limping. Let's go see if he's okay."

Sybil headed over with Wesley following slowly behind. He was sitting on the grass again, holding his right ankle and grimacing in pain.

"Hey, bud. You okay?" asked Sybil.

"Nah, I think I wrenched it pretty good."

Wesley came up to them and knelt on the grass beside him. "Sorry, man," he said under his breath, then again a little louder. "Sorry, Hamish. Are you all right?"

"No, my ankle is bad. It wasn't your fault, Wesley. I slid into you. Runners are pretty worn. See…" He flapped the sole at the toe where it had let go from the bottom of the shoe. "They're shot."

"I see that," said Wesley. "Can you stand?"

"Just give me a minute or two."

"Sure," said Wesley, hesitating. "You need anything?"

"No. It'll be all right in a bit." He sat for a few moments, but his ankle began to swell.

Quelling the nausea, he called out, "Simon, think you and Wes can get me back to the school for first aid?"

"I'll help, too," said Marc, standing over his friend in concern. "We can take turns."

"Let me have a look first," said Sybil. He took off his shoe and sock and she winced at the bruising and swelling.

"Want to try standing up, Hamish?" asked Sybil. "But don't put any weight on it."

Wesley and Simon put their arms around Hamish's back and hoisted him to standing position while he balanced on his left leg. "Lean on us, Hamish," said Simon.

"Ow, ow," moaned Hamish. "It hurts too much."

"Make a chair," said Wesley. He linked his arms with Simon's and told Hamish to sit. He relaxed on the make-shift chair with his arms around their necks and was carried to the school. Hamish's mother was called and he was taken to Emergency for x-rays.

"Poor Hamish," said Sybil. "Just before Christmas. Rotten luck. Good thing soccer season is over."

"Yeah, sorry. I got pretty mad," said Wesley. "Can't help it sometimes."

"You'll work on it," said Simon. "Got'ta remember, not everyone is out to get you, Wes. Sometimes things just happen. Can't be helped."

"I s'pose you're right," he said, feeling a little relieved.

After school let out for the day, Sybil found Wesley. "Want to walk home with us. It's not much out of your way. You can use the walkway between our subdivisions to get home."

"Sure, thanks. You hear anything about Hamish? Hope nothing's broken."

"Yeah, I got a text message from his phone. His mom says it's a bad sprain. No broken bones."

"That's good," said Wesley. "Don't need that for Christmas."

"We hear you are interested in astronomy," said Sybil, probing for some common interest.

"Yeah, I am. How'd you know that?"

"Heard talk on the schoolyard," replied Simon.

"Ever seen the Perseid meteor showers in August?" asked Sybil.

"You kidding? Course I have," replied Wesley. "Watch 'em every year."

"Want to go out to the Vedder River dyke with us next time?" Simon was warming up now that he had Wesley's interest.

"I s'pose that'd be okay. Used to take my telescope out there with my Dad…" The conversation dwindled.

"We don't have to wait for August to go star watching," said Sybil. There are other showers, like the Quadrantids in January and the Lyrids in April. Lots of others, too."

"Got'ta be a night owl," replied Wesley, remembering the first time he fell asleep in a lawn chair while his dad watched.

"So, when do you want to go?" asked Sybil.

"No use going without a telescope. No meteor showers."

"We could still check out the constellations. Binoculars don't work very well but we can try them. Maybe you know some we don't," said Simon. "What's your favourite?"

"I think I like the Big Dipper best. It's part of Ursa Major.

What do you like?"

"No brainer," laughed Simon and Sybil. "We like Sirius and Orion."

"Oh yeah, the hunter. He's cool." said Wesley. "And Sirius is the brightest star in Canis Major."

"I like Cassiopeia," said Sybil. "The vain queen."

"One of the first I learned," replied Wesley.

"Our star sign is Leo. What's yours?" asked Sybil, watching for Wesley's reaction.

"Capricorn," replied Wesley, without missing a beat.

"So, when's your birthday?" asked Sybil.

"Christmas Day."

"On Christmas Day? No way! That's cool," said Simon.

"Nah, never had a birthday party. Everyone's having family Christmas."

"You never had a birthday party with friends?" asked Sybil.

"Nope, just Dad…and Mom before she died." Conversation stopped and silence opened between them. Then Sybil found her voice.

"Your mom died? So sorry, Wesley."

"Yeah, man. That's sad," said Simon.

"It was a long time ago. Before we moved here."

"It's still sad. Sorry, Wes," said Simon.

"I kind'a like that."

"What do you like?"

"When you call me 'Wes.' "

"A little like Simon calling me 'Syb.' I like that, too."

"Well, what do you say? Friday is our last day before Christmas break. Let's check out the night sky," suggested Simon.

"Gets dark early now. Winter solstice is coming up. How about 8:00 p.m., and hope we get a clear sky," said Wes.

"Good. We'll come by your house," agreed Sybil.

"Here we are," said Simon. "This is where we live. Got time to stop for a snack?"

"Should get home. Dad expects me to get chores done and start dinner before he comes home from work."

"A cookie and a drink won't take long. Besides, we want to show you something," said Simon.

"If it doesn't take too long. S'pose I can run the rest of the way to make up time."

"Come around the side, Wes," said Sybil, leading the way. They were just through the gate when Sirius bounded toward them, a mass of wriggling fur leaping in circles around them.

"This is Sirius," laughed Simon. "He's very energetic."

"I see that. Hello, Sirius," smiled Wes, as the hound sniffed his hand. "He's a big one."

"Yes, and his heart is even bigger," laughed Sybil. "He loves everybody."

Wesley giggled. He was being subjected to a face-licking and it was plain to see Sirius liked him. "He's awesome! I can see why you like that star constellation."

"Enough now, Sirius. Come inside, Wes and meet Mom," said Sybil.

When they entered the kitchen, Franceska was just pulling the last pan of cookies out of the oven. "Hi, guys. How was school? The cookies on the table are ready to eat."

"Mom, we'd like you to meet Wesley Peters," said Sybil.

Franceska was taken aback but she never let on. "Wesley, it's very nice to meet you. You have never been here before. Glad you could stop."

"Have a cookie, Wes," said Simon, holding the plate out to him.

"Thank you, Simon, and thank you, Mrs. Huber," he said, looking down at his feet. Being in someone else's house made him shy and uneasy.

"Would you like a glass of milk to go with it?" asked Franceska.

"Ah, no thank you, Mrs. Huber. Can't stay long. Have to get home."

"Well, you can stay long enough to see our tree house," said Sybil. "Let's go."

They headed out the back door toward the rope ladder dangling from the trunk of the old tree.

"Up you go, Wes. You first," said Simon.

"This is cool!" said Wesley, as he neared the top and crawled inside. The leaves had all been shed, allowing him to see into surrounding neighbours' backyards. "Always wanted one of these."

"You can come over anytime," offered Sybil, as she and Simon crawled in beside him. "Now you know where we live."

"Thanks, that'd be great."

"You like to hike?" asked Simon.

"Haven't done much. Got too much work at home."

"We have jobs after school now, a couple days a week and have to work Saturdays for a while. But after the Christmas rush we could come and help you. Then you can come hiking with us sometime."

"You'd do that for me?"

"Sure, why not?" said Sybil. "There's two of us. We can get our chores done twice as fast and have plenty of time left over."

"It'd be fun," said Simon.

"Not sure what Dad will say. But I guess we can ask him."

"Okay, after Christmas, then. Before we go back to school we'll go up Tea Pot Hill."

"Heard about it. Never hiked it, though. Strange name for a hill."

"Story goes that some early explorers found a teapot up

there. That's how it got its name."

"Cool! Guess I'd better be going or I'll be late," said Wesley. He crawled down the ladder and hopped off. "Thanks for the snack and showing me your tree house."

"Sure, stop by anytime, Wes."

"Sirius is the best," laughed Wesley, as he knelt to hug the big hound. "See you guys tomorrow."

"Come by our house in the morning and you can walk with us. Marc will be here, but Hamish with his bunged up ankle... Doubt he'll be at school."

"Thanks, that'd be nice."

Life at school was a whole lot easier. Wesley still had moments when old habits, his former ways of reacting to things, came forward. But he was learning that people would give him a chance to prove himself. Many found that they actually liked him, especially when they saw him treat Sybil with respect. It had been a notorious relationship around school. They had been only too glad it was her and not them. Everyone, except Alex, had avoided Wesley. That deadly duo had been fractured after the last incident at the bus loop. And it came as a surprise when Alex's family had suddenly moved away.

The school counsellor called Sybil in one day and asked how it was going. She had noticed the difference in both her and Simon. Most importantly she had seen changes in Wesley.

"What has happened, Sybil? You and Wesley seem to be getting on much better."

"You'd have to ask Wesley about that, I guess. Simon and I figured he could use a friend or two. He's all right."

"Wesley has made some changes in his life, that's for sure. It's good to see."

"I have another class starting. Have to run," said Sybil. She was not prepared to discuss it further.

"Okay, see you another time, Sybil."

The end of the week came and school let out for Christmas break. Sybil and Simon were concerned. Wesley had never had a birthday party with friends and Christmas was only a few days away. They decided to approach their parents.

"Mom, would it be okay to have a birthday party for Wesley? His birthday is on Christmas Day and he has never had one with friends."

"Never had a birthday party?"

"No, his mom died when he was very young. Before they moved here. Everyone has Christmas Day with their families."

"How tragic for them…" Franceska's brow puckered in concern. "I suppose I can see the logic, but to never have a birthday party. Even before or after, on a different day."

"His dad must have found it pretty hard after her death," said Sybil.

"Do you think we could throw him a party and ask a few of our friends from school?" asked Simon.

"Who would you ask? Many people travel away for Christmas and want to be home for turkey dinner," said Franceska, becoming more aware of the situation. It was one thing to say, 'Never had a birthday party.' It was altogether different when planning one for Christmas Day. "I see the dilemma," she conceded.

"We can work something out, can't we?" said Sybil. "Let's have our Christmas on a different day and hold Wes's birthday on December 25th."

"You know, that might just work," said Franceska. "Let's ask the McRorys and the Leesoms if they would like to be part of it."

"Oh yes! I know Hamish and Marc would love it," said

Sybil.

"We've discussed the problems at school many times. I am sure they will be on board," said Franceska. "And we'll ask Wes and his dad to have Christmas with us this year. I hope his dad will agree when I explain what we have in mind."

"We can have Christmas turkey on Boxing Day instead," said Sybil. "Simon and I have been saving for a new telescope for Wes. His got broken."

"Yeah, and we are to blame for that," said Simon, explaining the whole thing.

"That's rather a mean thing to do. Probably scared the wits out of him," said James, coming in part-way through the conversation. He saw the merit in what they were planning and whole-heartedly agreed.

"There's just one thing. We don't have quite enough saved for the telescope. We're short by about $150. We can order it on line and have it delivered by courier to arrive on time."

"Say no more," said James. "Your mom and I will loan you the rest but we expect reimbursement for $100. We will give you the $50 as part of our birthday gift to Wesley."

"Oh, thank you! We'll place that order right now. Come on, Simon. We'd better get cracking," said Sybil. "Let's order it and start making plans for decorating."

"We can bake the cake," said Simon. "Can we get party favours, Mom?"

"We'll give out movie passes to Cottonwood 4 Cinemas, here in Sardis," said Franceska. "You can all see a matinee one day over the Christmas break."

"Super idea, Franceska," said James. "You buy the passes and I will provide popcorn and a drink combo. There's sure to be some good Christmas movies playing."

"I am going over to the McRory's place right now and will ask the Leesoms as well," said Franceska. "You want to come,

James?"

"Sure, you go ahead and I'll be right over."

"Anything else you need before I go?" asked James, looking at Sybil and Simon. "This is a great idea. I am proud of you two."

"No, I think we can manage," said Simon. "I've just placed the order. Courier service will deliver within two days."

"Wes will be surprised," said Sybil. "Can't wait to see the look on his face when he opens it!"

Franceska and James returned home shortly. "It's all planned. We are holding Wes's birthday on Christmas Day. After gift opening in the morning we are getting together for Christmas dinner on Boxing Day at our house."

"Here?" laughed Sybil. "How will we manage that many people?"

"No problem. It will be pot luck. Your father and I are doing the turkey and stuffing. And we'll supply the dessert. Hamish and Marc's family are doing the rest."

"Now all we have to do is convince Wesley and his father about the merits of not having to cook a turkey. Do you know his name, James?"

"Seems to me it is William. Goes by Bill, I heard."

"Will you give him a call and ask if we can drop by this evening to see him?"

"Sure, I'm on it."

"Let's get those errands done, Sybil," said Franceska. "Simon, do you want to come?"

"Sure, I don't want to miss all the fun," he laughed.

They piled in their jeep and headed off to pick up movie passes, then stopped to buy a card and decorations at a Dollar Store.

"We need wrapping paper for the telescope," said Simon. He picked out a colourful one with planets and stars.

"Perfect," said Sybil. "What kind of cake are we making?"

"Chocolate. What else? He liked those cookies with chocolate."

"But that's so plain," said Sybil.

"Why don't you two make a Black Forest cake? It's jazzed up with cherries and whipped cream," said Franceska.

"Add candles and it will be a fine birthday cake," agreed Sybil. "Almost forgot. We need to buy candles."

After the meeting with Wes's dad, things were a little subdued. "Bill doesn't seem too enthused about the whole idea," said James. "He thinks it will be too much of an inconvenience to us."

"We told him we wanted it to be a surprise for Wesley, and it was not an inconvenience at all. We asked him to come on Boxing Day for Christmas dinner as well. Told him there were two other families joining us," said Franceska.

"It took a bit of convincing, but he finally agreed," said James.

"Guess he hasn't had much to be social about since he lost his wife," said Franceska. "It can become a way of living. Work, home, sleep, work, home, sleep."

"And he agreed to keep it a secret from Wesley," said James. "That's the main thing."

"What time are they coming over that day?" asked Sybil.

"We asked them to be here by 1:00 p.m. That will give us enough time to prepare everything in the morning. We can decorate the night before."

"Can we make pizza?" asked Sybil. "Simon and I will help. There'll be veggies and dip, chips and juice. That should be all we need."

"Yes, three large pizzas should do it," said Franceska.

"I've asked a few other kids from school. There's Ashley, Kiana and Dana. I really like them a lot. Dylan and Carlos, too. When they told their parents why we are doing it on Christmas Day, they agreed. So they are all coming!"

"Maybe we should make four pizzas. Good thing I bought extra movie passes. Can never have too many of those on hand."

December 25th arrived. The house was decorated in a space theme with planets clustered around a giant sun hanging from the ceiling. A *Happy Birthday* sign was strung above a window in the large sunroom where they planned to hold the party. They could close the double doors and allow guests to dance and have fun.

The morning was a flurry of activity with Simon and Sybil assembling chocolate cake layers, filled with cherries, creating the delectable confection of Black Forest Torte, Simon's favourite. With a flourish of her decorating tube Sybil added a final ruffle of whipped cream with artistic flair. She stood back and admired her handiwork. "What do you think, Simon?"

"Awesome! You could start your own business," teased Simon.

"I'll business you one. Stick out your tongue, smarty-pants." He did as ordered and she squirted the last dollop of whipped cream in his mouth.

"Yum! Gimme more, please."

"None left. You'll have to wait for the party. Take the cake to the fridge in the basement, will you please, Simon?"

"Sure, no problem. Can't guarantee I'll be back."

"Touch that cake and we'll lock you down there," said Sybil. "No party for you!"

"Aww, no fair, Sybil."

They turned to the business of assembling pizzas while mom rolled out crusts. James stood ready to pop them in the wall ovens and keep an eye on them. When the first two were in the warming oven, the last two went in to bake.

The last of the guests arrived at 12:45 p.m., ready to surprise Wes when he came through the door. Promptly at 1:00 p.m., the doorbell rang and a bewildered Wes was ushered into the sunroom. His face registered shock at the shout of 'Surprise!' A big grin morphed to a delighted laugh and he said, "What the heck! You guys! Why did you do this?" He continued to laugh as a tear escaped down his cheek. "This is too much. Way too much! Wow! My first birthday party. Thank you!"

His friends gathered around him and clapped his back. "You can't go through life without a birthday party," said Simon.

"Nope, it's high time you had one," said Sybil. "Can't think of a better time than now."

"Who's ready for pizza?" said Simon, bringing in a tray. "Help yourselves. There's one with ham and pineapple and the other has pepperoni and mushroom. I will bring a vegetarian in next."

"Anyone want a juice?" asked Sybil. "There's plenty in the cooler on ice. Grab whatever you like." She cranked up the volume on her iPod. Soon they were all moving to the music of Queen. It didn't matter how old the music was, her generation still loved the up-tempo beat of *We Will Rock You* and *Crazy Little Thing Called Love.* When *We Are the Champions* played, they joined in at the top of their lungs. They were brought together under unusual circumstances and felt the momentum of the day. The power of change that came to them gently was felt by everyone in the room.

"Open your presents, Wes," said Sybil. They led him to a corner table with brightly wrapped packages. She handed each gift to the person who had brought it so they could present it themselves. There was the usual electronic stuff and gift cards for stores. She saved theirs until last and handed it to Simon.

"Here, you give it to Wes," she said.

"No, I think you should be the one to give it," replied Simon.

She smiled, held the gift out to Wes, and stood watching as he read their card. 'To Wes. We hope this makes your day. Sorry, for the unusual display. Happy Birthday from Sybil and Simon.'

Everyone wondered about the strange message. Wesley had long since attributed that incident to the bump on his head. Now, he threw them a sidelong glance. It was still a bit of a blur, but the moment passed when he ripped the paper off his gift and saw the picture on the box. He stopped and stared at it a long time, speechless. He opened the box and lifted out a beautiful instrument swaddled in bubble wrap.

"A telescope! You're joking. This is one of the best. Had my eye on it a long time."

"Hope you like it," said Sybil.

"Like it? I love it. But it's way too much. I can't accept it."

"Of course you can," said Sybil. Her penetrating glance warmed him inside.

"How'd you know?" he said, a little bewildered.

"Oh, pretty easy to guess you'd enjoy something like this," said Simon.

"All those astronomy talks we had," laughed Sybil. "We should start an astronomy club at school."

"That's a cool idea," said Wesley. "Think our science teacher would go for it?"

"Don't see why not. We can ask."

"Anyone else interested?" asked Wes.

"You bet," answered Carlos.

"Count me in," said Dana and Dylan.

The party ended with final plans to get together for a

movie in between Christmas and New Year's Day.

Bill had stayed in the kitchen visiting with Franceska and James.

"I can't thank you enough for this," he said. "Wes has not had an easy time. We've had to go it alone for many years."

"You're not alone, Bill. You have neighbours," said James.

"What happened to his mother?" Franceska was afraid to ask.

"Had cancer, very young. Died on Wesley's birthday when he turned five. We moved here shortly after."

"Where were you before that?" asked James.

"Came from the east coast—lived in Nova Scotia. Job transfer, then a lay off. Eventually, I started a business. Designed and built a water cannon to fight fires."

"That sounds like a good idea, especially with so many fires in the province this year," said James.

"Takes me out of town a lot. It was touch and go for the first while, but things have picked up this last year."

"Well, you can call on us anytime. Wes is welcome to come over after school and on weekends. Whenever you need to go out of town on business, we'll be here for him. He can stay with us."

"Thank you very kindly. That was always my main concern. How to provide for Wes when I had to go out of town. Had to put him in emergency respite a few times. I had no one."

"You need to work. I can see how hard that would be," said James.

"I don't think Wes understood that. My leaving him with strangers. He was angry and started acting out more."

"Well, no need to worry, now. We're here and we've got your back. If we can't do it, I am sure our friends, Hamish's or Marc's families would help out. Those two boys were here today. Been friends since forever," said James.

"We'd best be going," said Bill, rising to his feet. "Can't thank you enough, Franceska, James. Your two kids have made a big difference. Wes seems a lot happier these days."

"No problem. Glad it's working out," said Franceska. "We shall see you tomorrow, then. Come over whenever you have finished gift opening. Have a bit of brunch with us. Nothing like the smell of turkey cooking to work up an appetite. You will meet the McRorys and Leesoms, those families we just spoke of."

Wes appeared in the kitchen. "Guess what, Dad! Sybil and Simon gave me a new telescope! You should see it. Can't wait to try it out."

"A telescope?" Bill looked startled. "That's too much. We can't accept it."

"Of course you can," said James. "Simon and Sybil have been working after school and on weekends. They owed Wes for the broken one."

"You know about that?" asked Bill.

"Yeah, the kids confessed. They scared Wes one night. That's what caused the problem."

"Oh? I had no idea. Wes never said anything." Bill was at a loss. "Well, in that case, I guess it would be all right. On one condition. Sybil and Simon get to use it whenever they want to. That okay with you, Wes?"

Sybil and Simon watched the changing expressions rippling across Wesley's face. He stared blankly, then a niggling doubt clouded his vision as he considered the comment. Sybil and Simon had confessed to scaring him. What *did* he see that night?

He winced and shrugged it off. They were friends now and it felt good. Whatever it was, he was okay with it. He came back to the present with a start when he realized everyone was staring at him.

"You bet. And thank you, Mrs. Huber, Mr. Galowin. It was such a surprise! No one has ever done anything like this for me." He turned to Sybil and Simon. "How can I ever repay you? This party, the telescope. It's way too much."

They stood grinning at Wes. "Nonsense. You deserve it. Our first night out sky-watching is pay enough."

Discussion Questions

1. Is bullying a learned behaviour or is it a personality disorder?
2. Was Wesley really a bully? Why or why not?
3. Why were other students in the school not willing to step in; glad it was Sybil and not them?
4. Is it difficult to stand up for others?
5. Is there a difference between the characters of Wesley and Dimondus? In what ways are they alike or not alike?
6. What is the difference between problems on the school grounds and problems in Aquadria? How are they alike or different?
7. Did Wesley find it easy or hard to relate to kindness? Why?
8. Do you think there are people who are incapable of responding to kindness? Why or why not?
9. Do you think Simon and Sybil were justified in playing that prank on Wesley?
10. Is there a difference between personality and character? If yes, what is the difference?
11. What role does upbringing have in forming character?
12. Does mutation in Aquadria and the Duplicating Chamber compare to conditioning of society? How is it similar or different?
13. When you read a story, is it helpful to read and understand from multiple characters' points of view?

Made in the USA
Lexington, KY
29 November 2019